WE NEED A LITTLE CHRISTMAS KISSING

"Scott?" she said, knowing he'd turn his head.

She could thank him for being here, for making this past week so much easier than it would have been without him. Or she could just do what she wanted to do.

So, when Scott turned his head, she leaned toward him, hearing the sudden clamoring of her own heart, and it seemed the temperature of the air between them changed. She brushed his lips tentatively with hers, afraid he'd pull away, thinking, *This is how he felt the other night.* It was scary, going out on a limb. Heat shimmered through her as their lips connected, and she hung suspended, waiting to see if she was about to be humiliated. Whether she'd get back what she'd given him the other night.

Instead, his arms fit easily around her, as if he were catching her from a fall. He pulled her closer, his lips meeting hers, joining them together. So gentle, yet so wonderfully solid. She wrapped her arms around his neck, and his arms folded more firmly around her, and now her heart pounded not from fear, but something else entirely. He deepened the kiss, and Liv forgot all about the cold. All about the attic. All about anything but the way it felt being in his arms and letting time stop . . .

Books by Sierra Donovan

NO CHRISTMAS LIKE THE PRESENT

DO YOU BELIEVE IN SANTA?

WE NEED A LITTLE CHRISTMAS

Published by Kensington Publishing Corporation

We Need a Little Christmas

SIERRA DONOVAN

ZEBRA BOOKS
KENSINGTON PUBLISHING CORP.
http://www.kensingtonbooks.com

ZEBRA BOOKS are published by

Kensington Publishing Corp.
119 West 40th Street
New York, NY 10018

All Kensington titles, imprints, and distributed lines are available at special quantity discounts for bulk purchases for sales promotion, premiums, fund-raising, educational, or institutional use.

Special book excerpts or customized printings can also be created to fit specific needs. For details, write or phone the office of the Kensington Sales Manager: Attn.: Sales Department. Kensington Publishing Corp., 119 West 40th Street, New York, NY 10018. Phone: 1-800-221-2647.

Zebra and the Z logo Reg. U.S. Pat. & TM Off.

First Printing: October 2016
ISBN-13: 978-1-4201-4150-4
ISBN-10: 1-4201-4150-3

eISBN-13: 978-1-4201-4151-1
eISBN-10: 1-4201-4151-1

10 9 8 7 6 5 4 3 2 1

Printed in the United States of America

For Tammy, the best big sister I ever had.

AUTHOR'S NOTE

We Need a Little Christmas is a love letter to my family. While it reflects the jumble of feelings you tend to find in a roomful of women, it's also a work of fiction. Any attempts to take the characters and events literally will only lead to confusion.

However, just for the record, anyone reading this book should know:

—My older sister isn't type-A like Liv. And I could never be that organized.

—Our mother has never chipped her kneecap. (Although I have, by tripping over the dog.)

—Our grandmother, rather than a mere eighty-three, lived to be almost a hundred and two.

But we really did have one of those silver aluminum Christmas trees. I still love them, in all their kitschy glory.

Chapter 1

It shouldn't be hard to recognize her own sister.

But as Liv Tomblyn scanned the faces in the crowded baggage claim area, she was starting to have her doubts.

She couldn't find Rachel in the post-Thanksgiving throng of travelers at the airport. Maybe she'd gotten a haircut, or changed the color, or something else to throw Liv off. She found herself trying to picture Rachel's Facebook photo, wondering how recent it was. Her clearest mental image was the way her sister had looked four years ago, the last time Liv had come back to California. Rachel had been straightening the curl out of her strawberry blond hair then . . .

When you tried to picture your little sister from her Facebook photo, you'd been away too long. And it shouldn't take your grandmother's memorial service to bring you home.

Liv checked her phone again for messages or texts. Nothing. Giving up for the moment, she turned to the baggage carousel as it made another round. She sighted the larger of her two red suitcases—she'd chosen the luggage because it was easy to spot—and stepped forward to reach for it.

"Here, let me get that." A male voice spoke behind her, to her left, and a hand reached past her to snag the suitcase.

"Hey—" she began, then followed the hand up its arm to the face of the owner. It was a long way up, but she recognized the face, the sandy brown hair and the blue eyes that regarded her with what looked like mild amusement.

"Hi, Liv."

"Scotty?"

She hadn't seen him since graduation, but there was no mistaking Scotty Leroux, the class clown for all her years growing up in Tall Pine. The fact that he was about six-foot-five helped. Which meant he must have just gotten here, because he would have stood out even in the holiday mob. His eyes held the same glimmer, as if he were about to laugh at something. Back in the day, Liv had never been sure whether the joke was on her.

"Rachel sent me." His resonant voice cut through the rumble of voices around them. "She hit a snag on her way out the door."

"What—"

"Nothing major. Let's get out of this mess and I'll tell you about it. How many bags have you got?"

"Just one more." A frown creased her forehead. "Another red suitcase. But—"

Setting the first bag on its end, Scotty shifted his focus over her head and past her to the carousel. "That one?"

She followed his nod to the smaller bag now rounding

the corner of the conveyor belt on its way toward them. Yes, sir, red luggage did the trick. Liv stepped forward. "I'll get that one."

Scotty passed her with one easy stride, taking advantage of his longer arms to reach the suitcase before Liv could get to it. "Whoa." He hefted the bag. "The little one's heaver than the big one. What have you got in here?"

She answered reluctantly. "Shoes."

"What are you, a centipede?" Scotty's mouth lifted in the teasing grin she recalled from nearly ten years ago.

She tried to ignore the embarrassment that rushed in. Why did she feel the urge to explain herself? "I like having options."

"I guess so." He raised his eyebrows, looking from the two suitcases on the floor back to Liv. "How long are you staying?"

"Through Christmas. There's a lot to do." Liv steadied her voice. "Mom and Rachel and I need to sort through Nammy's whole house. And she lived there for sixty years."

"I know." Scotty's voice softened, and this time there was no trace of kidding in his expression. "I'm sorry about your grandma. She was a nice lady."

"Thanks." Liv's eyes prickled, but no way was she going to break down in an airport. Breaking down wasn't something she tended to do anyway. It never did any good, and there was always something more useful to do.

Scotty surprised her by giving her arm a quick squeeze, and Liv tried to figure out this strange new world she appeared to have landed in. She'd known

Scotty the way everybody knew everybody at Tall Pine High: this one's a brain, this one's a cheerleader. She remembered him as lean and gangly, on the goofy side. Not a grown-up, and certainly not someone to call in a sudden emergency. He'd filled out physically, gotten more solid. And for some reason, her sister had called him.

What was the emergency? A *snag*, he'd called it. She needed details.

She opened her mouth to ask again, but he turned to lead her through the automatic sliding exit doors, carrying the small suitcase in one hand, pulling the large one along on its wheels with the other. Liv followed as she tried to formulate her questions. She wondered how well he'd known her grandmother. Why her sister wasn't here.

And why, of all people, had she called Scotty Leroux?

Outside, he came to a stop next to the wall of the building and set her suitcases on the sidewalk. There was somewhat less confusion out here; the jumble of voices gave way to the sound of cars and their doors as people pulled up to the curb to load and unload.

"So what's going on?" Liv asked.

Again, no trace of teasing in the usually-laughing blue eyes.

"Your mom fell," he said. "Rachel says it's not a big deal, and not to worry. She wanted me to make sure you understood that. She didn't call or text you because she didn't want you to have extra time to stress before I got here. She says your mom just landed hard on her knee, and she couldn't put any weight on it. So Rachel

4

took her to the walk-in urgent care center and called me to get you."

"She fell? How?" Random falling was what old people did. Her mom was only fifty-seven. Her grandmother had been eighty-three, and she'd never fallen once.

Not that Liv knew of, anyway.

"I didn't get all the details. Rachel just kept saying for you not to worry."

"Okay." Liv took a second to close her eyes and re-assimilate.

Don't worry sounded like a surefire cue to worry, especially when your grandmother just died, you were already rattled, your mom fell, and your sister sent a former classmate instead of coming to pick you up at the airport herself.

Liv pulled out her cell phone and dialed Rachel's number. It went straight to voice mail. She considered leaving a message, reconsidered and hung up. Rachel probably had her hands full. She lived in San Diego, a three-hour drive from Tall Pine, so she'd been staying with Mom while they waited for Liv to join them. It had taken Liv two days to get here. Booking a flight the week after Thanksgiving hadn't been easy, and she'd been trying to tie up loose ends at the office before she left Terri to handle the business for four weeks.

Still, she should have gotten here quicker.

"The hospital might have made her turn off her cell," Scotty said after she hung up without speaking. "Plus, the reception is always hit-or-miss in Tall Pine."

He was trying to reassure her.

Don't worry, her sister had said.

Right.

She faced him again, tilting her head back to look up farther than she felt comfortable doing. Liv was taller than average, but Scotty's extra height made her wish she'd worn shoes with some kind of heel, rather than the practical sneakers she'd worn for traveling.

"Okay," she said. "Let's get up the hill and see what's going on."

Scott had run out the door when Liv's sister called, aware that Rachel was already behind schedule to pick Liv up at the airport. He hadn't thought to grab anything as he left. If he had, he might have tried to find a CD labeled *Music for Driving Down the Freeway with Someone You Barely Know.*

Not that Liv seemed like she was starving for conversation. At the moment, she sat with her head turned toward the window of the passenger seat of Scott's faithful, battered F-150.

She ran a hand through her hair, still the same rich chestnut color. It tumbled past her shoulders in disorderly waves that were all the more attractive because she obviously wasn't thinking about it.

He shouldn't be thinking about it.

Liv's eyes, when she'd been looking at him, had worn a preoccupied, slightly out-of-focus look that made perfect sense in a woman who'd just lost her grandmother. He needed to respect that. And he felt that loss as well. Olivia Neuenschwander had worked her way into his heart. He knew he wasn't alone. Eighty-three years old or not, her absence left a hole, and the rest of Tall Pine would miss her, too.

Almost as if she'd heard his thoughts, Liv turned to him. "I didn't know you knew my grandmother."

"Everyone knows Nammy." He felt her double take at his use of the nickname and wished he could rewind. Olivia had been *her* grandmother, not his, even if Liv had moved away.

Olivia. It occurred to him, belatedly, that Liv must have been named after her.

"I did some repairs around the house for her," he explained. "It's what I do. I'm the local rent-a-husband."

He paused. Usually when he told people that, it was an opening for *Insert Wisecrack Here*, but she didn't bite. Then again, Liv Tomblyn hadn't been the wisecracking type. More the student-council, straight-A, overachiever type. After graduation, she'd lit out for college somewhere out of state, and he didn't think she'd been back much since.

He didn't really know her, but the aura of quiet radiating from her told him she might regret her long absence.

"Your grandmother talked about you a lot," he said. "She was really proud of you. You would have thought you were a Fortune 500 mogul." He glanced over to make sure she was still with him. "Although I'm not quite sure what it is you do. Something about home remodeling?"

"Not quite. Terri and I are home organizers. We help people manage their storage, their clutter, sometimes their schedules."

Scott frowned. "I wonder how she got *remodeling* out of that."

"Well, I specialize in closets."

He almost swerved the truck. "Closets?" he repeated.

It was hard not to laugh. He managed to keep a straight face, but he sensed her stiffen beside him.

"Seriously," she said. "It's a real business."

Scott bit his lip and kept his eyes on the road.

"It's a service," she insisted. "When your living space is jumbled, your life is jumbled. Your stress level goes up, you lose valuable time looking for things . . . it even affects people's concentration."

Sounded like a serious first-world problem to him. "Well, anyway. From what Namm—what your grandmother told me, it sounds like you've done really well with it."

He didn't mean to sound patronizing, but he did, even to his own ears.

She crossed her arms. "What about you? Rent-a-husband? *You* sound like a gigolo."

A little late, but a wisecrack after all. Scott didn't miss a beat.

"Only when business is slow. A guy's gotta eat."

A moment of silence. Then a short burst of laughter escaped from her, and he felt the tension diffuse. A step in the right direction.

"Okay," she said. "You've used that one before, haven't you?"

"There are no old jokes," he said. "Only old audiences."

He glanced sideways at Liv as the truck continued up the hill. Her job still sounded ridiculous. Granted, Liv's skills might come in handy for the work her family had ahead of them, but he wondered if they'd be getting a consultant, when what they really needed was a daughter and a sister.

Then he detected a flaw in the picture.

"Wait a minute," he said. "Your job is helping people deal with their clutter, and you brought along a whole suitcase just for shoes?"

From the corner of his eye, he caught an embarrassed smile. "I never said I was consistent."

After an hour and a half of mostly-silent driving, they made the turn off the highway onto Evergreen Lane. The street was decked out in its customary Christmas finery, with arches of lights stretching from one side of the street to the other, garland wrapped around all the lamp posts. Scott wondered if the festive decorations felt incongruous to Liv for this rather somber homecoming, but if so, she didn't comment on it.

However, within a block, he saw her back straighten. Soon she was craning her neck, taking in the shops on either side.

"Oh, gosh, there's the pizza place . . . and the T-shirt shop . . . they painted, didn't they?"

Scott grinned. "*I* painted, actually."

He wasn't sure she heard him. "And the Christmas store's still there. And the Pine 'n' Dine . . ." They passed a vacant space, and Liv stiffened. "Is the ice cream shop gone?"

Scott almost chuckled at her near alarm. "No. They just moved. It's another block up, on the left."

When Scott pointed out the pink-and-white awning of Penny's Ice Cream Shoppe as they drove by, he could have sworn she visibly relaxed.

"We've got another important landmark coming up," he said. "Coffman's Hardware."

She frowned. "Why's that important?"

"For one thing, I'm there about twice a day to pick up something for a job. For another thing, it's one of our most dependable cell phone hot spots. Well, a warm spot, anyway."

He'd seen her peeking at the phone in her lap ever since they lost reception on the highway that climbed up the mountain. Scott saw that look all the time on tourists in Tall Pine—checking for signal bars as if they were stranded aliens hoping for communication from the mother ship. If Liv was going through similar withdrawal, she'd have to get used to it. For now he gave her the benefit of the doubt. The last she'd heard, her mother was in urgent care. Watching for some word from her sister would be the natural thing to do.

At Coffman's Hardware, he pulled to the curb and tried not to eavesdrop, although that was hard to avoid from less than two feet away in the cab of a truck.

"Rachel?" Liv held her cell phone to her right ear, away from Scott. "How's Mom? What happened?"

And then there was nothing to hear for a couple of minutes, as Liv sat stock-still and listened. She brought her left hand below her temple, rubbing in small circles. Her breathing was slow, quiet, schooled.

"So it could have been a lot worse," she said. Then quickly added, "Thanks for taking care of her. We're not far away. Right by the hardware store. We'll be there in . . . ten, fifteen minutes, I think." She glanced at Scott.

Of course, from his side of the conversation, he didn't know where they were going. He shrugged. "Close enough." After all, it was hard to be more than fifteen minutes away from anything in Tall Pine.

When Liv hung up, she turned to Scott. "They're back at my mom's house. I can direct you."

No point in mentioning he'd been there himself. With Tall Pine's quirky roads, it would still be easy to botch a turn. He sat silently behind the wheel and let Liv's directions take them to Faye Tomblyn's house, about three-quarters of a mile off Evergreen Lane. The little clapboard home boasted a nice coat of fresh-looking white paint, with deep green trim. Scott gave a mental nod of approval to whoever did the upkeep or had chosen paint durable enough to withstand the intermittent rain and snow of their mountain winters. On the other hand, he wasn't sure he cared for the creepy-looking plaster gnome that guarded the front porch—

He'd barely come to a stop in the driveway before Liv was out of the truck, rushing up the walkway at a near run.

Her sister, apparently, was like-minded, because the front door opened before Liv reached it, and Rachel burst out.

Watching the reunion between the two sisters, Scott quickly decided he didn't know Liv Tomblyn as well as he thought.

Chapter 2

As Rachel came running out to meet her, Liv's heart caught in her throat. Again.

Her frantic visual scans through the airport would have been much easier if she'd been able to keep in mind the fact that Rachel was seven months pregnant.

"Liv!" Rachel cried, and crashed into her.

"Rachel!" Liv cried, and crunched her little sister into her arms.

Her *big* little sister, because Rachel's pregnant stomach bulged between them, as firm and round as a basketball. Liv giggled and sobbed at the same time as she stepped back.

"I can't believe it," she said. "My little sister . . ."

"Big as a house?" Rachel interjected, and they both laughed, sobbed, and hugged again.

Words welled up in Liv's throat and mind, too many to keep up with. *I'm sorry I was gone so long. I'm sorry about Nammy. I'm sorry . . .* She set the warring emotions aside and went to something useful. "How's Mom?" As if they hadn't covered it already on the phone ten minutes ago.

"She said she was in a hurry getting ready and she didn't see the throw rug in the kitchen and she just—fell. Hard, on the kitchen floor. I know, it's like one of those bad old commercials. 'I've fallen and I can't get up . . .'"

Liv's stomach clenched. Her grandmother dead and her mother falling down in her own kitchen—it was too much to take in. "But she's okay?"

Rachel patiently repeated what she'd said on the phone. "It looks like a sprain. But the urgent care physician said she should see her regular doctor for a follow-up next week."

Liv became dimly aware that Scotty Leroux had followed her out of the truck and now stood behind her, tall and silent as an oak tree. She should thank him and let him know he was free to go, but that felt rude.

She turned and got no clue from his expression. Once again, he looked more serious than she remembered.

"I need to go in and see my mom," she said. "Want to come in for a minute?"

Like Liv, Scotty seemed unsure. After a moment he nodded, and they went inside. Liv was assaulted, as she had been on the drive through town, with a sensation of the familiar and the foreign. The living room carpet, still dark brown, maybe a little more worn looking than the last time she'd seen it. The walls, that honey tone they'd helped Mom pick out after their father died, when it was important to find something to do that would occupy their minds. Her mom, sitting in the easy chair that had always been her favorite.

Seeing her little sister pregnant had been a shock, an adjustment. Seeing her mother—

Faye Tomblyn sat with her right foot propped up on a kitchen step stool that now served as a makeshift footrest. A pair of crutches leaned against the arm of the couch beside her. She started to stand, but both daughters immediately shouted her back down into her chair.

"Mom." Liv bent down, engulfing her mother in a gentler version of the crunch she'd given Rachel outside. With her mom's chin hanging over Liv's shoulder, she knew her mother couldn't see the insistent tears prickling at her eyes.

Liv *had* to get a grip. Half an hour in Tall Pine, and she was turning into a leaky faucet.

But Mom looked so much older than she had when Liv flew out for Rachel's wedding four years ago. Rachel and Brian lived just a few hours away in San Diego, and Liv knew her sister visited often, so for Rachel, the change would have been more gradual. For Liv, it was jarring. The scattered strands of white she remembered seeing in her mother's auburn hair had turned into a full-on dusting of gray; it made up nearly half of her hair color now. Her jawline was a little blurred, a little softer, as if the ten or fifteen extra pounds she'd gradually gained over the years had finally started to show in her face. And those crutches, propped against the sofa . . .

Just a silly accident, Liv reminded herself. Mom had been in a hurry. It was a wonder she'd wanted to come with Rachel to the airport at all. Her mom had always hated airports, with all their turmoil and confusion.

Liv blinked hard and pulled back resolutely. She focused on her mom's familiar gray-blue eyes. They still looked the way Liv remembered, the same way they'd looked all the times Mom had scooped Liv up after *she* fell down.

"Mom," she said, mock scolding. "What did you do to yourself?"

"The rug was in my way," her mom said. "I tried to show it who was boss. I lost."

Liv melted into another hug, no longer caring that she was crying, until she remembered Scotty standing behind her like a long, tall shadow. Poor guy. She shouldn't have brought him into the middle of all these female hormones.

She stood again and wiped her eyes before she turned in his direction. Sure enough, he stood a few steps back, as if waiting to be of service. "You know Scotty, right?" she said to her mom.

"We all know Scotty," Mom said. "Thanks for getting Liv here."

Scotty nodded awkwardly, and Liv once again had the feeling she'd missed some developments at home while she'd been gone.

"I'm sorry about Nammy," he told her mother, and Liv did another mental double take at his use of the family pet name.

"She appreciated you," Mom said.

Okay. Liv had missed *way* too much.

"I'll be right back," she told her mother. "Let me walk Scotty back out."

Silence engulfed them as they stepped outside the house Liv had grown up in. Yet she felt as if she was more out of place here than Scotty.

"It's okay," he said. "You don't need to walk me—"

Liv led the way to the battle-scarred truck, and Scotty followed, his long legs catching up with her easily. When they reached the truck, he cracked the door open. But his eyes were on her, and once again Liv wished for the couple of extra inches her shoes usually gave her.

She breathed in the dry, bitter cold that surrounded them, seasoned with the scent of pine trees. So different from the air in Dallas. It was midafternoon in late November; it would get colder still in the next few hours.

"Scotty, I'm sorry," she said. "I never said thank you, did I?"

He gave her a warm smile, and this time she didn't suspect him of laughing at her. "You're welcome. I was glad to do it. And I'm glad your mom's going to be all right. I know it's a strange kind of homecoming for you."

Liv nodded mutely, reminded once again of her reason for being here. She'd forget for minutes at a time, and then Nammy's loss would hit her again, catching her off guard.

Tomorrow was the memorial service. Then maybe it would *really* be real.

"Well, I'm sure I'll see you around," Scotty said. That lazy smile toyed at his lips, then vanished. "For one thing, you guys will probably be needing the truck. Nammy accumulated a lot of stuff."

They stood facing each other like a customer and

a store clerk who weren't quite sure how to end a transaction. For a second she thought he might try to give her some kind of consoling hug. But they'd barely known each other before; common sense must have prevailed. He turned toward the truck.

"Thanks again, Scotty."

Keys in hand, he turned back. "No problem. Just do me one favor." One corner of his mouth tipped up at her. "Call me Scott."

"What?"

"Nobody calls me Scotty anymore, except . . ." His smile widened ruefully. "Well, everybody. But I keep trying."

She nodded. "I'll try to remember."

"That's all a guy can ask." He swung up into the front seat, barely *up* at all for him. "Maybe one of these days it'll take."

Liv discovered their old bedroom was now a guest room, and Mom had traded in the two twin beds for one double. The top of the long dressing table on the left wall held a tidy display featuring eight-by-tens of Liv and Rachel's senior portraits, a wedding photo of Rachel and Brian, and the marble-mounted pen set Liv had been awarded as class valedictorian.

"Roommates again," Rachel said.

"It looks nice." Liv contemplated the slightly unfamiliar room. "A lot less cluttered than it was when we were both crammed in here."

But without even closing her eyes, she could see the dressing table littered with clutter, most of it

17

Rachel's: nail polish, makeup, spare change, ticket stubs, drinking glasses that left water rings and drove Liv nuts. Keeping their things cleanly divided and separated had been impossible, and it had been a bone of contention between the two of them the whole time they were growing up. When Liv went to college and shared a dorm room with someone who wasn't her sister, she'd needed to keep all her belongings condensed on her own half of an even smaller room. It had taught her the value of making the most of space.

Four years of college had sharpened her business sense, but as it turned out, living in a dorm had been the training ground for her livelihood.

"So, what's up with Mom, really?" Liv asked. "*Why* did she fall?"

Their mother had managed to stay awake another half hour after Liv came back into the house. But then the pain pills from the urgent care doctor had kicked in, and she'd started nodding off. Liv and Rachel had sent her to the master bedroom to lie down.

"As far as I know, just what Mom said," Rachel answered. "She was in a hurry, she tangled with the rug, she fell."

"Does it sound right to you?"

"It's the kind of thing that could happen to anybody."

Liv frowned. "I know she's just laughing it off. But it seems strange to me. Did you ask the doctor—I mean, is she having some kind of balance problem or anything?"

"I didn't think to ask. I mean, Mom was right there. She can talk."

"Unless she didn't want to bring it up. Sometimes people can get defensive when they're . . ." Liv's voice faded away. She couldn't say it.

"When they're what?"

Liv gulped. "Getting old."

"Liv!"

"Sorry." Liv rubbed her aching jaw muscles with her fingertips, trying to get rid of the tension. "She just looks a lot grayer than she did the last time I saw her."

Four years ago. *And whose fault is that?* She didn't know if Rachel was thinking the same thing, but Liv winced inwardly anyway.

"Mom's a long way from old," Rachel said.

Liv was silent, not wanting to put her foot in her mouth, but thinking that fifty-seven wasn't far from sixty. Wasn't sixty officially senior-citizen territory? She didn't want to think of their mom that way, either.

"Well, the urgent care doctor did want her to see her regular doctor," Rachel said. "We can ask more questions then."

Visions of brain clots and other unknown maladies reeled through Liv's mind. "When can she get in to see him?"

"At this point, you know what I know." Rachel lifted her shoulders. "We only got home about fifteen minutes before you called. It's Saturday. We could phone his answering service, but I don't think there's much point. It doesn't seem like something he'd drop everything for on his weekend, and tomorrow afternoon is

Nammy's memorial service. I say we call first thing Monday morning."

Rachel sounded a little edgy, like a witness being cross-examined, but her tone stayed even. Liv decided not to press. Even if she did wish Rachel had found out more.

"Sorry," Liv said again. "You've been dealing with this for the last few hours, and I'm just catching up."

Rachel's shoulders relaxed, and she turned to survey the room again. "Looks smaller, doesn't it?"

"You've had it to yourself the past few days. I imagine it just got smaller with me in it."

"Brian and I stay over together sometimes." Rachel bit her lip and grinned. "Yeah, this is smaller."

Liv returned the grin, feeling the tension evaporate. "You'd better not snore. Anymore."

"Are you kidding? I'm pregnant. I sleep with three pillows to keep from getting heartburn, and Brian says I snore like a buzz saw."

"Where is Brian, by the way?"

A shadow crossed Rachel's face. "He couldn't get away. They put him on a crew of firefighters to go up and put out that wildfire way up in Bakersfield, and they're still at it. Only twenty percent contained."

And Liv felt like a beast. Rachel's husband was five hours away, putting out fires. She had to be worried sick. That, on top of Nammy's death, and taking their mom to urgent care today. No wonder Rachel hadn't thought of all the questions to ask.

"I'm sorry," was all Liv could think of to say.

"He'll be okay." There was a stronger set to Rachel's

shoulders than Liv remembered as she gave a resolute shrug.

Last time Liv had seen Rachel, she'd been a bride, and that had been hard enough to wrap her head around. Now she was the wife of a firefighter, and a mother-to-be. Time had moved fast since Liv had been gone. Everyone seemed to have changed so much. Even Scotty Leroux.

Which brought another question to mind. "What's the deal with Scotty? How'd he get to be the first person you called to pick me up?"

"He helped Nammy a lot. You know, little repair jobs. She got pretty attached to him."

"That's what he said." It made sense, Liv supposed. With their father and grandfather both gone, Nammy would have needed someone for help with heavier work.

"Mom thought of him," Rachel added. "By the time I got here she'd pulled herself up into one of the kitchen chairs, and she pointed me to his business card on the fridge. He's done some work here, too. He got that ceiling fan in the living room to stop going *whump, whump, whump.*"

"Really? It's done that ever since I can remember."

"I guess Nammy got tired of hearing it when she came over. She's the one who sent him to fix it."

And he'd already volunteered his truck to help when they started clearing Nammy's house. It looked like she'd be seeing quite a bit of Scotty—or Scott—while she was here, unless they found some alternative. Liv had mixed feelings about that. He seemed nice enough.

But she didn't like hitting people up for favors any more than she had to. And after her last breakup, she wasn't anxious to deal with anything male.

Rachel broke in on Liv's thoughts. "Do you want to lie down for a little while, as long as Mom's napping? You're probably bushed from the trip."

Liv shook her head. "I'm pretty wound up. I'd rather—do stuff. What's going on with the memorial service? Is there anything we should do to get ready?"

"It's one o'clock tomorrow at the church. There's going to be a lunch, but they've got volunteers to set it all up. So, Pastor Tom is going to say a few words. He was here the other day, and it's supposed to be pretty upbeat. I guess Nammy talked to him at some point, let him know that when she—went—" Rachel looked away and blinked. "She didn't want a *funeral*. Some of her favorite songs, but happy ones. And they're doing an open microphone thing where anyone can come up and . . ."

Rachel's voice faltered, and Liv nodded. "I get it."

Liv almost risked another hug, but that would probably get both of them bawling, and from what Rachel said, that was *not* what Nammy wanted. Liv grabbed a tissue from a handy floral box on the corner of the tidy dresser and thrust it in front of Rachel's face so she could see it.

"Thanks." Rachel dabbed her eyes and blew her nose with a honk that made them both laugh. Better.

When Rachel looked up at Liv, mascara was delicately smeared under Rachel's eyes. Everything about Rachel was always dainty. Several inches shorter than Liv, she'd inherited their mother's fine-boned build, one of the things that made the pregnancy look so incongruous. Liv was tall, like their dad. He'd died in a car accident when Liv was a senior and Rachel was a freshman.

Compared to that, losing a grandmother should be easier. Given Nammy's age, it wasn't a total shock. But it still felt a long way from easy.

"How are *you* doing?" Rachel asked. "Are you okay?"

Liv's eyes prickled. "Yeah. Probably about the same kind of *okay* as you. It's got to be so much worse for Mom."

Unshed tears blurred Liv's vision, and she wondered if maybe that was why Mom tripped. Blurry eyes were to be expected at a time like this. Liv just didn't want them.

She blinked hard and sniffed. Rachel reached past her, snatched another tissue, and waved it in front of her. They both gave another shaky laugh.

"Okay," Liv said, once she'd stopped the leakage before it could really start. "The memorial. Is there any kind of a photo display?"

Rachel contemplated her own crumpled wad of tissue. "Mom lent Pastor Tom a couple of framed pictures when he came over. One is that *awful* one of all of us in front of the Christmas tree, when I had that hideous perm—"

"And I'm wearing the sweater that made me look like a linebacker?"

"No, you didn't," Rachel said, unconvincingly.

"Anyway. What if we raid the old pictures and try to put something together? You know, something people can look at in the lobby. We can start while Mom's lying down. I don't know how hard it'll be for her. After we get some photos picked out, we can show her what we've got and see if she wants to change anything."

"Like *that's* going to keep us from crying."

"Maybe not. But at least it'll keep us busy."

Chapter 3

Scott contemplated the board of photos propped up on a table in the front lobby of the church. In the pictures, Liv's grandmother progressed from a bride on black-and-white film to the woman he'd known these last few years. The display hadn't been here a couple of hours ago when he arrived to help set up tables and chairs in the fellowship hall. Liv and her family must have brought it. He had a feeling they'd been up most of the night putting it together.

The last photograph showed Nammy poised behind a birthday cake, candles aflame, trying to wave the camera away. Her eightieth, he guessed. People didn't usually go in for *that* many candles every year.

She hadn't colored the gray out of her hair, but she wore a red dress, and her eyes sparkled. Two things older people often lost: color and sparkle. Nammy never had.

Scott cleared his throat and stepped back. In the lobby behind him, people were filing into the church's main sanctuary for the service. A *lot* of people; he'd better go in and find a seat. He turned and crossed the gray slate floor of the lobby to accept a single-sheet program—was that the word for those things?—from Millie Bond, another older lady who didn't look her age. Unlike Nammy, Millie colored her hair a pale blond that was probably her original shade; it looked good on her. Of course, it ought to. Millie ran the hair salon just off Evergreen Lane.

"Scotty." How anyone over seventy could so be perky was beyond him, but Millie managed it. "Nice of you to come."

"Thanks, Millie."

He noticed that she wore a bright green scarf—one that she'd knitted herself, if Scott knew Millie. The splash of green reminded Scott that this was the Christmas season, and that Nammy had let it be known that she didn't want somber, drab clothes at her memorial. He'd taken her to heart and worn his blue pullover sweater, hoping he wouldn't stand out like a sore thumb, so Millie's scarf was encouraging.

He stepped in through the sanctuary's oak double doors and stood aside so he wouldn't block traffic while he got his bearings. It felt a little like going to a wedding where you weren't sure whether to sit on the bride's side or the groom's. He didn't know where he fit here. But then, most of the people at the service didn't appear to be family. They were faces he saw around town every day. A lot of them were older folks, but by no means all.

He saw Sherry Poehler from the Pine 'n' Dine walking down the center aisle by herself, apparently searching for a seat. That might be a good way to go. They'd graduated in the same class, and they knew each other pretty well. Or maybe that would kick up a new rumor. He didn't need that.

Sherry sat down with Tiffany and Chloe, two other waitresses from the diner, rendering the point moot. Tiffany had broken up with Scott in March. There weren't any hard feelings, but it would make for an awkward seating arrangement.

If his parents hadn't left last week on a holiday cruise, like a couple of crazy kids, this would be easier.

Reluctantly, Scott moved forward and made the obvious choice: there was still an empty seat next to his uncle, Winston Frazier. Winston would talk his ear off if he got half the chance, and of course he'd sat near the front, where Scott's head had more chance of blocking someone's view. His uncle did, however, have the distinction of being the one person in town who actually called him Scott.

"Hi, Winston." Scott noted that his uncle had gone with a stern gray suit.

"Scott." Winston turned without surprise as Scott took his seat, and Scott grinned at the old man's concession to Nammy's wishes: an electric-green tie with a cartoon image of Frosty the Snowman. "Fashionably late, I see."

"I'm not late, I—" Scott turned to see that the crowd filing into the church had slowed to a trickle. "What time is it, anyway?"

"One-o-two. You'd know that if you ever wore a watch."

"They kept breaking." Or getting lost. Or he'd forget and wear them into the shower. He'd finally settled for keeping time on his cell phone, but that involved getting the thing out of his pocket. If it stayed in his pocket, he was less likely to lose it.

"The flowers are nice," Winston said. It was always refreshing to hear his uncle say something positive. "She didn't want people to buy anything they'd just have to throw away."

Scott followed Winston's eyes to the front of the church. The stage was clustered with potted plants, mostly poinsettias because of the time of year. Scott hadn't realized poinsettias came in so many colors. Most were the traditional red, and several were the pale yellow-white variety, but he also saw some streaked with pink, blue, or even lavender. Other potted flowers dotted the stage in shades of red, orange, and purple. Very little white. It looked as if Nammy had gotten her message across.

No casket, of course. That would have been at the top of the list of things Olivia Neuenschwander didn't want.

On the center of the communion table at the front of the church, someone had set a Christmas cactus between two framed photos of Nammy: a larger version of the wedding picture and a photo of her with Liv, Rachel, and their mother in front of a Christmas tree.

The family photograph made Scott's eyes go where he realized they'd wanted to go all along: the front row of pews.

Nammy's little family sat in the front row of the center section of pews. Liv was at the end, with their mom in the middle and Rachel on the other side, flanking their mother like two red-haired sentries. From his seat a few rows back, Scott was close enough to see Liv's profile as she gazed toward the photos on the table, her features composed and serious. Her rich chestnut hair spilled down the back of her dress, which was a deep plum color. Her mother had worn dark green and Rachel, a pastel blue.

Scott's eyes swept over the rest of the church and saw a slightly muted rainbow of shades scattered through the rows of pews. With Pastor Tom's help, the town of Tall Pine had definitely gotten the message.

Well done, Scott thought, glancing once again at Nammy in the center of the group photo.

Liv turned and said something to her mother, whose crutches were propped awkwardly between them. Faye Tomblyn smiled and dabbed her eyes with a wad of tissue.

Pastor Tom stepped forward, apparently satisfied that enough people had found their seats, and started to speak.

The service didn't turn out to be as difficult as Liv expected. Pastor Tom had known Nammy for a couple of decades, after all. He had plenty of stories to tell, and he kept the tone lighthearted and positive.

It had been harder to deal with the friendly concern from everyone they ran into before the service started. Liv quickly lost count of the number of times someone asked her *How are you doing?* or *Are you okay?* She heard it from everyone from Nammy's friends to Liv's former classmates. Every time someone asked how she was, it felt like an invitation to crumble.

She couldn't crumble. Mom needed her. Rachel needed her.

So far Mom seemed to be doing as well as Liv or Rachel, but she supposed mothers were conditioned to put up a strong front for their kids. Or maybe the pain medication was acting as a buffer.

At the pulpit, Pastor Tom sounded as if he was wrapping up, and Liv realized she'd missed the last ten minutes of what he'd said.

"Ecclesiastes isn't one of the feel-good books of the Bible, so I'm not sure if Olivia would want me to quote it. But I think a few of the verses apply today. 'To every thing there is a season . . . a time to weep and a time to laugh; a time to mourn and a time to dance.' Most of you probably don't feel like dancing right now. However, Olivia wanted every one of you to know, emphatically, that this is *not* a time to mourn. While she was here, she brought all of us a bit of her joy. And I know it's her joy that she wanted to leave behind."

Liv closed her eyes, forced herself to relax, and wondered why she hadn't stashed an extra tissue in her coat pocket. Oh, wait, she had. She'd given it to Mom.

Finally they rose as Pastor Tom invited them to join in a few more of her grandmother's favorite songs. When the worship leader started on "Leaning on the Everlasting Arms," Liv knew she was in trouble. Because she knew exactly why Nammy had picked it.

The song showed up in *Night of the Hunter,* a movie their family had watched with Nammy when Liv and Rachel were little girls. It was sung, menacingly, by Robert Mitchum, who played an evil preacher in the movie. Afterward, Liv and Rachel could never hear the hymn the same way again. They'd think of Robert Mitchum lurking in the shadows, and they'd elbow each other and giggle. And Nammy knew it.

Liv did all right until they got to the chorus. Then she made the mistake of looking at Rachel, whose eyes gleamed with humor, because she got the joke, too.

Crying at your grandmother's funeral was understandable. Getting the giggles—no.

Liv bit vigorously into her lower lip, but she knew it wouldn't be enough.

She stood with as much decorum as she could, gave her mom's arm a squeeze so she wouldn't be worried, and headed for the nearest exit. To her relief, there was a side door on the right side of the room, not far from their row. She pushed her way through it and got as far as she could down the hall before the laughter escaped.

She held her hands to her face, hoping to muffle the sound. The door had felt heavy; hopefully that would help, too.

She stood against the wall, laughing until tears came, aware that those tears could turn into something else if she didn't watch out. Nammy's private joke was just the tip of the iceberg. So many emotions were close to the surface, she couldn't name them all. So she bit her lip again, wiped her eyes, and started pulling in slow, deep breaths.

At least no one had followed her out to ask her if she was okay.

She strained to hear the music through the sturdy wooden door she'd escaped through and realized she couldn't. Hopefully, that meant no one on the other side had heard her, either. But how many songs would

31

come after "Everlasting Arms," she wasn't sure; probably just one or two. She hurried to the ladies' room to patch up her makeup before the service ended.

On her way out of the ladies' room, she heard rapid footsteps and voices from the kitchen, just off the fellowship hall.

"Kelly! It's the last song!"

"This platter's almost full. But we still need at least . . ."

Liv couldn't make out the rest, but what she'd heard didn't bode well.

She walked through the kitchen's open side door and found two young women, a large bowl three-quarters full of what looked like chicken salad, several loaves of bread, and one platter laden with sandwiches. Based on the crowd she'd seen in the sanctuary, those wouldn't be enough to last five minutes in the buffet line.

"Liv." With her shorter haircut and a few extra years, it took a moment to recognize Kelly Billone from high school. "Are you doing okay?"

"I'm fine. How about you guys?"

The second woman looked a couple of years younger, and Liv remembered Kelly's little sister. Ramona, that was it.

Ramona's words rushed out. "We came to set up the sandwich platters before the service, but there weren't any sandwiches, and so Kelly ran out to get the stuff for the chicken salad—"

"Who was supposed to bring the sandwiches?"

"Jenny Ritter. She was fine when I made the reminder

call last week. But we found out this morning that she had to have her appendix out—"

"And so you two have been back here making sandwiches by yourselves for an hour?"

"An hour and a half."

"Good Lord," Liv said, then hoped that didn't count as taking God's name in vain. Especially in God's kitchen.

"Everything else is ready," Ramona said. "We took care of the table settings, and I got the side dishes set out while Kelly ran to the store."

"Okay," Liv said. "We can do this."

No point asking why they hadn't hollered *Mayday* an hour and a half ago. Liv's wheels started turning, because this was what she did best. *Organize.*

"You guys need reinforcements," Liv said. "Keep doing what you're doing, and I'll see who I can round up. Then maybe we can get an assembly line going. Thanks for your help."

"I'm sorry about your grandma," Ramona said as Liv spun for the door.

When the last song ended, Liv was nowhere in sight.

Scott had seen her make a quick exit out the side door and wondered if she'd broken down. Now he rose from his seat with the others and watched as the ushers escorted Faye Tomblyn and Rachel down the center aisle toward the exit. *Not my business,* he reminded himself. He wasn't family, after all, even if Nammy had almost made him feel like he was.

Faye's newly acquired crutches made their progress slow. When the two women and their escorts passed the last row of pews, the other attendees began to work their way to the center and side aisles. Winston was buttonholed by his old pal, David Radner, and Scott took the opportunity to break free. He'd probably end up having lunch with the two old men anyway, but for now, his steps drew him toward the main exit, weaving his way over to Faye, Rachel, and their ushers.

Just before Rachel and Faye reached the open double doors at the exit, Liv entered the sanctuary like a salmon swimming against the current. Scott saw her catch each of the two women in a brief hug, say a few words to them, and continue upstream into the exiting crowd.

She didn't look broken up. She looked like a woman on a mission, and she was heading straight for Pastor Tom, who'd stopped to chat with Millie. Then she veered off to talk to Sherry, of all people, while Tiffany and Chloe stood by. As Liv spoke and gestured, the word that came to Scott's mind was *purposeful*. After a brief conversation, Sherry nodded and moved quickly for the exit, both of her friends in tow.

Scott caught up to Liv just as she caught up to Pastor Tom.

"Pastor Tom—" Liv broke off and started over. "Thank you. That was a wonderful service. I know my grandmother would have loved it."

The pastor nodded pleasantly, as if waiting for the rest.

Liv paused to take a breath. "We hit a snag in the kitchen. The sandwiches aren't ready yet."

We? Liv was running the kitchen now?

"Can you make an announcement that lunch is on the way? I rounded up a few extra volunteers, and I'll get some appetizers on the tables while people are waiting." Liv meshed her fingers together, the fidgety gesture the only indication that she was nervous. Her nails gleamed deep burgundy; when in the world had she found time to paint them? "We can start the open mic and . . . could I ask you to speak a little more? To fill some time?"

Pastor Tom blinked, then shrugged amiably. "I'll give it my best shot. But fair warning: I used up my best material in the message just now."

Scott knew Pastor Tom was rarely at a loss for words, but asking him—or any preacher—to ad lib was generally not a good idea. It could get a little . . . well, talky.

Scott stepped forward. "I can help you fill."

They both turned, startled, to look up at Scott. With his height, it wasn't often he went unnoticed for this long.

"You?" Liv said.

"Well, if you want, I could see if Conan O'Brien is available."

"I'm sorry," she said. "I didn't mean—"

"Trust me. I have a big mouth."

He saw confusion in her serious hazel eyes and felt a tug at his heart. She might be all business on the outside, but Scott suspected the outside was a pretty thin crust at this point.

As she hesitated, he played his trump card. "Or I could have *you* go up and fill."

"Good—grief, no." Liv shot an uneasy look at the pastor. It was pretty obvious what she'd been about to say.

Good save, Scott thought, and winked at her. Liv reddened and bit her lip.

If Pastor Tom noticed Liv's near slip, he didn't react. He turned his attention to Scott instead. "Thanks. You're hired. I'll make the announcement and turn it over to you to start the open mic. People are usually a little hesitant about coming up first anyway—"

Both of them turned toward Liv, but she was already winging her way to the kitchen, making surprisingly good time on an improbable pair of deep purple high-heeled shoes.

Chapter 4

Liv found some crackers and dip on the buffet table, put them on smaller plates, and started distributing them to the guests seated in the fellowship hall. In the kitchen, Kelly, Ramona, and the waitresses—Liv's new heroes—were whipping up sandwiches at an impressive rate.

By the time Liv brought out the second load of cracker platters, Scotty was at the microphone.

"I learned a lot from her," he was saying. "She taught me some new expressions. 'You'd complain if they hung you with a new rope.' 'You're blind in one eye and can't see out of the other.' And my favorite: if you said 'excuse me' to Olivia, she'd say 'I excused a pig once and it died.' I'm still not sure what that one means."

He really *had* spent a lot of time with Nammy.

"She also taught me that no home is complete without a cross over the mantel and a horseshoe over the door. Sorry, Pastor. Olivia did like to hedge her bets."

Liv leaned against the kitchen doorway, riveted, while Scotty told how good Nammy's potato cheese soup had tasted when he came in from the cold after fixing a leak in the roof. The way Nammy had left her husband's painter's cap hanging on the coat rack after he passed away. The kinds of things Liv would have talked about herself, except there was no way she'd ever be able to step up to the microphone to get the words out.

This was harder than Pastor Tom's message. Harder than "Leaning on the Everlasting Arms," at that tipping point where she'd teetered between laughing and crying.

When tears threatened again, Liv took that as her cue to check on the sandwiches.

Thankfully, the platters were nearly full. Liv brought out the first big tray of sandwiches and set them at the head of the buffet table. Sherry followed, setting a second platter on the other side of the long table, so the guests could form two lines going down both sides of the buffet. As Sherry set her platter down, she smiled across the table at Liv.

She knew the ash-blond hair color Sherry wore now wasn't the same shade she'd had in high school. What had it been? Dark brown or light brown?

"Thank you *so* much," Liv whispered.

Sherry waved her off. "Anything for Olivia."

Liv turned to catch Scotty's eye and signal that the sandwiches were ready. He was already looking right at her. Liv's heart gave an unexpected lurch.

Behind her, Sherry asked, "Hey. Are you okay?"

Scott's voice cut through on the microphone, saving her from trying to answer. "I'm getting a signal from the kitchen," he said, his eyes still on her. "It either means lunch is ready, or it's time for me to sit down and shut up. Probably both."

A light chuckle rippled through the crowd, and Scott asked them to let the family serve themselves first. Mom would need someone to bring her a plate. Liv skimmed over the potluck side dishes set out on the buffet table, making note of some choices to relay to her mother, and headed over to join Mom and Rachel.

Rachel stood as Liv reached the family table, thoughtfully reserved for them near the microphone. It offered a great vantage point to see and hear people speak; not so great if you wanted a short walk to the buffet.

Liv hugged Rachel. "Go get started on your plate. I'll find out what Mom wants."

Once again, her little sister had been holding down the fort. As Rachel left, Liv turned her eyes to her mother, who looked fragile and tired once again.

The words escaped Liv's mouth before she thought: "Are you doing okay?" The same question she'd been tired of hearing all day.

"I think so." Most people wouldn't catch the quaver in Mom's voice, but Liv recognized it, even though she'd rarely heard it. The way Mom sounded when things *weren't* okay, and she wasn't able to hide it. Like when Liv's father died. Or the night they'd rushed Rachel to the hospital with a high fever. And today.

"I wish Bob was here," Mom said.

"You know he would be if he could." Mom's older brother, their uncle Bob, was in Minnesota recovering from gall bladder surgery. Liv lowered herself onto the edge of the folding chair next to Mom's and took her hand.

Mom's free hand went for her napkin. She dabbed her eyes, then gestured with the napkin toward the microphone Scotty had vacated. "That was really nice," Mom said, her voice fragile but steady.

They'd be hearing more reminiscences from the crowd once everyone filled their plates. Cheerful memorial or not, this would be an emotional afternoon.

"Everyone loved Nammy." Liv squeezed her mother's hand again, hoping she wasn't making it harder for Mom to fight back tears. "What can I get for you? They've got the sandwiches, pasta salad, potato salad—"

"You know what I like," Mom said, and Liv realized she did. Why press her mother for any decisions today?

"I'll be right back," she said, and hurried to the buffet table.

She dished up a plate for Mom. Took it back to the table. Realized Mom and Rachel didn't have drinks yet, and brought back two cups of punch. By that time, Sherry was taking her turn at the open microphone.

"If Olivia ever didn't show up Saturday afternoon for pie and coffee, I would have called 911," Sherry was saying.

Liv went back toward the kitchen to make sure the other two waitresses had been set free from their sandwich-making duties. What were their names again? She needed to find out and get them some sort of thank-you gift.

On her way, she crossed paths with Scotty Leroux, who was coming out of the buffet line, a plate of food in hand. His blue eyes caught hers again, the way they had so effectively even from across the room. It must be the sweater, she decided. It matched the color of his eyes almost exactly.

"Liv. Haven't you sat down yet?"

"I'm getting there."

"What are you doing?"

"Checking on the kitchen." Liv thanked God for her high heels; at least this time she didn't have to crane her neck to look up at him.

"I'm sure the kitchen's fine." He was studying her, and Liv had the feeling he was seeing a little too much. Maybe being nearer his eye level wasn't such a good thing after all. "Go sit," he said softly. "Sit down with your mom and sister. The crisis is over. You handled it. Everyone else can take it from here."

She nodded, her eyes drifting past him to her family's table. Mom and Rachel looked like a solitary little island. Mom's only sibling was in Minnesota. Rachel's husband was stuck fighting fires in Bakersfield. And she was running her shoes off trying to be *useful*.

Of course she needed to get back to them. What had she been thinking?

Scotty squeezed her arm, a gesture undoubtedly meant to reassure her. But for some reason Liv's legs wobbled.

He was still searching her face. "Are you okay?"

That question again. This time, with Scotty's eyes on her, it brought a huge, aching lump to Liv's throat. She swallowed hard and tried to will it away.

"I'm fine." Her eyes dropped to examine the texture of the knit stitches of his sweater. "Thanks for helping us fill time there at the beginning. You did a great job. Mom loved it."

"It was no problem."

She bit her lip. She didn't know how to end the conversation. Finally, she just stepped back. "Well, I'll see you."

She started back toward Mom and Rachel.

"Liv?"

She gulped and swiveled to face him again.

Scott asked, "Did you get any food?"

She hesitated, trying to remember. A plate for Mom, punch for Mom and Rachel . . . no, she hadn't. Liv eyed the dwindling crowd in the buffet line and debated whether to join it.

"Here." Scotty handed her his plate, squeezed her arm, and let go. "Go sit down," he reminded her, and he returned to the end of the line before she could argue.

The open mic went on for another hour.

"I tried teaching her to knit," said Millie Bond, who was at least ten years younger than Nammy. "But I just couldn't get her to hold still for that long."

"She could never resist buying anything with a little red-haired girl on it." That was Mrs. Swanson from the little Christmas shop, The North Pole. "Faye, Liv, Rachel—she always called you her girls. All three of you."

"I'll miss Olivia. For one thing, she was one of the few people who made me feel young." So Winston Frazier did have a sense of humor. Liv knew he'd been on the town council forever; somehow she'd completely missed the fact that he was Scott's uncle.

"She would have been happy to see the church was decorated for Christmas today . . ."

Good heavens, you'd think the woman was never home. She'd never given up driving, Liv knew, although Mom had worried about her on the mountain roads. Self-reliant to the end, Nammy had had her stroke in the public parking lot on Evergreen Lane a few days after Thanksgiving. An ambulance had been there in minutes, and she'd died quietly at Tall Pine Memorial Hospital shortly after Mom got there. All with a minimum of fuss.

One of the items Nammy picked up on that last shopping trip was bittersweet: a crib mobile of woolly little sheep, obviously for Rachel and Brian's baby.

Pastor Tom dismissed the gathering at four thirty, probably mindful of the fact that it would be dark soon. Mom looked tired, and Liv suspected another pain pill might be in order when they got home. But first, they had to wait through a procession of people who stopped by their table on the way out to give their condolences. And to ask if they were okay.

Finally, the crowd thinned. Liv and her family joined a slow cluster of people going out the church exit doors, which thankfully led straight to the parking lot without any stair steps. The cold air startled Liv, and she realized she hadn't thought to put on a jacket when they left the house this afternoon.

The half-dozen people in front of them halted just outside the door. Liv stopped short and rested a hand on her mother's arm, hoping to prevent a collision.

At first Liv couldn't tell why everyone was looking up at the sky, although it *was* pretty. The blue color was just beginning to deepen toward night, and she was surprised that the stars were already coming out.

Then she saw that the sparkles of white overhead were drifting slowly downward, and she heard hushed sighs around her. The sighs that came with the first snow of the season.

Liv gazed up at the glinting flakes. It wasn't coming down heavily, not yet, and their aimless twirling seemed to cast a spell. No one spoke. For the first snow to fall now, at the end of Nammy's memorial, seemed significant, almost holy. Liv didn't want to be the first one to move, even though she was shivering.

Mom and Rachel must be cold, too. She should take them back inside to wait while she brought the car up to the door.

Something warm settled over her shoulders. Liv reached up to find a brown corduroy coat draped around her, the bottom hem falling far past her hips. She didn't move. Without turning, she had a feeling she already knew whose coat it was.

"Wait here." Scotty's deep voice behind her was quiet, as if reluctant to break the silence. "I'll get the keys from Rachel and bring the car up."

Chapter 5

The next morning, Liv, Rachel, and their mother stood two inches deep in the snow that coated Nammy's front porch. Snow and crutches. Not a good combination.

But when they weren't able to get an appointment with Mom's doctor until tomorrow, Mom had insisted on starting the formidable task of sorting through Nammy's belongings. Liv could relate. She knew Mom wanted to *do* something. Sitting around wasn't in her nature.

Guess that's where I got it.

But going inside for the first time might be the hardest task of all, and Mom had the keys to the house buried in her purse.

"Hold on," Mom said, digging into another compartment while Liv wondered how long it had been since Mom cleaned out her purse. The organization gene didn't run strong in her family; no one was sure where Liv had gotten it.

She and Rachel each kept an arm linked through one of Mom's, which probably didn't aid with the purse rummaging, but they weren't about to see their mother do another face-plant on the snowy pavement.

Finally Mom fished out the keys on a ridiculous pink pig keychain and handed them to Liv. Liv dug her teeth into her lower lip as she unlocked the door, trying to pretend it was just any old lock in any old door. It was no use. The wash of memories hit her as soon as the door swung inward, and the indefinable scent of Nammy's home rushed out at her. What was it made of? A touch of potpourri, maybe, with some composite of Nammy's favorite soaps and cleaning products thrown in.

And sadly, it was already a little bit musty. How long since anyone had been inside? Less than a week. Maybe five days?

Liv took a deep breath, mindful that her mom's arm was still hooked through hers, and stepped across the threshold. Her mom and sister followed, like a human chain.

The assault of memories continued. The oval-shaped braided rag rug on the living room floor. The fake potted fern on its stand in the corner, because Nammy vowed she'd killed her last houseplant more than ten years ago. The wallpaper with ducks on the wing, because Liv's grandfather had liked it, so Nammy had never wanted to change it.

And, yes, her grandfather's painter's cap, hanging from the coat rack on the wall by the door.

Never mind Mom's crutches. Thirty seconds in the house, and Liv's own legs could barely hold her up.

"Let's get Mom a seat—"

"Mom, you need to sit—"

Liv and Rachel spoke at once, and they steered Mom to the nearest armchair. This wouldn't be a very efficient process; they'd need to work out a system where their mother could work from a central spot.

Mom propped her crutches against the arm of the chair. She was just beginning to get the hang of her new companions. "It's freezing in here."

She was right. Maybe literally. The snowstorm had ended somewhere during the night, and the day had dawned bright and clear. But it was still cold outside, and with all the snow on the roof, the house would hold a chill for a long time. Liv hurried to the thermostat in the hallway to switch the heater on, then went to find the stash of boxes she knew Nammy would have in the garage. Nammy had always hated letting a good box go to waste.

"I'm *still* freezing," Rachel said an hour later.

Deciding that the living room furniture could wait, they'd moved their operation into the combined kitchen and dining area, where the tile floor made things colder still. Despite all the moving around they were doing, the house was taking an inordinately long time to warm up. Liv went back to the hallway just off the dining area to check the thermostat. She frowned.

"It still says forty-two," she called to the kitchen, just a couple of steps down the hall from her. "I don't think the heater's kicking on."

"I never heard it," Mom called back. "It makes that clicking noise when it first comes on."

"Well, my fingernails are turning blue," Rachel said. "I think we'd better call Scotty."

Scotty, again. Liv should have seen *that* one coming. She fished out her cell phone. There were no reception bars. She walked back into the kitchen, but the display on her screen didn't change. "Where *is* there any reception around here?"

"Mom's house," Rachel said helpfully. "Sometimes when you get higher up it's a little better."

"So, what, I should climb on the roof?"

"No," Mom said. "You should use the regular phone, the way people have been doing for the past hundred years."

Liv sighed. Mom had never owned a cell phone and probably never would. Up in Tall Pine, the reception was so inconsistent, there just wasn't much use for them. She wondered if they'd even be able to reach Scotty. He was probably out working. Fixing someone else's heater.

As Rachel dialed the old black rotary phone on the kitchen wall, Liv had the feeling she'd fallen into a technological time warp.

She pulled up a dining chair alongside the one Mom sat in. They'd found an old needlepoint footstool for her to prop up her leg.

Liv caught herself asking, "How are you doing?"

"Not too bad," Mom said. "I like the Motrin better than that other stuff. It doesn't make me woozy. But all this—" She gestured around the kitchen.

"I know," Liv said.

With clients, it was easy to go into ruthless-with-discards mode. She taught them to ask themselves basic questions: *What will I use it for? Would I buy it again if I lost it? What's the worst possible thing that could happen if I throw it out?*

But generally, she was helping clients deal with their own clutter, not a lifetime of someone else's belongings. Just about everything in Nammy's house held memories for at least one of them. Even the pots and pans had been hard, although everyone had a set at home. Rachel had kept a cast-iron skillet, and Mom had decided to keep the baking sheets.

Rachel was speaking into the phone now, but her voice had the recitation-like tone of someone leaving a voice mail. There was no telling when Scotty would hear the message.

"Maybe we should break for lunch?" Liv asked when Rachel hung up. "Go somewhere warm?"

Liv didn't usually procrastinate, but this seemed like a great time to start.

"It's not even eleven o'clock," Mom pointed out. "And we wouldn't be here if Scotty calls back."

"We could call back and leave him my cell—" Liv slapped her forehead. Her cell phone number wouldn't do any good if they were in a dead spot.

Rachel grinned at her. "Hang in there. You get used to it after a while."

Nevertheless, Liv took one more glance at her phone. There were no messages on the display, but did that mean anything? She realized she hadn't heard anything from Terri about the business since she got here. Hopefully that meant the holiday doldrums had set in, as expected. If an emergency did come up, it might be hours before Liv heard about it.

"Okay." Liv sighed and pocketed her phone. "Where were we?"

They'd started two piles in the living room: one to keep, and another one, nearer the door, to go. The to-go pile was bigger, but not by much. Liv girded her loins and pulled open the hall closet. Nammy's coats—not easy. Liv kept a bright red car-coat for herself, and Mom kept a cardigan sweater she'd given Nammy for her eightieth birthday. Clenching her teeth, Liv finally packed up the rest.

The boxes on the closet floor and on the top shelf all appeared to contain Christmas ornaments. "I'm surprised she hadn't started decorating yet," Liv said.

"She had a rule," Mom said. "December first. When I was little, I had to wait till December before I could put on the Christmas records. I would have driven her crazy otherwise. I played 'Rudolph the Red-Nosed Reindeer' all month long."

Liv grinned. Then her heart twisted. She'd heard the same story countless times from Nammy.

Rachel must have seen her falter; bravely, she reached past Liv and pulled out the two metal canisters Nammy had used for her tree decorations.

"Liv?" Rachel said uncertainly. "Maybe you keep one and I keep one? And Mom, you could go through and pick out your favorites?"

Mom nodded, her eyes glistening. "Let's don't open them right now."

"That's what I was thinking," Rachel said.

Liv silently hauled the two canisters to the to-keep pile. The growing stack would catch up to the to-go pile if they weren't careful. But she wasn't ready to sift through the Christmas ornaments either.

When Liv returned to the hallway, Rachel had dragged out a box containing Nammy's artificial tree and was reaching into the back of the closet. Her muffled voice exclaimed, "Holy cow! Is this what I think it is?"

Rachel hauled out a long blue-and-white box that Liv recognized immediately.

Liv gasped. "I didn't know she still had it." A surge of childhood nostalgia hit her. Taking over where Rachel left off, she pulled the box the rest of the way into the dining area.

"Look, Mom." Liv brought the box to rest at their mother's feet. "The silver tree."

For Liv, just looking at the closed box conjured up a host of warm memories. Inside would be the branches and base for Nammy's old silver aluminum Christmas tree—the kind that came with a color wheel to shine different shades of light on the branches. Four panes of plastic rotated in front of a bulb aimed at the tree, making the metal branches reflect red, blue, orange, and green. Nammy used to put the tree up when Liv and Rachel were little, and the two of them would sit on her living room floor for what seemed like hours at a time, watching it change colors.

Mom viewed the box with a little more reserve. "You're kidding. She kept it?"

At her less-than-joyful tone, Liv and Rachel exchanged a mutual look of betrayal. "Mom!"

Rachel added, "You mean you didn't like it?"

Mom flushed, as if she'd been caught in a guilty secret. "Not that much. But I knew you girls loved it."

Liv remembered her mother helping Nammy set up the tree for them, year after year. She didn't remember any complaints. "I never knew you didn't care for it."

"Maybe just because it was the first tree we had when I was growing up. Sometimes you want what you don't have. I was always kind of jealous of kids who had real trees. When I was older we started getting them from the tree lot at the home store, and I was glad. Nammy started putting up the old silver tree again for you kids when you were little. You got a big kick out of it." Mom nodded at the box with a rueful smile. "You've got to admit, it's pretty cheesy."

Liv lowered her eyes and studied the box reluctantly. Through the eyes of an adult, she supposed, it was sort of hokey. But still . . . "I wonder what kind of shape it's in by now."

She hadn't seen the silver tree since she and Rachel were in their teens. By that time Nammy had switched to a typical green artificial tree, most likely the first one Rachel had found in the closet. But what were they going to do with the trees now? None of them really needed either of the Christmas trees. They needed to start getting more practical, or they'd never make it through this.

The doorbell saved her from continuing the discussion.

"I'll get it." Liv nodded at Rachel. "You sit down."

Rachel hadn't complained about anything except being cold, but to Liv, it looked like her sister was tottering under all that extra weight around her middle.

Sure enough, Rachel plunked into the chair next to Mom with no argument.

"Coming," Liv called.

She opened the door and stepped aside to let in Scotty Leroux. Today he definitely looked the part of the handyman, wearing a warm-looking tan winter vest over a plaid flannel work shirt. Liv quickly closed the door after him, although the air outside didn't seem any colder than the air inside.

Were Nammy's ceilings lower than normal? Either the small home made Scotty seem even bigger, or he made the house feel smaller. Liv held herself up as straight as she could.

"I got Rachel's message," Scott said. "She wasn't kidding. It's like an igloo in here."

"You got here fast."

"I check messages every time I stop by Coffman's Hardware. It's a decent system." Scott looked over her head into the dining room. "Hi, Rachel. Hi, Mrs. Tomblyn."

"Call me Faye," her mom said. Scott already called her grandmother Nammy. Now he was going to call her mother Faye?

Liv walked past him to lead the way to the thermostat. It had to be her imagination, because he'd just come out of the cold himself, but the air around him felt warmer as she brushed past. "The thermostat's right here," she said unnecessarily. Scotty flipped down the plastic cover of the little wall-mounted box and gave it a cursory glance. She went on, "And I think the main unit is on the right as you go into the garage."

"That's the water heater. But thanks for playing." He

quirked a smile at her as he took one long step down the hall to the door that opened to the garage. The rush of air that came in from the garage was definitely colder than the air in the house.

"Wait here," he said as Liv started to follow. "You guys can—burn some kindling or something."

Liv stared at the door as it closed after him, hugging herself against the chill. Like Mom and Rachel, she hadn't taken her coat off. She returned to the dining area, arms still folded.

"He knows his way around here, that's for sure." Her lips felt almost numb, and she wondered if they were as blue as Rachel claimed her fingernails were.

"Well, he would," Rachel said. "He's been here a lot."

Liv wrapped her arms more tightly around herself—not just against the cold this time, but a strange, niggling feeling she couldn't put a name to. Except that Scotty had been here—for Nammy and maybe for the rest of her family, too—when she hadn't.

She shouldn't hold that against him. Holding it against herself . . . that was a different matter.

When you were six-foot-five and wore size fourteen shoes, sometimes it was hard not to stumble into the wrong spot. So Scott did his best to tread lightly when he came back into the roomful of women.

They were huddled around the kitchen table, as if for warmth. Liv was still standing, and his eyes went down to her shoes. Sneakers today. Patterned with blue roses.

"I think I got it going," he said.

Faye Tomblyn nodded. "I heard the click."

From overhead, Scott felt the initial rush of air from a vent in the ceiling, cold against the back of his neck. It would take a minute or two for the chilly air to clear out of the ducts; longer than that before the house felt habitable.

"It might be a good idea for me to wait a few minutes and make sure the heater keeps behaving itself," he said. "Do you have anything ready for me to take out? For donations or anything?"

He hated to ask, but after all, that was what they were there for.

"There's a stack over here," Liv said.

Arms folded, back straight, she led him toward a modest-size pile of boxes near the front door. Of course, they'd barely started. They'd been working just long enough to give the always-orderly home the disheveled look of a house where someone was moving in or out. A heck of a way to spend the Christmas season.

Scott loaded the boxes into the back of his truck, waving off Liv's offer to help. Three women, one of them pregnant, the other one on crutches—no wonder they'd hardly made any headway.

By the time he finished transferring the boxes, Liv and Rachel were boxing up dishes from the cabinet, embroiled in what sounded like a series of momentous decisions over coffee mugs. He wondered how and when they were going to deal with the furniture, but decided this wouldn't be a good time to bring it up.

Instead, he nodded at two stray boxes in the dining room near Faye's feet. "What about those?"

Glances between the women bounced around the room like an unleashed ping-pong ball.

"They're Christmas trees," Rachel said, looking uncertainly from Liv to her mom, and Scott could feel emotional undercurrents as surely as the warmish air that was beginning to spread its way through the house.

Women were always filled with undercurrents—unspoken thoughts that Scott had spent the past several years of his adult life trying to keep up with. Take those currents, multiply by three, then add in the grief over losing Nammy and the stress of sorting through her belongings. It was the perfect storm.

Nammy had been free of undercurrents, as far as he could tell. What you saw was what you got. Did women have to live that long to get rid of all those complex, unspoken nuances? It seemed like a waste of time to him.

While Scott waited for a judgment call, he noticed that Faye and Rachel's eyes had landed on Liv, as if they'd elected her their new, unofficial team captain.

"Okay." Liv closed her eyes. "Let's think about this. A Christmas tree spends eleven months out of the year boxed up in a closet . . . and you already have one, right, Mom?"

Faye nodded.

"Rachel?"

Rachel bit her lip. "Brian likes getting fresh ones."

"Okay. And I don't need one either. We can donate the green one, all right?"

Two nods. What other colors did Christmas trees come in? He supposed he'd seen some trees flocked with fake snow, but . . .

Liv nodded toward the older, blue-and-white box on the floor. "Now, what about the silver tree?"

A thick silence fell, and Scott did his best not to move.

"Well, I can pass," Faye said. "Do either of you girls want it?"

"Rachel?" Liv prompted gently.

Rachel slowly shook her head. "I guess not."

Liv sighed, and Scott thought he saw her shoulders drop as she bent to pick up the box, preparing to carry it to the door.

"I can get that," he said, taking it from Liv as she straightened.

It weighed practically nothing. Strange, for something that seemed to be a topic of such heavy debate. But then he realized she hadn't completely let go of the box, and something was swirling in her hazel eyes as they locked with his. Not as simple as tears; he'd seen signs of those yesterday.

If this house was the perfect storm of female turmoil, Liv was the epicenter. Liv, with her straight posture, practical thinking, and determination to get this job done.

They stood facing each other, supporting opposite sides of the long cardboard box. Liv didn't want to let it go, and Scott held on to his end as if, by doing so, he could help to hold her up. He didn't want to sway her and make what was obviously a hard decision harder. Then inspiration struck.

"I have an idea," he said. "There's a new little Christmas hotel in town. It just opened over the summer, and they're trying to put a tree in every room. Last I heard, they were still taking donations. I'll bet they could use these trees. That way you'd know someone was enjoying them."

Liv's lips quirked up a little. "A Christmas hotel?"

It was as close to a smile as he'd seen on her today, and some of that cloudy look seemed to clear from her eyes.

Liv's mom said, "It's really cute."

Liv turned toward her mother, her lips widening into a definite smile. "And what are *you* doing hanging out at hotels, Mom?"

She'd loosened her hold on the box; Scott set it down, gently, on top of the box that held the green artificial tree.

"They had a big grand opening this summer," Rachel chimed in. "Brian and I went there with Mom and Nammy. It was kind of a big deal around here."

"A Christmas hotel that opens in the summer?"

"It's a long story," Scott said. "But it's pretty cool."

"You really ought to see it," Rachel said.

And just like that, for some reason, his big old feet blundered ahead, probably straight into his mouth. "Want to see it now? You could ride along while I drop the trees off."

Rachel and Faye looked at Scott; Liv looked at her mom and sister.

"Go ahead," Faye said. "We'll wait here."

"I shouldn't leave you guys," Liv said, but Scott didn't hear any conviction.

"No, you should go," Rachel said. "It's adorable."

Liv cast her eyes around the room, and that invisible weight seemed to return to her shoulders. "We've got so much to do."

"No, go," Rachel said again. "We're good. The house is warming up, and we've got that pasta salad we brought from the memorial." She grinned. "We won't work too hard while you're gone."

Liv's shoulders relaxed a little, and Scott knew the battle was won.

Chapter 6

What had he been thinking? Scott wondered.

Once again, Liv sat in the passenger seat beside him, long hair cascading down her shoulders, a faraway look in her eyes. But he'd had the feeling Liv needed to get out of that house for a while, and the weakness of her protests had confirmed it.

He only knew one way to deal with it. The way he dealt with most things in his life: try to lighten the mood.

He broke the silence. "So, did you find any gold bricks yet?"

Liv turned from her weighty contemplation of Evergreen Lane. He wasn't sure she was really seeing anything outside her window. "What?"

"I was just thinking, with the amount of time Nammy lived there, you could run across just about anything in that house. Like buried treasure, or . . ." He trailed off. "Sorry. Lame joke."

Liv answered as if she hadn't heard him. "You really don't have time for this," she said. "We really appreciate everything you're doing. Be sure to let us know what we owe you."

"It's not about money. You know that."

He got the feeling Liv would have been more comfortable if it *were* about money. Something that clearly delineated what she owed him. One thing about her that clearly hadn't changed: she was an orderly, organized, list-making kind of gal. She probably didn't like balances left outstanding.

What this *was* about, Scott wasn't sure anymore.

Helping Faye and Rachel by picking Liv up at the airport was a no-brainer. It was what neighbors did for each other, and the fact that they were related to Olivia made the decision even more clear-cut.

Liv . . . not so clear-cut.

She was a complicated mixture of vulnerable and resolutely self-reliant. He couldn't tell which side tugged at him harder. He did have a soft spot for vulnerable women. But the way she'd taken over yesterday's kitchen crisis—that had been impressive. Even so, he'd caught that glimpse of the vulnerable girl trembling under the weight of it.

This morning, with her tousled hair and oversized college sweatshirt, it was obvious she hadn't expected anyone besides her mom and sister to see her today. She looked tired, distracted, and frazzled. And gorgeous. Probably even more so today than yesterday, because she wasn't even trying.

"Seriously," Liv was saying. "We're cutting into your time."

He waved her off. "Forget it. You know how things

work around here. Next time I'm in a pinch, I'll hit your family up for . . . I don't know, a casserole or something."

That got a smile out of her.

"You want casseroles?" she said. "We've got casseroles. Mom's fridge is full of them. She says people were bringing them in all week. Then last night, we spent an hour trying to fit in a bunch of leftover side dishes from the potluck. It was like a jigsaw puzzle."

Scott remembered. By the time he pulled Rachel's car up to the front of the church last night, several women had caught up to the three women to offer them a small arsenal of casserole dishes and Tupperware containers. Liv and her family had been visibly weary, but gracious, as the well-wishers loaded down the backseat.

After a moment of silent contemplation, Liv said, "I shouldn't have left them at Nammy's like that."

"You know something? I think they knew you needed a break."

"We just barely started, and there's so much . . ."

"Know something else? I think they needed a break, too. Unless they were just really dying to get into that potato salad."

"Pasta salad."

Whichever. "It's a lot to take on, Liv. It's okay to pace yourself."

"It needs to be done."

"I get that. But remember, your grandmother's memorial was *yesterday.*"

She looked out the window again. "You think I'm pushing too much?"

Scott fingered the steering wheel. He wasn't trying

to be hard on her. Just the opposite. "I think you're pushing *yourself* too much. Just remember, you're only human. And the first day is probably going to be the hardest. I imagine it'll get a little easier as you go."

"At least Rachel balances me out a little bit. She's so supportive with Mom."

At the word *supportive,* Scott saw the two younger women flanking their mother on the way out to the church parking lot, ready to steady her at the first wobble.

"You don't have any brothers or sisters, do you?" Liv asked.

"Nope. My folks decided to quit while they were ahead."

She sent him a puzzled frown.

"I was a hard act to follow," he said. "I think my mom's exact words were, 'Never again.'"

That surprised a laugh out of her. Good.

"I weighed eleven and a half pounds," he said. "And when I started walking and talking, I was even *more* trouble."

He felt her eyes on him. "When did you outgrow it?"

"Who says I did? *Outgrow* implies that somewhere along the line I grew up."

She was still studying him, he was sure of it. Then again, it was easy to get convinced someone was staring at you when you were trying so hard not to look at them. He was afraid she was going to say something embarrassingly serious.

Instead, she said, "I remember the senior prank."

Good. He was used to defending himself on that

one. "It wasn't just me," he protested. "The other guys just . . . left me holding the goose."

While the other seniors were doing something innocuous like toilet-papering houses, Scott and a couple of his friends had been thinking big. And talking bigger. So they'd kidnapped the rival school mascot, the goose of Mount Douglas High.

And ended up setting it free.

"It wasn't my fault," he protested. "When we got it back to Tall Pine High, we were going to put it in the principal's office. Two birds with one stone, so to speak."

Liv started to laugh.

"But when we got into the principal's office and opened the cage, that sucker fluttered out so fast, right for the door, like he'd been waiting for that moment all his life . . ."

"And you didn't think to close the door behind you first?"

He slapped the steering wheel. "That was Dane's job. He had *one job*."

She was laughing again. It felt good to hear her laugh.

"And who in the world knew the thing could really *fly*? I figured he had his wings clipped."

She tried to get her breath. "So, you had how many accomplices?"

"Three. You'd think four guys could've handled one goose. Ron was standing lookout, fat lot of help *he* was—"

"But you were the only one who got in trouble."

"Code of honor. I didn't name names. It was my car

they picked up on the security cameras, and the picture was pretty fuzzy . . . but I was a lot taller than the other guys. It was pretty obvious."

"The clown car. I remember."

Six-foot-four by the time he was sixteen, and he'd picked an orange VW bug for his first car. He had to admit, it was partly the ridiculousness of the size that had won him over. It was also a car he could afford on his salary from the local burger joint—and he'd been told Volkswagen Beetles were easy to work on.

"Yep. I took the rap. They almost didn't let me walk at graduation. My folks finally talked them into letting me work it off by doing landscaping work for Mount Douglas High over the summer. But you don't know the worst of it."

Scott glanced at her, and of course she was watching him.

He said, "People hold me personally responsible for the goose population at Prospect Lake."

"What? There were *always* geese at that lake. One of them chased me when I was four."

He nodded. "Still. Whenever that happens to anyone around here, they let me know one of *my* geese went after them. Now, am I wrong? You have to have at least *two* geese to make more geese. Unless I kidnapped a pregnant goose. And the Mount Douglas goose was male."

"How do you know?"

"Well, his name was Harold, for one. And I heard they made sure to get a male goose, because who wants to hassle with the eggs?" Scott shrugged. "I did my homework. You can't say I didn't case the crime scene."

They reached the turn onto the main highway, the one that had brought them from the airport. This time Scott continued up the mountain. The next town, Mount Douglas, was nearly an hour away.

"How far is it?" Liv asked. "I don't want to be gone too long."

He sensed a little tension returning as she twisted in her seat, as if to look back at the responsibilities she was leaving behind.

"It's not much farther." He slid a glance her way, enjoying her puzzlement and the slight element of mystery.

They were leaving Tall Pine proper behind, as the businesses alongside the highway grew farther apart. They passed a lumber yard, an ancient gas station, and the town's one and only car dealership. Then, open fields on either side of them. Last night's snow, still pristine and unbroken, shimmered in the late morning light. Scott squinted, wishing he'd brought his sunglasses.

Liv showed a fresh interest in the world outside her window. She blinked against the bright glitter of sun on the snow. "Wow."

"Nothing like this in Dallas, is there?"

The atmosphere in the cab of the truck shifted again with a new silence from Liv.

Women. It was too easy to say the wrong thing. *Give her another fifty years,* he thought.

A moment later a large sign with an arrow showed up on the right, marking a turn that otherwise would have been easy to miss. Fashioned from rustic wood—

pine, what else?—it looked as if someone had already gotten out here to brush away any snowfall that might have obscured the letters last night.

"'The Snowed Inn?'" Liv let out a laugh that was half a groan.

He could really get used to hearing that laugh.

"Not my idea," he said. "That's one bad joke you can't blame me for."

From the sign that marked the turn, it was just a few hundred yards to the inn itself—a long two-story building reminiscent of a ranch house or a ski lodge. It was flanked by pine trees that, ironically, had needed to be transplanted to the spot. Before that, the land had been a large vacant field. Scott watched Liv to see if she recognized the location. The uniform blanket of new snow surrounding the building would make it harder. The tall trees neatly outlining the far outer edges of the property would be the best clue.

Scott pulled up in the wide front driveway. "Any idea where we are?"

Liv frowned, then looked past the hotel to the trees that once would have formed a barrier to keep the people outside the property from seeing the big outdoor screen. "It's the old drive-in movie theater, isn't it?"

"A cigar for the lady," Scott said, and one of the wide double doors of the inn swung open.

He'd hoped Mandy would be the one to greet them, but it was Jake Wyndham who stepped out, wearing a pullover sweater over a collared shirt. Barely over thirty, Jake had come to Tall Pine from back East a couple of years ago and managed to get this place built literally from the ground up. People in town—the females, especially—often remarked that Mandy Reese had landed quite a catch when she and Jake got married.

Like most of the women in Tall Pine, Liv looked suitably impressed as the brown-haired, brown-eyed East Coast transplant walked up to the truck. Scott groaned inwardly. Not that it should bother him.

Then she murmured, "He looks really . . . preppy."

Scott laughed out loud as he climbed out to help Liv out of the truck. Not one to wait, she already had her door open. "Hold on," he said. "The driveway could be pretty slippery."

But by the time he reached her side of the truck, to his mild annoyance, Jake had beaten him to the gentlemanly act of giving Liv a hand down. It wouldn't do, of course, for The Snowed Inn to be held liable for a visitor taking a spill from the snow and ice in the driveway. But Scott knew Jake didn't think that way. No, Mr. Ivy League just had really good manners.

"Welcome to The Snowed Inn," Jake said, releasing Liv's elbow once she stood steadily on the ground. "I'm Jake." He cast a questioning glance past her to Scott.

"We come bearing Christmas trees." Scott rested his hand on the back of the pickup. "And I thought you might be able to give Liv the nickel tour while we're here."

"Absolutely. And thanks." Jake nodded to Liv before turning back to Scott. "Let's grab the trees and get out of the cold."

Scott picked up one box while Jake took the other, although it was hardly a two-man job. Scott winked at

Liv as she followed them inside, hoping his instincts were right and she'd like what she saw. Maybe that's what this errand was all about. His gut told him she needed some distraction and Christmas cheer. Especially this Christmas.

Chapter 7

Liv followed the two men as they set the Christmas tree boxes on top of the check-in counter in the hotel lobby.

Lobby didn't really describe the front area of The Snowed Inn.

With everything that had happened this week, Christmas had only peripherally entered Liv's mind. That changed when she walked through the door. The scents of pine, cinnamon, and crackling logs embraced her. Pine garland, red berries, and white lights served as accents on every available surface, from the mantel of the fireplace on the left wall to the banister of the curved staircase in the center of the room. A big Christmas tree stood next to the stairs, tinsel shimmering from every branch. Strung popcorn wrapped around the tree from top to bottom. Without thinking, Liv reached out and fingered one of the puffs of popcorn. Sure enough, it was real. She couldn't help but smile.

"I think she likes it." Scotty's voice pulled her attention past the tree, where he and Jake still stood by the gleaming dark wood check-in counter.

Liv stepped forward to join them, but she had trouble

keeping her eyes still. A six-foot nutcracker figure stood guard on the other side of the stairs, and the half of the lobby to the soldier's right was filled with cozy-looking chairs and sofas, as well as a second fireplace. Reluctantly, Liv dragged her eyes away from the unexplored half of the inviting room, joining Scotty and Jake by the counter.

"Thanks for the trees," Jake was saying. "How did we luck into two?"

She tried to think of the simplest way to condense the story. "We were going through my grandmother's things. Scotty said this would be a good home for them."

"This is Liv Tomblyn," Scott said belatedly. "She's—"

"Olivia Neuenschwander's granddaughter. Of course," Jake said, as if he should have known all along.

"You knew Nammy, too?" She was just about positive she'd never seen him before. And somehow, as friendly as he seemed, he didn't quite feel like a Tall Pine native.

"Mandy did. Mrs. Neuenschwander was one of her best customers at the Christmas store."

The Christmas store. Mandy Claus. Memories started to take shape in Liv's mind.

"I'm sorry about your grandma," Jake was saying. "I know she was over eighty, but things like this are never easy."

Yesterday so many people at the memorial had told her how nice it was that Nammy had stayed active up to the end, that she hadn't been sick. Other than her family, Jake and Scotty were the only people who hadn't tried to gloss over her grandmother's death with a well-meaning platitude.

71

"Thanks," Liv said, and meant it.

"So," Scott said. "About that nickel tour."

A door behind the counter opened, and a pretty dark-haired woman came in through it.

"Mandy," Jake called across the counter. "Two more trees."

The woman's face lit up in a ready smile, and Liv recognized her. Yes, it was *that* Mandy. They'd been in the same grade all through school. Somewhere around third or fourth grade, Mandy had made the local news when she told everyone she'd seen Santa Claus in her living room. Years of teasing had followed, and Liv remembered her as sweet but shy.

Mandy still looked sweet, and she might still be shy, but her smile was warm and easy as she came around the counter to join Jake. "Are these from you?" She looked from Liv to the boxes. Then back to Liv as recognition filled her eyes.

Liv said, "Hi, Mandy."

"Liv." Mandy abandoned the boxes and headed straight for Liv. "I'm so sorry about your grandma. I would have been there yesterday, but Mrs. Swanson asked me to fill in for her at the Christmas store. She didn't want to miss the memorial."

Mandy reached Liv, and they had that awkward moment of *Do-we-hug-or-don't-we?*

"Thanks," Liv said, and then took the hug.

"I worked at The North Pole shop until last year," Mandy said as she stepped back. "Olivia could never resist anything with a little red-haired girl. She talked about you and Rachel all the time. You've got—what is it, an interior design business?"

Apparently Nammy had a *lot* of trouble getting Liv's line of work across to people. "Home organizing. It's a little hard to explain."

Mandy looked puzzled, but beside her, Jake was nodding. So, at least one person in Tall Pine had heard of such a thing. Definitely not from around here, Liv decided.

"She specializes in closets," Scotty put in, although Liv was pretty sure he was still unclear on the concept. At least this time he wasn't making fun.

"I think she said you were opening a chain of them?" Mandy asked.

"We just opened a storefront about two years ago, that's all." It seemed Nammy had gone around telling people she could fly.

"Everybody always knew you'd do well," Mandy said.

Liv felt her face warm. She'd heard a lot of *that* yesterday, too. Voted most likely to succeed in the yearbook, alongside Mark Knopp. He'd been accepted at UC Berkeley and, as far as she knew, he hadn't been heard from since. Maybe he'd invented some kind of new computer superconductor that people relied on every day without ever realizing it was there. Or maybe Mark had just figured that it was easier to meet expectations when you weren't around.

"About that grand tour," Scott said again.

"About the Christmas trees," Liv began, at the same time.

Scott nodded at her, as if yielding the right-of-way. "Go ahead."

"What kind of trees are they?" Mandy asked. "Why did she have two?"

Liv stepped forward and fingered the brittle old blue-and-white box. If anyone could appreciate this tree, it was probably Mandy. "It's one of those old silver aluminum trees—"

"With the wheel that makes it change colors?" Mandy looked fascinated.

Liv caught a glimpse of Jake's face behind Mandy, his brow furrowing dubiously.

The nickel tour of The Snowed Inn turned out to be well worth the trip.

Jake and Mandy led them through each of the guest rooms upstairs, all currently vacant following the weekend crowd. Each room had a different decorating theme. The "Reindeer Room" featured reindeer figures and fabric patterns. "White Christmas" had a snowflake motif, with pine cones and gold accents to add color. "Heart of Christmas" was accented with red hearts on blankets, throw pillows, and a lovely quilted bedspread. At the far end of the hallway, a honeymoon suite was decorated in white lights and antique lace.

"Most of the rooms have Christmas trees," Mandy said. "But we're still short a few, and I really wanted to have one for every room in time for Christmas, so you're a lifesaver."

"After Christmas, will you take down the trees?"

Mandy and Jake exchanged glances.

"We're still talking about that," Jake said. "Obviously, Christmas never ends here. But having trees up just in December might keep the Christmas season a little more special."

"But since the guests aren't here year-round, the trees would be special year-round," Mandy said.

Jake smiled; it was obviously an ongoing discussion. "We'll talk about it in January."

Through most of the tour, Scotty hung back. Of course, he'd seen it before. And, as Jake and Mandy frequently pointed out, he'd installed a lot of the inner workings: wood-burning stoves, old-fashioned pedestal sinks, and all of the bathroom flooring, using brick or stone instead of the usual tile.

Another Mandy touch: decorative air fresheners gave off holiday scents like cinnamon, cider, pine, cookies, or apple pie.

"I can't handle the cookie or pie scents for too long," Jake said.

"They make him hungry," Mandy said.

They didn't quite finish each other's sentences, but the connection between them was obvious. Coming back down the stairs, Mandy led them to a set of double doors leading off the lobby. "This room is Jake's baby. We call it the Man Cave."

"I got to thinking some people—husbands, especially—might like a place they could go that's a little less Christmas-centric. So we did this."

The doors opened onto a large room where red and green gave way to earthier tones: a brown leather sofa, two easy chairs to match, and a bookcase on one wall loaded with volumes that didn't look like the usual *Reader's Digest* condensed books some people used as decorating props. A cabinet in the center of the bookcase wall held a flat-screen television. Another cabinet door opened to reveal a movie collection that filled several shelves.

In one corner stood a single concession to Christmas: a tall, skinny artificial pine tree decorated only with pine cones.

"Another handy feature," Jake said, "is it's really easy to get a conference table in here to use it for a meeting room."

"And do *you* hang out here a lot?"

"I thought I might, back when we were planning it. But in point of fact, no. For one thing, I'm usually too busy. For another"—he shrugged, casting a look Mandy's way—"the hotel's a home away from home. We wanted to give it that Christmas warmth, and I think we succeeded. I like it here and—no, I really don't burn out."

Jake led the way out to the unexplored section of the lobby, with all the tables and cushiony chairs. "Now, in here, we have Mandy's pride and joy. We just started this up last week."

A counter ran along the back of the room with several tall stools and a window for taking orders. "A hot drink bar," Mandy explained. "For coffee and hot chocolate. Jake didn't start off to go into the restaurant business, but I thought it would be a cozy touch."

"And Mandy makes the world's best hot chocolate," Jake added, standing next to his wife. "We just got this part going last week. We learned a lot about food service regulations." They exchanged a visible shudder.

"Care for a cup?" Mandy offered. "On the house?"

And Liv remembered, reluctantly, to check the time on her cell phone. No reception bars in here either.

But the time made her cringe with guilt. She'd left Mom and Rachel for too long, and surely Scotty had work to do, too.

"We'd better get going," she said reluctantly.

She directed a look up at Scott, who nodded. He'd been so gregarious in high school, always joking. It surprised her how quiet he could be. Had he changed, or had she known him that little?

On their way out, Liv took one more look back at the blue-and-white box on the counter, next to the other tree's much-newer box. It looked like a cast-off.

If there was a right place to leave the silver tree, it was here. It was just hard to leave it at all. Liv reminded herself of what she told her clients: *You can't keep everything.*

But for the first time in an hour, she felt melancholy grip her again. The little side trip to the Christmas inn had been a refreshing break, but she didn't know if it would make getting back to work any easier. A lot of tough decisions lay ahead at Nammy's house. Tough not just on her, but on Mom and Rachel, too.

She turned away resolutely and walked out through the door Scott held open for her.

She tried to concentrate on the present. "Thanks for bringing me," she said. "It sounds like you're responsible for half the innards of the hotel."

"Thanks." He tipped up a crooked grin at her. "Nobody notices the insides. Except when they're out of order."

They started back toward the truck. "How long have Mandy and Jake been married?" Liv asked.

"About a year and a half, I think."

"Is Mandy pregnant?" Something about the way she looked reminded Liv of Rachel, and that clichéd glow that pregnant women were supposed to have.

"Not that I know of," Scott said. "Although people around town are always taking bets on how soon that's going to happen."

He pulled the passenger door open for her, and she tried not to look back at the rough wooden door of the hotel. It didn't help. In her mind's eye, she could still see the abandoned box on the counter.

Hopefully The Snowed Inn and its clientele would get some enjoyment out of it. But they wouldn't have the memories. She could still see the way the tree had looked from her vantage point on Nammy's living room floor, the changing colors washing over the fake silver needles, the mysterious boxes of presents underneath. And Rachel beside her, always goading her to peek . . .

She didn't need the tree.

Where would she put it?

Staring straight ahead, she bit her lip.

"Liv?" She heard Scotty's voice beside her and realized he hadn't started the truck. "Are you okay?"

It must be the thirtieth time she'd heard that question in two days. It was the second time she'd heard it from Scotty.

It must have been one time too many.

All at once, the snow-frosted roof of the hotel outside Scotty's windshield blurred, and a sob rushed out of her. Liv's hands flew up to cover her face. But once the first sob escaped, she couldn't hold the others back. She bent forward, as if she could hide. She couldn't make herself stop. But she hated to have people see her cry.

"Hey." She felt Scotty's arms fold around her, pulling her against the soft down of his vest, and she buried her face there, surrounded by her own muffled sobs. Every time she tried to stop, they came back harder. It was like trying to hold your breath when you'd just run ten miles.

Eventually, that was what slowed her down: exhaustion.

She finally reached a point where she stopped to catch her breath, still pressing her face to Scotty's vest, mortified. How long had he sat there while she blubbered all over him? All without squirming or, heaven forbid, making some trademark Scotty Leroux joke.

She felt him lightly stroking her shoulder. "Better?"

She rested her cheek against his jacket, glad he couldn't see her face. "Just don't ask me if I'm okay again." A weak laugh sputtered out of her; she stopped it before it could turn into another sob.

"It's a deal." His arms loosened around her slightly, but he didn't seem in a rush to let her go or push her away.

She took another deep breath. "I'm sorry."

"What have you got to be sorry for?"

Probably he meant the question to be rhetorical.

But it brought another sob welling out, and to her horror, she heard her words spilling out with it. "I should have been here. I haven't seen Nammy in four years, and now I'll never see her again. And my mom's getting old and—"

"She's not old," Scotty said. "Remember, sixty is the new forty."

"She's only fifty-seven."

"See?"

She sobbed out another laugh, then rested against Scotty's vest as the truck filled with quiet. She felt drained, wrung out.

"Everything changed while I wasn't looking." She barely knew him, but she couldn't seem to keep the words from coming out of her. "I don't belong here."

Liv's stomach clenched as a half-formed thought rose to the surface: "You belong here more than I do."

"Hey." His arms tightened around her, just a little. "If you mean Tall Pine, that's because I never left. If you mean your grandmother's house, with your family— that's nuts."

She caught her breath with a shudder and waited for him to go on. Because if he had a way to make her believe that, she wanted to hear it.

"You know what I saw when you got to your mom's house?" he said. "I saw you and Rachel running at each other like a couple of speeding trains. I saw you jump in to help take care of your mom. If anyone can keep you three on track going through all that stuff, it's going to be you. And that's got to be one ugly job." She felt him smoothing her hair. "Just go slow. Don't push too hard, and don't expect too much. Not from your mom and sister, and especially not from yourself."

Just for a moment, Liv let herself relax against him. A feeling seemed to seep into her, a sense of strength that had nothing to do with how big he was.

Then Scott loosened his hold and cupped her face in his hands, brushing away tears. "You're doing *fine.*"

A shaky breath escaped her. She closed her eyes and willed herself not to cry any more.

"Now," he said softly, "do you want me to go in and get that tree back?"

She'd almost forgotten what set her off to begin with. But that was *exactly* what she wanted.

She nodded vigorously.

Scott walked back into the lobby to find Mandy and Jake contemplating their bounty. Facing three-quarters away from the door, they didn't hear him come in.

Mandy fingered the picture of the green tree on the side of the newer box. "I'll bet this tree is going to be perfect."

"Uh, Mandy, you're ignoring the obvious." Jake was looking at her with a wry grin. He tapped the blue and white box that contained the silver tree. "Where are we going to put *this* one?"

"Maybe we could give one of the rooms kind of an early sixties look." There was just a touch of uncertainty in her voice. "Call it the Retro Room or something."

"Sweetheart, the whole hotel is retro. But *antique* retro. If we change a room around to fit that thing, we'll have to call it the Kitsch Room."

Mandy wasn't convinced. "I'll bet it looks really nice lit up."

Scott cleared his throat. "Uh, guys. I think I've got your solution."

They turned. Mandy wore a guilty look, as if they'd been caught saying someone's baby was ugly.

Scott said, "Liv's seeing it as more of a centerpiece. Right here in the middle of the lobby. Maybe with a big brass plaque dedicating it to her grandmother. You know, about this big." With his hands, he formed a shape and size roughly equivalent to a tombstone.

For a moment they stood with frozen faces.

Mandy cracked a smile first.

Jake looked relieved. "Yeah, right."

"Actually, she was having second thoughts," Scott admitted. "Sentimental value." He paused. "Her little sister was pretty attached to it."

Jake stepped aside, gesturing expansively toward the box. Scott picked it up and tucked it under his arm.

"Tell her I'd really like to see it when it's set up," Mandy said.

When he returned to the truck, Liv was sitting up straight. Only her faintly red-rimmed eyes bore any evidence of the state she'd been in just a few minutes ago. He should have known it wouldn't take long for her to pull herself together.

He loaded the tree back into the truck and joined her in the front seat.

"Thanks," Liv said. No more sniffling, no more apologies. So they were back to normal.

Scott felt a vague, selfish disappointment. Of course he didn't want her falling apart and miserable, but it was perversely reassuring to see a chink in the armor. He'd seen Liv master her emotions time after time these past few days, but no one should be in control *all* the time. It couldn't be healthy. Could it?

And in that moment when she'd been sobbing in his arms, he'd had a feeling that was undeniably compelling. Protective? Concerned? Okay, those were part of it.

He'd felt needed.

Chapter 8

Liv braced herself as Scotty stopped the truck in front of her grandmother's house. The little one-story home, with icicles slowly dripping from the roof, didn't look formidable. The memories inside it were good. The task of sorting through them—*that* was formidable.

She'd kept Mom and Rachel waiting too long, and it was time to buckle down and do what she'd come here to do. Still, she didn't move. Not yet.

As she stared at the windows, Scott began, "Are you—"

She darted a look at him. Not *that* question again.

He broke off, then finished, "—ready to go inside?"

His arm rested on the back of the seat behind her, not touching her, but looking ready to catch her if she had another meltdown. She wouldn't. She'd checked the visor mirror a few minutes ago, and her eyes had just begun to lose their red-rimmed look.

On top of it all, Liv didn't know how she was going to explain the fact that, after all the discussion and careful reasoning, she'd come back with the silver tree.

"I'm fine," she said. "I'm sorry I—"

"Let's make a deal," Scotty said. "I stop asking if you're okay. You stop saying you're sorry. Or I get to clunk you with a great big stick."

Now, *that* was trademark Scotty Leroux.

Belatedly, she remembered that two days ago she'd promised to start calling him Scott.

"Deal," she said. She looked at the lace curtains of the house again, unable to see inside. But she thought she saw the lace move, as if someone had been peering out the window a moment ago.

"Just one thing," Liv added. "Can you put the tree in the trunk before we go inside?"

Inside, the temperature in the house was actually comfortable. Almost too warm, in fact, after the bracing air outside. Rachel was rinsing lunch dishes when Liv came in, so maybe she hadn't been watching at the window after all.

"Hey." Her sister turned away from the kitchen sink to greet them. "Come look what we found."

Mom fumbled for her crutches as she started to rise from her place at the kitchen table. Liv rested a hand on her shoulder, and her mother sank back down into her chair.

Liv and Scott followed Rachel down the hallway to a small wooden cabinet Liv didn't recognize. She certainly didn't remember the contents. Cans of new paint. A set of blue-and-white-patterned tiles. Another set of tiles, these in a mock-brick pattern. Several rolls of wallpaper. Liv pulled out a roll and unwound it slightly to get a good look at the pattern.

"Apples," Liv said. "These are cute." She called down the hall to the dining area. "Do you remember any of this stuff, Mom?"

"No. I don't know when she would have gotten any of those things."

"I do," Scott said.

All heads turned toward him. Hands in his jeans pockets, he leaned awkwardly against the wall of the hallway.

"It's a little hard to explain." He passed a hand through sandy hair. "You know I did some work for her around the house. But about half the time, she'd ask me to take her on a run to Coffman's Hardware or the home store next door." He nodded toward the cabinet. "She'd pick up some little thing like tile or paint. Never much at once. She talked about remodeling the kitchen, or the bathroom, or whatever. But she never got around to scheduling me to do the job. It was always 'one of these days.' I felt half bad letting her spend her money, but it was *her* money . . ." He shrugged. "There didn't seem to be much point, but I didn't have the heart to try to talk her out of it. I think maybe it was good for her to plan something."

Liv looked down at the wallpaper in her hands. Dear Lord, the apples were starting to look blurry.

Added together, the things in the cabinet probably hadn't come to more than a few hundred dollars, a little at a time. But what had Nammy been thinking?

Liv blinked carefully, and the apples sharpened again. Only then did she raise her head to look at Scott. "Do you think maybe she was . . . slipping?"

"No," Scott said without hesitation.

"No," Mom called, just as quickly, from the kitchen.

Maybe it was good for her to plan something. Scotty might have something there. She knew Nammy had stayed active with the church, with her garden, and she and Mom had spent a lot of time together. But with her children and grandchildren grown up and Liv's grandfather gone so many years, the hours alone in the house had probably seemed long.

Blinking once more and clearing her throat, Liv rerolled the wallpaper and returned it to the cabinet shelf where she'd found it. "It's all brand-new," she said. "Maybe sell it online?"

Silence greeted her words. She dropped the subject for now.

The mysterious cabinet was relatively small, it was self-contained . . . it was one more decision that could wait until later.

After Scott left, Liv and Rachel resumed the job of boxing up the dishes. Liv wasn't about to bring up the fact that while she'd been touring hotels and ostensibly dropping off Christmas trees, she hadn't eaten lunch. She'd have some of the pasta salad after she got some work done.

"You were gone quite a while," Mom said. "We were getting worried about you two."

"Worried?"

At Liv's puzzled look, Rachel smiled mischievously. "Didn't you know? Scotty gets around."

Liv felt her face go red. *"What?"*

"I wouldn't put it like that," Mom said. But she was

smiling, too. "He's just been . . . friendly with quite a few girls."

"Friendly." Rachel nodded. Her eyes gleamed. "That's a good way of putting it. He's just *sociable*."

"Scotty? You're kidding."

Not that he wasn't easy on the eyes. But it didn't sound like him, somehow.

Liv frowned. "And you sent me off with him?"

"We're just messing with you," Rachel said. "He's a nice guy. He's just dated quite a few girls the past few years."

Liv tried to remember if he'd dated a lot when they were in high school. Not that she could recall. Then she remembered the way his arm rested behind her on the back of the seat. Maybe his sympathy wasn't as unselfish as it seemed.

Not that it mattered. She'd be going home right after Christmas. Besides, it had barely been a month since she broke up with Kevin. After *that* fiasco, she wasn't in a hurry to deal with anything male.

She'd barely thought about Kevin these past few days, but with Nammy's death, the trip out here and the memorial, she supposed that wasn't surprising.

Liv let it go and concentrated on boxing dishes. Maybe they were past their first hurdle, and they could start making some headway on the house.

"Can you fix it?"

Scott looked up from his crouched position in front of Mel Kruger's dishwasher. "You cut me to the quick. Have a little confidence."

"I'm just not sure how much damage I did trying to fix it myself. If you could get it going again before Gloria gets home, I'd really appreciate it."

Scott grinned. Retirement made work for idle hands. "If it weren't for all the repairs I did to fix a job somebody else started, it'd cut my business in half."

He picked up his wrench and spun it between his fingers. "Now, if I get out of here before Gloria knows what happened, there's an extra twenty-dollar confidentiality fee."

Mel's eyes lit. He played along with the joke. "That's blackmail."

"Tomato, to-*mah*-to."

Less than half an hour later, the job was done. "Thanks," Mel said. "You saved my hide."

Scott closed his toolbox and stood to leave. "Another appliance repaired, another marriage saved."

If only everything in life could be that easy. A new motto for his business cards: *I dream of a world where everything could be fixed with a wrench.*

Maybe he'd stumbled onto something at that. Of course he liked fixing things; that was why he'd gotten into this line of work. To take it to another level, he liked the way it felt to make things better. Maybe that explained his history with women, too. He did have a way of gravitating toward girls who were nursing a broken heart. And when they were feeling better, they did have a way of moving on.

How Liv fit into that picture, he wasn't sure. He just knew he was thinking about her way more than he should. Wondering how she was faring with her mom and sister, and how they were progressing on that house.

Liv didn't seem broken to him. Her troubles were the kind that time would heal. She didn't really need him, and that was fine. He was trying to break the habit of rescuing damsels in distress, anyway.

He loaded his toolbox into the truck and slammed the tailgate, wondering if that heater at Nammy's would be giving them any more trouble.

At one time or another, this man had seen all three of them naked.

Granted, for Liv, the last time would have been when she was about ten, and it was probably a similar story for Rachel. Still, it was one of the drawbacks to living in a small town.

Dr. Melendez stood in the examining room, regarding the X-rays from urgent care with a frown. "You say this happened Saturday?"

"Right," Mom said. "But it's only Tuesday."

Dr. Melendez wasn't much older than Mom, which must make things twice as awkward for her. To spare her the indignity and inconvenience of undressing and paper gowns, Liv and Rachel had found a loose pair of sweatpants for her to pull on over a pair of shorts. Not that there was much dignity in Mom having to sit on the papered examining table in those shorts, her legs out in front of her as if she'd mistaken December for summer, and the table for some kind of elevated beach towel.

Dr. Melendez looked from the X-rays to Mom's knee with vague disapproval. "I could X-ray it again," he said. "But I'd really like Dr. Driscoll in Fontana to take a look at it, and I'm sure he'll want to run his own set of X-rays there."

"Who's Dr. Driscoll?" Liv asked, half a beat ahead of Rachel.

"He specializes in sports medicine, believe it or not." Dr. Melendez lifted his graying eyebrows at Faye. "I know you didn't exactly do this by skateboarding. But he sees a lot more of this type of injury than I do, and we want to be sure it's healing properly. I don't like that swelling."

Liv had hoped they'd have a few minutes with Dr. Melendez away from Mom, but she wasn't sure they'd get that opportunity before he ducked into the next examining room. So she spoke up in front of Mom.

"But *why* did she fall?" Liv turned toward her mother, half apologetically. But something about this still didn't seem right, and if she didn't speak up now, she might not get an answer. "Was the knee giving you trouble before? Or did you lose your balance?"

Mom looked a little like the way Liv used to feel when she'd been caught at something. "I—got a little dizzy." Her face turned pink.

Dr. Melendez frowned at her. "Have you been having trouble with your vertigo again?"

"Her *what*?" Liv exclaimed.

Mom went from pink to red. "It's nothing. I mean, it's something I had a few years ago. I haven't had any trouble with it since. I just got dizzy for a minute the other morning—"

"How did I not know?" Rachel sounded dismayed.

"It was right after you and Brian got married." Mom

gave a small, knowing smile. "You weren't up here too often that first year."

Liv asked Dr. Melendez, "So, what do we need to do?"

"If it doesn't give her any more trouble, probably nothing." He turned to Faye. "But *you* need to let someone know if you're still having symptoms."

"I'm not. I'm not even sure that's what it was." Mom shifted her gaze away. "And I didn't want to get the girls worried."

Liv fought back the urge to lecture her own mother in front of the family doctor. Mom was entitled to some dignity, and the shorts didn't help much with that.

Fifty-seven *wasn't* old. Liv knew that in her brain, but her heart was having a hard time listening to reason.

Back at the house, Liv noticed Rachel was quiet while they had their lunch, another warmed-up casserole from someone at the church. They talked Mom into lying down after they ate. Talking her mother into lying down was another new experience for Liv. Mom had always been the one to take care of *them*.

"You were right," Rachel said as they loaded the dishwasher.

"About what?" Liv rinsed a glass and handed it to her sister.

"You know what I mean. The vertigo thing. How did you know?"

"I didn't know anything. It just felt wrong to me," Liv said. "I guess I wanted there to be a *reason*."

Not that vertigo was great news. But according to

Dr. Melendez, it wasn't age-related, and Liv took a shallow comfort in that.

"She said she tripped, and I bought it." Rachel closed the dishwasher. "You're still the responsible one."

An air of discontent hung around Rachel, and Liv tried to pinpoint the source. "Hey, this isn't about who's right, or who's responsible," Liv said. "We just want Mom to be okay."

"I know. I . . . Sorry." Rachel went for a kitchen chair and sat, her legs splaying less than gracefully in front of her. Liv wondered if she'd ever get used to seeing her sister waddle like the pregnant woman she was.

Part of Liv wanted to let the conversation drop. The other part knew she had to look this thing in the eye, and she had a feeling she knew what was bothering Rachel. Liv pulled up another chair at the dining room table. "Let's have it."

"What?" Rachel looked at her, eyes round and guileless.

Liv sighed. "I *know* I've been gone forever. You've been here for Mom and Nammy when I haven't been. I should have made the time."

"I didn't say that."

"But it's the truth."

"The truth," Rachel said, "is I *like* coming to see Mom. Brian is gone so much, and when I get here Mom always puts food in front of me. Sure, I help her with things. We help each other out. But then you walk in and right away I'm the kid and you're the grown-up."

A silence welled up across the two feet of kitchen-table-corner that separated them.

"You got Mom to the doctor Saturday," Liv said quietly. "I should be thanking you for that."

"You did," Rachel said. "You also heated up the casserole. And served it."

"Like that was hard to do. Besides, Mom's hurt, and you're . . ." Liv looked down at Rachel's round middle and risked the word: "Huge."

A smile tugged up at the corners of Rachel's mouth. "With nearly two months to go." She rested a hand on her stomach. Her whole face softened, and their rough moment seemed to be over. Rachel never had been one to stay in a bad mood for long. But Liv didn't want to get off the hook that easily.

"I've got a lot to make up for," Liv said. "Work me like a dog while I'm here."

"Like I could stop you." Rachel smiled ruefully. "Don't think I've forgotten all the times you did my chores for me when I was backed up on my homework."

"Yeah, but what you really wanted was for me to do the *homework*."

"I've grown up since then."

Impulsively, Liv stood up and hugged her. "I noticed."

Chapter 9

"Have you got me on speed dial yet?" Scott caught himself grinning as Liv opened Nammy's front door.

She regarded him with one of her serious looks. "This is only the second time."

Put me on speed dial anyway.

He couldn't help it. The more dressed-down Liv got, the more she got to him. Today she'd tugged her long chestnut waves up into an impatient ponytail. She wore jeans again with a different sweatshirt, this one with an anchor logo. In what was quickly becoming a habit, Scott looked down at her shoes. Tennies again. With little anchors.

She stepped back to usher him in, and Scott entered with a sense of déjà vu. A new to-go pile stood stacked near the front door, so they'd made some progress since he was here last. The living room furniture was still untouched, but as he followed Liv, he saw the kitchen was taking on a stripped-down look, with more boxes and chaos.

He greeted Rachel, and Faye, who sat in the same chair with her foot propped on a footstool. Scott turned off to the hallway leading to the garage and the heater. He was pretty sure what he'd find, and the method he'd tried before was clearly a temporary fix at best. He'd have to own up. He hated that.

Scott made a note of the manufacturer's name. He'd contact them first. That way he'd have something more concrete to tell Liv and her family.

He got back into the dining area in time to hear the *whoosh* as the heater kicked on.

Liv stood waiting near the stove. "Now, Scotty, we're not taking no for an answer this time," she said. "We really appreciate your help. But you need to tell us what we owe you."

She wore her best serious, all-business expression, and Scott suspected she was trying to make him forget the way she'd crumpled up in front of him the other day. He could understand that. But she did have a way of overcompensating.

"I didn't really do much of anything," he said, more truthfully than she knew.

"We're taking time away from your work," Liv insisted.

Scott leaned against the frame of the doorway between the kitchen and the hall. "We went over this the other day. You know the answer. You don't owe me anything."

He wanted to add, *Don't make me clunk you with a stick.* It might startle Liv into a smile. But out of context, it wouldn't sound right to Faye and Rachel.

Rachel joined the debate. "Scotty, picking Liv up at the airport is one thing. This is your livelihood."

Liv sent her sister an appreciative nod.

"Seriously, Scotty—" Liv's mother began.

Scott put up his hand. "Here's the story. Olivia was my favorite customer. Anything I can do for you ladies, I feel like I'm doing for her. So I'd appreciate it if you'd stop giving me guff about it." He smiled to lighten the jibe. "Besides, with all the business she threw my way, I'm halfway to retirement already."

He hoped they wouldn't see through that one. In point of fact, he hadn't taken money from Olivia half the time either. Especially when he ended up taking her on one of those home-improvement store runs. More often than not, when they got back to the house, she ended up feeding him. Food was always fair game in lieu of payment for a favor, especially for a guy who'd never learned to cook. Olivia made a mean homemade soup, and her brownies were sinful.

With that thought in mind, he added, "Now, if you happened to get any of Millie Bond's lemon bars in that fridge full of food from the church, maybe we'll talk."

Three red heads, one of them graying, all turned toward each other.

"What?" Scott asked.

"Lunch." Liv slapped her forehead. "We forgot the casserole we were going to bring."

Well, it got them off the subject of money, anyway.

"One of us can run back to the house later," Rachel said.

He didn't want to spark a new debate by volunteering now for a food run. He'd just make it a point to drop back by the house around lunchtime.

* * *

Maybe she just wanted a break.

Maybe she just had a yen to hear a voice that didn't sing soprano.

But somehow, Liv wasn't surprised to find herself riding to the Pine 'n' Dine with Scott a few hours later, picking up lunch to take back to Nammy's.

She *had* to stop this. But dropping off another load at the thrift shop had been a tempting break, and a hot takeout meal sounded better than another reheated casserole. Plus, she'd picked up thank-you gifts yesterday afternoon for the waitresses who'd helped her at the memorial. This was a chance to drop them off.

They walked past the PLEASE WAIT TO BE SEATED sign and stood at the register.

All right, who was she kidding? Some deep-voiced, blue-eyed companionship had been too tempting to turn down, even if her sister claimed he'd turned into the local Casanova when she wasn't looking. As he stood beside her in the vest she'd scrunched her face against the other day, it still didn't seem likely. But what did it matter? She wouldn't be here long enough to get involved.

All she really knew was he made her feel better, and she would have been disappointed if he hadn't happened to drop by at lunchtime.

"Is their fried chicken still as good as I remember?" she asked.

"If you've gotten used to fast-food fried chicken, it's way better," Scott said.

A girl with short dark hair came out of the swinging doors that led to the back kitchen. Liv recognized her as one of the sandwich-making waitresses. What was her name again?

"Hey, Tiff," Scott said behind her.

"Tiffany." Liv held out a little gift-wrapped box. "Thanks again for helping with those sandwiches the other day. It meant a lot."

The girl's dark eyes, richly coated with mascara, darted from the box to Liv to Scotty, then back to Liv. At last she stepped forward and accepted the box. "Thank you," she said. "You didn't have to do that."

"I wanted to. I've got something for Sherry, too, and your other friend . . ."

Tiffany was looking upward, past her again, at Scotty. A little slow on the uptake, Liv began to catch an undercurrent.

". . . Chloe. That was it," Liv persisted, trying to bring Tiffany out of her paralysis.

"Right." Tiffany's eyes returned to Liv. "She works nights. But she's my roommate. I can give it to her."

Liv handed her a second box. She'd gone out after Mom's appointment yesterday and picked up some little Christmas necklaces at The North Pole. The owner, Mrs. Swanson, had spoken so fondly of Nammy at the memorial, Liv was glad for the chance to throw a little business her way.

"Thanks again." Tiffany's glance flicked up past Liv again, more briefly this time. "I'll get Sherry." She spun to retreat to the kitchen. "Hi, Scotty," she said, over her shoulder, as she walked away.

Sherry came out a moment later. "Liv! You're still here! I thought you already went back to Texas for your"—Sherry's brow furrowed as she floundered—"home improvement business?"

"Home organizing," Liv said.

"Oh." The frown vanished, but the slightly puzzled look remained. "Well, it's great to see you again. You must have a terrific staff to keep things going while you're gone."

Let's see. That would be Terri and me. And a silent partner who just flew the coop.

Liv dredged up a smile. "It'll be fine. It's our slow season."

And she gave Sherry her gift-wrapped necklace, glad to change the subject. Then, at last, they ordered the chicken.

In the parking lot afterward, Scotty opened the truck door for her. "You know, when you can't explain your line of work in ten words or less, it might be a little *too* specialized. What do you put on your business cards, anyway?"

"Home organizer. They know what it is in Dallas." That sounded more brusque than she meant it to. She undercut it with, "But it says 'y'all' underneath."

Scott chuckled, so apparently she hadn't offended him. Liv climbed into the truck, and he came around to slide behind the wheel.

"Seriously," Liv said, "I wonder if I'll even know what my job is by the time I get back. What in the world did Nammy tell people?"

Scott handed her the bag of chicken, and its delicious aroma wafted up to her. "I think she told me you help people redo their houses. But she made it sound really complex. And important." His eyes glimmered at her. "With offices in Taiwan, Beijing . . ."

She closed her eyes, as if cringing from a blow. "Stop, stop."

She knew Scotty was kidding. She also knew that somehow, somewhere along the line, her reputation had exceeded her. Being the class brain had carried a certain level of expectation, but it all seemed to have magnified since she'd been gone. With a lot of help from Nammy.

"Relax," Scott said. "She was proud of you, that's all."

"She might be a little less impressed if she knew about all the ramen noodles and peanut butter sandwiches I ate those first couple of years."

"Or maybe she'd be that much more impressed."

His voice held a warmth that told her he meant what he said. He hadn't started the truck yet, and when she turned his way, he was regarding her with something that might be admiration. Or it might be a little more. Liv fought the urge to shift in her seat, not sure how to react, if in fact there was anything to react to. But the discomfort and uncertainty she felt wasn't unpleasant. It felt like something she'd been missing for a long time. Something different, something exciting. She couldn't remember Kevin ever looking at her this way.

The devilish thought popped into her brain: *Kevin who?*

Closely followed by: *Scotty Leroux and me? Really?*

It didn't seem nearly as preposterous as it would have just a few days ago. For a moment it seemed almost tempting. Liv drew a long, slow breath and looked down at the white bag in her lap. Taking her eyes off Scott helped her think more clearly. She could be jumping to conclusions, in which case she could really make a fool of herself.

And, she remembered, it wasn't what she was here for. Take care of Nammy's loose ends. Be there for Mom and Rachel. Then get back to Dallas and the business with Terri, who still hadn't called or texted, and hopefully that meant things were going fine without her.

Nope, she and Scott weren't in the cards, and she'd better remember that.

When she raised her eyes to his again, this time a little concern had crept into his expression.

"Are you"—he stopped before the forbidden question came out, then gave her a crooked grin— "hungry?"

Liv grinned back, and things were back to normal. "Absolutely."

Good thing she hadn't made a fool of herself. As they started back down Evergreen Lane, Liv remembered something else. Another reason she and Scotty Leroux weren't such a great idea. It was really none of her business anyway, but she couldn't resist asking.

Liv waited a few minutes. Then, as offhandedly as she could, she asked, "So what's the story with Tiffany?"

Scott hesitated briefly, then answered in a similar light tone. "Tiffany? We dated for a while a few months ago. We're still friends. Things are just a little . . . awkward."

It doesn't matter. Leave it alone. But for some reason, Liv couldn't stop herself. She made her tone playful. "Oh. I heard about that."

Scott's head jerked her way, eyebrows raised. Quickly,

he turned back toward the road. "You heard about me and Tiffany? Not much to tell there."

"Not just Tiffany." She didn't know what made her want to needle him. Still facing the windshield, she cast a sidelong glance at Scott for his reaction as she added, "Rachel told me you get around."

It got a bigger reaction than she expected.

Scott's head jerked in her direction again. Then he pulled to the side of the road and hit the brakes. The sudden stop didn't exactly give her whiplash, but Liv felt herself shift forward and back again.

He leaned back on the headrest and let out a long sigh before he looked at her again. "You're kidding. *Rachel* said that? Your sister, who lives a hundred miles away?"

"Well, she's up here a lot."

She tried to read his expression. As she watched, exasperation seemed to be warring with amusement.

"Okay," he said. "I've heard that one, too. Scotty Leroux, serial dater. But people aren't getting a good look at the stats." Still leaning back in his seat, he started to tick off on his fingers. "Tiffany. Broke up with Adam Gerard, started going out with me. Started dating Steve Pagano two months later. Vicki Martinez. Broke up with Todd Davenport, dated me three months, got *married* to Robert Quinn six months later. Angie Cleghorn. Broke up with—"

"Okay. I think I get it."

"—Oh, yeah, and she's married now, too. I'm not a serial dater, Liv. I'm a bus station."

"Sorry."

"Forget it." He started the truck again and cast her

the familiar lazy grin. "Just saying. For some reason I keep ending up being the transitional guy around here. So unless you broke up with somebody lately, don't worry. You're totally safe."

She decided not to mention Kevin. Instead, she raised her chin. "What makes you think I was worried?"

His grin didn't falter. "Wishful thinking?"

His eyes rested on hers a moment longer before he drove forward.

Liv didn't answer. But her stomach fluttered.

Chapter 10

Scott followed Liv back into Nammy's house, carrying the big white bag of fried chicken.

"I know that smell!" Rachel practically yanked the bag from his hands.

"Not much trouble with morning sickness, huh?" Liv said.

"Not on your life."

"I wasn't thinking," Faye said. "Didn't we pack away all the dishes?"

Liv frowned, but Rachel resurfaced from the chicken bag with a wide smile. "Taken care of." She held up a handful of paper plates from the bag.

"Sherry thinks of everything," Scott said.

And saw three curious glances dart his way. *No, as a matter of fact, Sherry and I never dated.* But saying it would just sound defensive. He was used to defending himself on the old goose story. That was ancient history, and it was fun to tell. The whole serial dater thing, though— that was getting old.

He figured the only way to put it behind him was to

keep moving forward. So Scott said, "Something I need to talk to the three of you about—"

"Drumstick?" Liv interrupted, fishing one out of the bag. It looked crispy and delectable.

"Ladies first," he said.

Liv held the drumstick up in front of Rachel and her mother. "Age before beauty? Or—"

"Pregnancy trumps," Faye said.

Rachel didn't argue. She nabbed the drumstick and put it on her plate.

Scott cleared his throat. "As I was saying—"

"Let's eat first," Liv said, and pressed a plate into his hand. He felt absurdly pleased at the wordless invitation. Although sending him out the door without any Pine 'n' Dine chicken . . . that would have just been cruel.

So Scott waited until everyone had their plates dished up. Then it was confession time. He had to stop putting it off.

"That heater," he said. "I didn't fix it. It's probably going to do the same thing tomorrow."

Once again, three pairs of female eyes settled on him. He noticed that Rachel and Faye's eyes were the same shade of light gray. Only Liv's had that hazel blend of blue and green, flecked with brown.

And he was studying those eyes too long, he realized. The way he'd caught himself doing in the truck a little while ago.

"What do you mean?" Faye asked.

"I mean, I couldn't find anything wrong with the heater." He turned a chicken wing in his hand. This was embarrassing. "Sometimes, when something doesn't work and you can't tell why, you try what I call the Captain Obvious method."

They looked at him questioningly. Scott sucked in his breath and gritted his teeth.

"I switched the unit off and back on again," he said.

"Oh," Liv said, and suddenly he felt several inches shorter.

"Well," Rachel said, "since it worked again today, maybe you could show us how to do that so you don't have to keep running over here?"

"Right, and that might work. As a stop-gap method. But something must be wrong with it, and if you're planning to sell this house eventually . . ."

They all nodded slowly.

"So, I called the manufacturer after I left this morning," Scott said. "I left a message on their voice mail. Maybe they'll know of a solution they can explain to me over the phone. Otherwise"—he hated to say it—"I'll have them send out one of their own representatives to look it over."

It felt like admitting defeat. But they all nodded again. Obviously they didn't know a man's pride was at stake.

"Okay," Liv said.

Okay. If they could overlook it, surely he could get over it, too. "I'll show you how to work the switch in case it happens again tomorrow morning."

After lunch he showed Liv, the most able-bodied of the three, where to find the switch on the unit in the garage. One less reason for him to come around. He hoped they'd keep coming up with others.

As he and Liv came back into the kitchen, Scott asked, "By the way, what did you decide to do with the tree?"

Faye and Rachel looked at him blankly. Liv threw him a sharp glance, as if he'd tattled on her.

"The tree?" Faye asked.

All attention turned Liv's way. She lowered her gaze. "It's still in Rachel's trunk."

Rachel brightened. "You saved the silver tree?"

Liv blushed.

Rachel stood and caught her sister in a hug. "I'm glad. I was so depressed seeing it go out the door."

"I got a little . . . depressed myself," Liv admitted.

She darted another quick look at Scott, as if daring him to say something about their little scene in the truck. As if he ever would. Especially if he valued his life.

"Why didn't you tell us?" Rachel asked.

"I wasn't why I wanted to keep it. I didn't know what I was going to do with it."

"I do." That was Faye.

The girls turned to her as one.

"Let's put it up at my house." Faye indicated her propped-up leg. "I don't see myself running out and buying a fresh tree this year."

Liv's expression went from discomfort and embarrassment to something softer. "That's a great idea."

"We could use Nammy's ornaments." Rachel glanced toward the living room, where the "keep" pile had continued to grow. "It'd be a fun way to sort through them, and decide who wants to keep which ones."

"And you girls could decide how much you really like the tree," Faye said. "You've never had to put it up before. You'll get a ton of shocks from those metal branches."

Liv pretended to glare at the naysayer. Then she bent down and hugged her. "Thanks, Mom."

Faye put her arms around her girl, and it was only when Liv's chin was over her mom's shoulder that Scott noticed the misty look in Faye's eyes.

Women were complicated, all right, and emotions tangled among the three of them like a ball of yarn. But Scott wasn't so dense that he couldn't read the simplest and most overriding one in this room: love.

It felt like the right moment to bow out. Scott started quietly toward the front door, planning to say his goodbyes when he was safely at the exit.

"Scotty," Rachel said before he was halfway across the living room.

He turned.

"Do you want to come over tonight? And help us set up the tree?"

Straightening from her mother's arms, Liv aimed a look at Rachel. Scott fumbled for an answer.

He'd probably be intruding. It probably wasn't a great idea. But the invitation touched him almost as much as it surprised him. He watched Liv for some kind of a cue, but she was busy sending one of those female-only telepathic messages to Rachel.

Faye chimed in. "That'd be nice. Unless you have other plans. My mom was really fond of you."

How could he say no to that?

Except that there was a lot going on behind Liv's hazel eyes, and he couldn't decipher any of it.

"If you think you can deal with a room full of us," Liv finally said enigmatically.

But she *was* smiling, and smiles from Liv weren't too easy to come by. At least not these days.

He edged toward the door. "I'll bring eggnog," he said, his hand on the knob.

An evening with this little family could be an eventful one.

Liv gathered paper plates and chicken bones until she heard Scotty's truck pull out of the driveway. Then she turned to Rachel. "Where did *that* come from?"

"Don't be a Grinch." Rachel smiled serenely as she held the big white takeout bag open for Liv to deposit the trash. "Scotty's doing a lot for us, and he won't take a dime. Besides, you heard him at the memorial. He was pretty attached to Nammy himself."

Okay, she couldn't argue with that. But she still wondered if Rachel had something else in mind.

"And if we've got him around while we're putting up the tree, we might not get so—soupy," Mom said.

She couldn't argue with *that*, either. Liv remembered the way he'd made her laugh with the goose story, when laughing had been the furthest thing from her mind.

But she still envisioned wheels turning behind Rachel's guileless eyes.

Chapter 11

When Liv opened her mother's door after dinner that evening, Scott looked as confused about his presence tonight as she felt. But he'd been game enough to show up, grocery sack of eggnog in hand, that slightly crooked smile at the ready.

And he looked good. He'd changed out of his work shirt and vest, into a red sweater that definitely said Christmas. He wore the same corduroy jacket he'd draped around her the evening it snowed after the memorial.

Remembering that, perversely, she shivered as she let him in and closed the door.

"It feels great in here," Scott said. "It's cold tonight."

Liv nodded as she led him into the kitchen to put the eggnog away. They'd spent the last hour and a half straightening the living room for their suddenly invited company. Her sister, in particular, had gone to extensive lengths to make things cozy. Rachel had started a fire in the fireplace, put Christmas music on the living room stereo, and she'd even asked Mom if she had any candles. They'd finally dug up a couple of tall red ones and put them on the mantel, although it felt like overkill to Liv.

And just where *were* Mom and Rachel right now? Once again, Liv smelled a rat.

Liv's heels clacked on the kitchen tile, and she felt Scotty's glance sweep down to her feet. She'd never decorated a Christmas tree in high heels before, but she was wearing them tonight. She didn't want to spend the evening craning her neck to look up at him. If there was one thing she never wanted to come across as, it was small and waifish.

"Thanks." She smiled at Scott as he handed her the eggnog, one carton at a time, to load into the refrigerator. Regular, low fat, and her favorite: vanilla spice.

Scott unloaded one more item out of the grocery bag. "I brought these, too." He held out a plastic-lidded platter of cookies dusted with powdered sugar.

"Pfeffernuss," she said.

"Is that what they're called?"

"Nammy didn't tell you that?" She'd loved teaching Liv German words, even though she probably hadn't known more than a dozen of them herself.

"No," Scott said. "I just know they were the cookies she used to give me after a run to the home store. I thought they were homemade until I spotted them in the grocery store."

Liv pulled open the lid and set the cookies on the kitchen island. "Know what *pfeffernuss* means?"

He shook his head. "I guess she knew I had enough trouble with Neuenschwander. Probably one reason she let me call her Nammy."

Although, as they both knew, *Olivia* wasn't hard to

say. Undeniably, he'd been special to Nammy, even if he tried to downplay it.

Liv heard herself chatter on. "*Pfeffernuss* means 'pepper nut.' Germans just love compound words. You know what the German word is for *thimble*?"

He shook his head, looking a little perplexed.

"*Fingerhut.*" She carefully pronounced the soft "g" sound, but landed hard on the "t." Scott looked even more puzzled. "It means 'finger hat.' I always thought that was adorable."

"I think the only German word I ever heard her say was a swear word. When she dropped an egg."

"*Himmel?*"

He nodded.

Liv grinned. "It means *heaven.*"

"Not the way she said it."

"You should have heard the way she said it to *us.*"

Liv picked up one of the white-powdered cookies and bit into it. She'd been served her fair share of them, too. The familiar flavor—a little like licorice, a little like gingerbread—brought another keen reminder of Nammy. It made her absence hit harder, too. But remembering was better than forgetting. That was what tonight was all about.

Feeling her eyes sting, Liv turned to the lower kitchen cabinet, where her mother usually kept the big platters, and found a Christmas plate edged with holly. Perfect. By the time she put the plate on the kitchen island, her tears had receded. She started transferring the cookies to the platter. "Thanks for coming."

"Thanks for letting me come."

He probably realized Rachel had put her on the

spot with her out-of-the-blue invitation. She held the Christmas plate out to him, although it was still less than halfway loaded. "Pfeffernuss?"

Scott picked up a cookie with a smile, blue eyes on hers. "Don't mind if I do."

How could a smile be serious? Pondering the answer to that one, Liv set the plate on the countertop with a clumsy clatter.

"Liv?" Mom's voice called from the living room. So her mother and sister hadn't gone completely AWOL.

German lesson over, Liv thought. "Coming," she said.

It didn't take long to assemble the tree. Liv was sure that on his own, Scotty could have put it together in about thirty seconds. But he hung back, as Liv noticed he had a tendency to do where her family was concerned, while Liv and Rachel carefully gauged the size of the branches they were inserting into the tree's metal tube of a trunk. Small ones on top, big ones on the bottom.

Unleashing the branches from their individual brown paper tubes was the best part. As the branches slid out, the fake needles blossomed into shiny silver plumes, at least twice as big around as the tubes that had held them.

The worst part, as Mom had predicted, was the static that came out with the branches. Sweet little Rachel actually swore when she got her first shock.

"I warned you," Mom said from her place in the easy chair, where they'd consigned her for Phase One of the project. Even if the crutches themselves hadn't excused Mom from tree-assembly duty, she said, she'd earned a free pass from all the years she'd helped Nammy put the tree together.

Rachel shook the hand the tree had stung. "Nobody likes an I-told-you-so."

Halfway through the undertaking, Scott stepped in to help, and the rest of the tree was built in no time. He stood back with Liv and Rachel to regard the tree, squinting faintly. Liv wondered what he thought of their artificial heirloom. It wasn't often Scott didn't have *some* kind of comment.

She had to admit, it didn't look like much. The tree stood shorter than she remembered—much shorter than Scotty and just a few inches over Liv's own five-foot-eight. The branches weren't dusty, but they didn't have quite the magical luster she'd pictured in her mind. Of course, the living room was fully lit. When the room was dim and the tree was lit up—

She and Rachel turned to each other at the same moment.

"The color wheel," they said in unison. Then they looked down at the rectangular box, now empty except for the brown shells of those paper tubes. Of course the color wheel couldn't have fit in there.

"I didn't think of it," Mom said, no longer teasing or smug.

"It wasn't in the closet," Rachel said.

"You're sure?" Scotty said. "Not even on the top shelf?"

Rachel shook her head. "We cleared the top shelf. There was gift wrap, some more decorations, a few board games—"

Realization sank in on Liv. "You cleared the top shelf while I was gone the other day?"

"Sure. I stood on a chair—"

"You stood on a chair?" Liv couldn't keep the alarm from her voice. She looked pointedly at Rachel's middle, then back up to her face, which took on a guilty look.

"Hey." That seemed to be Scott's universal word for smoothing things out. He rested a hand on Liv's shoulder. Not Rachel's, she noticed, although he directed a look at her sister. "No harm done. Just remember, no more climbing." One side of his mouth lifted in a crooked grin. "That goes for you too, Mrs. Tomblyn."

Mom's mouth quirked up in response. "Faye," she reminded him.

Scott nodded. "Remember, if you need to move something that's high up, I'm never too far away."

Belatedly, he lifted his hand from Liv's shoulder, and she released a breath she hadn't realized she'd been holding.

She spoke to Rachel again, her tone milder this time. "The color wheel's got to be in the house somewhere. After all, she held on to the tree. We'll find it."

"You know where it might be," Scotty said. "She had me take some things up to the attic a few times when I was over. She just didn't believe in throwing things away."

Liv frowned. "There's an attic?"

"Well, more of a glorified crawl space. California houses aren't much on attics. Not even way back when that house was built."

"How much stuff is up there?"

"A lot of boxes. No furniture or anything like that. But if I moved a box with a color wheel in it, I wouldn't have known what it was. I'm *still* not sure what a color wheel is."

A smile glimmered on Rachel's face. "You'll just have to see."

Liv gave Rachel a scolding look. "*You're* not going up there."

Then she bit her tongue. The big-sister routine *was* hard to shake.

"I'll help," Scott interjected.

"We can't keep—"

"Look," he said. "Here's what we'll do. The heater company's sending a guy out Tuesday. It makes sense for me to be there when he shows up. After all, I'm the one who put the heater in."

"You installed the heater?" Liv asked. "When?"

He shifted his feet. "About a year ago."

"It's a *new* heater?"

"Right. So I must have done something wrong, and I want to know what. I'll make it right. I promise."

Liv turned to her mother. "Did Nammy have any trouble with the heater last winter?"

Mom shook her head. "Never."

She turned back to Scotty. "So what makes you think it's your fault?"

"What else could it be? The truth is, I'd love to know it's not my fault. But I've *got* to know what the problem is."

Liv was silent. She understood that. She hated making mistakes, and when she did, she wanted to know what went wrong.

"So, anyway. While I'm waiting for the heater guy to show, I'll unload the attic." His eyes flicked from one woman to the next. "Safely," he assured them. "So we don't have any pregnant women jumping up on chairs like mountain goats."

"Did you say Tuesday?" Liv said. "That's when Mom has her appointment with the specialist."

"I can drive Mom," Rachel said. "She doesn't really need both of us there." She looked to their mother for confirmation, and Faye nodded.

Liv hesitated. Mom seemed to mean it. Maybe having both of them hover over her got a little overwhelming. And maybe Rachel didn't need Liv second-guessing her judgment. Maybe the most useful thing she could do was stay behind and go through the attic.

"Are you sure?" she asked, and Mom and Rachel both nodded.

"Meantime," Mom said, pulling herself up from the armchair, "we've got a tree to decorate. Let's get to work."

They uncapped the first tin of ornaments and got started, unrolling the decorations from their protective wrappings of tissue paper, paper towels and kitchen napkins. There were so many, and no two were alike. What one of them didn't remember, another of them would.

"Oh, gosh, Liv, remember these?" Rachel's face lit up as she unrolled another ball of tissue paper. "The gingerbread men we made that year we decided to make decorations for Nammy. This one was yours." Rachel handed a stuffed felt figure to Liv.

"No, the pink one was yours. The green one was mine."

"Are you sure?" Rachel squinted, studying the workmanship.

"Positive. Pink was your favorite color then, remember?"

"Either way, not a very natural color for gingerbread."

"Well, neither of us liked brown."

Rachel grinned. "I guess kids don't go in much for realism."

"And here's that bluebird." Liv gently pulled out a sequined glass bird with blue feathers to fill in the details of its wings and tail.

"Oh." Rachel sighed. "I love that one."

"That's mine," Mom said, but Liv was already handing it to her.

"What's the story behind that one?" Liv asked.

Mom held the ornament by its hook, letting the blue sequins catch the light. "I'm not sure. We had it from the time I was little. I always wanted to be the one to hang it."

Leaning on one crutch, she hung the bird with care on a prominent branch near the top of the tree, while Liv silently prayed she didn't topple over.

They couldn't keep Mom off her feet the whole time, so she spent half her time leaning on one crutch while she hung an ornament with her free hand. To make rest breaks easier, Liv and Rachel brought in a kitchen chair and put it close to the tree. They kept Scotty involved by handing off some of the more masculine decorations to him: a toy train, a nutcracker, a duck in flight.

119

"Is this as old as I think it is?" Scotty handed their mother a tarnished, flat gold bell. Mom, seated in the kitchen chair, brushed the ornament's surface lightly with her fingertips, as if to shine it.

"I don't remember that one." Liv stepped behind Mom and peered over her shoulder. Rachel joined her on the left.

"Nammy always hung this one." Mom's voice had that rarely heard shaky quality. A faint inscription was engraved on the surface of the bell. Liv could barely make out her grandparents' names, with the year below. "It was from their first Christmas," Mom said. "She told me she ordered it with cereal box tops. I don't think they even make that cereal anymore."

They helped Mom out of her chair and helped her find a prominent spot for it. Scotty slipped toward the kitchen. "More eggnog, anyone?"

It wasn't a man's world tonight, and he seemed to recognize the fact.

Half an hour later, the second tin of ornaments was still half full, but they were definitely running out of space on the little tree. Liv and Rachel stood back to view the results of their work, while Mom reclaimed her armchair, her foot dutifully propped up in front of her.

Scott, once again, stood to the side. "What do you think?" he asked.

"It needs the color wheel," Rachel said.

Liv nodded in agreement. It was wonderful to see Nammy's old decorations, but without the colored light to reflect off its branches, the silver tree itself wasn't quite as she remembered it. Of course, the last time she saw it was nearly twenty years ago. Maybe, through the

120

eyes of an adult, its dime-store origins were simply more apparent.

"We'll find the color wheel," Liv said.

They contemplated the tree in silence. With all the memories on the branches in front of them, it was a bittersweet moment. That had been the point, after all—to celebrate Nammy's memory.

Then, suddenly, Rachel was circling the room, gathering empty plates and eggnog mugs. She whisked them off to the kitchen before Liv had a chance to help. Her sister's sudden flurry of activity kept the mood from getting too somber, if nothing else.

Rachel returned from the kitchen, extending her arms over her head in an elaborate stretch. "Well, that was fun," she said. "But I'm beat. How about you, Mom?"

"It has been a long day," Faye agreed, and Rachel was by her side in an instant, helping her up out of the chair.

Before Liv could recover from her mental whiplash, her mother and sister had excused themselves and gone to get ready for bed. It was barely past nine o'clock. Scott stared down the hall after them, looking as startled as Liv felt. Unless he was a talented actor, he didn't appear to be part of the conspiracy. Because that was definitely the description that came to mind.

I should have seen this coming, Liv thought. Rachel's intentions to throw her together with Scott had been pretty obvious from the start. What wasn't clear to Liv was *why*. What was even more baffling was, what was she supposed to do now that they'd been so abruptly abandoned?

She could get Scotty's coat and hand it to him with a

cheery smile, but that seemed pretty rude. Michael Bublé was still playing on the stereo, for heaven's sake.

All evening long, Rachel had made sure the carols on the CD player never ran out. Right up until her quick exit, her sister had worked overtime to infuse the evening with Christmas spirit. Liv knew her heart was in the right place. Rachel always tried to keep everyone around her happy. It was an endearing trait, Liv told herself, one she could use more of herself.

This agenda to leave her alone with Scotty, both at the start and the end of the evening, was just a little . . . blatant.

My sister went from warning me about Scotty-the-Serial-Dater to setting me up with him.

Scott regarded her patiently, not quite smiling, with a bemused look in the blue eyes that contrasted with his bright red sweater. Looking at him didn't help her think objectively.

Offer him his coat? Or offer him more eggnog? Between the four of them, they'd already gone through enough eggnog to sink a battleship. She couldn't think of anything she could say or do that wouldn't point up the inherent awkwardness of the scene.

Did she want him to leave?

Of course she did. Anything else wouldn't make sense. She wouldn't even be in Tall Pine a few weeks from now.

Rachel had spirited away the plates, so Liv busied herself gathering stray tissue wrappings off the floor and off the couch. Maybe that was a nicer cue that the evening was, in fact, over. But Scotty, being Scotty, stepped in to help her.

"It's okay," she said. "You don't need to do that."

"Neither do you." He eased a bundle of tissue paper from her hand and deposited it into the empty tin. "This could probably wait until tomorrow. You've been going nonstop since you got here."

"No more than Mom and Rachel. And they're pregnant and wounded."

"And they just went to bed," he pointed out.

"Yeah," she said. "Funny, that."

Leave it to her to bring up the elephant in the room. As if this situation needed to get more embarrassing.

"Okay," Scotty said. "They weren't very subtle. But they meant well."

"I guess." Liv rubbed her arms as they stood facing each other. The flames in the fireplace were growing dimmer—one touch Rachel had overlooked in her hasty departure—and the room was getting cooler. "It's just sort of . . . borderline creepy, that's all."

"Thanks a lot."

"No offense. But doesn't it weird you out a little? Being pushed together like this?"

She made the mistake of meeting his eyes again and saw crinkles of amusement forming faintly at the corners.

"Liv, all they did was give us a little time alone together. I don't think they expect to come in here tomorrow morning and find our clothes all over the floor."

Now, *that* would serve Rachel right. "So what do we do?" she heard herself say.

"Whatever you want." Those eye crinkles edged upward into genuine smile lines, but this time it wasn't his trademark broad grin. "We could go out for a walk. Play gin rummy. Whatever."

That smile was almost enough to thaw away the awkwardness. Almost. Liv tried to steel herself. She was getting way too comfortable with him, and that didn't make sense either. *Three weeks. You're here for three more weeks. There's no point. Who ever heard of a winter fling?*

The silence stretched long enough for Scotty's half smile to dim. "Or I could go home. No biggy."

She could just let him go. But it didn't feel right. "Scotty—"

"Scott."

"Scott," she amended. "I'm sorry. It's just a lousy time."

"I know." He shrugged. "Like I said, no big deal. I've gotten the 'just-friends' speech quite a few times. Maybe I can even help you with the script."

Just friends. She should grab at that. Scotty certainly had turned into a friend, and a good one, in a very short time. But *just friends* was such a standard-issue brush-off.

"It's not that," she said lamely. "But—we keep getting thrown together. All this stuff with the heater, and now Rachel. And I keep jumping in your truck."

"Maybe because we enjoy each other's company? It's not exactly a crime, Liv."

"But there's no point. I'm leaving in less than a month."

"So what are you afraid of?"

"Who said I was afraid?"

"You act like it."

"I'm not. I'm just trying to save us both some trouble."

But maybe he wasn't so far off.

She couldn't think when he was looking at her. As if he was hearing more than she was saying. Maybe it wasn't so hard to see why he was such a hit with heart-broken women. But she didn't *want* him to hear what she wasn't saying. So she turned away and contemplated the tree.

It was . . . incomplete. Without the color wheel, and under normal lighting, it looked sad and spindly, even with the long-forgotten ornaments. Because nothing could bring Nammy back.

"Hey." There was that multipurpose word again. She felt his hand on her arm, felt tears threaten, and stepped away. If he touched her again, she was sure she'd cry. And she didn't want that. Behind her, she felt Scott move away, too, as if she'd singed him.

"I'm sorry," she said quickly. "Really. I know you're trying to help. I just don't want to start bawling again the way I did the other day."

"You don't have to be strong all the time, you know."

"I like being strong."

Scott looked at Liv in the soft living room light— the determined lift of her chin, the waver of vulnerability in her eyes—and felt a tug somewhere inside. He started to reach a hand toward her face, then stopped himself. He needed to quit reaching out when she kept pulling away. So he lowered his hand. But he stood his ground.

Finally she met his eyes. "It's not you. And it's not just Nammy. It's—everything."

"I know."

She looked at him questioningly.

"With women, it's never just one thing. It's like you're walking down the street and a big truckload of *everything* falls on you."

Usually, though, there was a guy at the heart of it. In his experience, *It's everything* always seemed to come after *It's not just Joe. Or Mac. Or Todd.*

This time, Nammy was at the heart of it, and that made Liv a different story. One he could relate to, because he felt that loss, too.

She was avoiding his eyes again, rubbing that area just below her temples.

"You know, you do that a lot," he said.

She looked puzzled a moment. "Oh." She lowered her fingers. "I carry tension in my jaw."

He couldn't help it. He reached up slowly with both hands and used his thumbs to rub that same area, from her jaw line to her temple, his fingers sliding into her hair. She didn't try to pull away this time.

The stereo had stopped, he realized, and the room was virtually silent except for the sound of the half-hearted fire on the other side of the room. Liv's eyes dropped shut, and the world seemed to pause. Scott tried for a cooler head. *She said she didn't want this*, he reminded himself. But she stood motionless, eyes closed, as if a spell had fallen over them both.

He smoothed his thumbs through the hair at her temples, more slowly. His eyes wandered down to her parted lips. He wanted to kiss her. But not unless she wanted him to.

"Is this how it starts?" she said, almost languidly.

"No," he admitted wryly. "Usually it starts with a girl venting to me about some so-and-so."

Her eyes stayed closed, and he let his thumbs come to a rest at her temples, holding her face cupped in his hands.

"At least in your case there's no so-and-so," he said.

That brought her eyes open. Her hazel gaze fixed on his, as if uncertain whether or not to speak. And he knew.

Oh, crap. He'd fallen right into his demographic again. Scott let his hands drop.

Liv blinked, as if coming out of their mutual trance.

"See?" she said. "I told you. It's a bad idea."

Scott made himself step back, but it wasn't easy. An invisible magnetic pull seemed to draw him toward her. Even though everything she said made sense. A little *too* much sense.

"Do you ever hate being right?" he asked.

And he left, before that invisible magnet made him reach for her again.

Chapter 12

By the time Rachel came down the hall the next morning, Liv's clothes were strewn over the living room floor.

Liv waited, listening, at the far end of the kitchen table, where the partial wall between the kitchen and living room kept her blocked from view. She heard Rachel's slippers shuffle down the hall—definitely Rachel, not Mom, because the crutches made distinctive sounds with the shifting of Mom's weight.

Liv sipped her coffee, savoring the flavor, drinking in Rachel's shocked silence.

Then came a tentative, "Liv?"

Liv lowered her mug, grinned, and waited a few more seconds.

"*Liv?* Where are you?"

"In here."

Rachel entered the kitchen, her round gray eyes at their roundest. Liv let her sister take in the sight of her in her robe, slippers, and pajamas.

"The coffee's warm." Liv took another placid sip.

Rachel sidled toward the coffeepot, still staring at Liv. "What happened last night?"

Liv was tempted to let the game go on a little longer, but decided it was better not to let wild images implant themselves too firmly in Rachel's imagination. "Nothing. Scotty left about fifteen minutes after you went to bed."

"Where'd you sleep?"

"In bed next to you, snore-meister. I got up half an hour ago."

"What about—" Rachel's head swiveled toward the living room, scattered with yesterday's clothes.

Liv shrugged. "Just an idea I got from Scotty. Didn't you wonder what happened to *his* clothes?"

"I was too busy freaking out." Rachel swatted Liv's arm and glared at her.

Liv took another sip of coffee, hiding a smile of triumph. Rachel heaved an exasperated sigh, then went to the cabinet and pulled out a blue coffee mug. Rachel had always liked blue.

"My turn," Liv said. "What was up with you last night? You and Mom took off like the room was on fire."

"We were tired." Rachel poured her cup of coffee, trying for those wide, innocent eyes again.

Liv tapped the tabletop with her fingernail.

"Okay." Rachel settled into her chair, across the table from Liv. "I was trying to do something nice. Scotty makes you smile. And we're all going through a lot of stuff right now. Literally and figuratively."

"Scotty Leroux, emotional first aid kit? You told me he was a big Romeo."

"I was kidding around. He's dated a lot of girls, but

I've never heard any of them say anything bad about him. And he's *nice*. Maybe that doesn't sound like much, but it can be awfully hard to come by these days. I never told you about the guy I went out with before Brian and I got engaged."

Kevin had seemed nice, too. Until, all of a sudden, he dumped her, and she'd felt like a fool.

Liv backtracked. "I missed something. You and Brian dated all through high school."

"Until we broke up the summer after graduation. Everybody expected us to end up together, but I wanted to see what else was out there, I guess."

"So you found out you were right the first time?"

"Basically."

Liv had always wondered how Rachel could be sure she was ready to get married when she was barely twenty years old. If Rachel's visible contentment was any indication, it was working out well. Well enough, apparently, that Rachel was worried about *her* now.

Her little sister wasn't supposed to be more together than she was.

"Brian's coming up tomorrow night, isn't he?" Liv asked.

Rachel nodded with a Mona Lisa smile that Liv tried not to read as smug. After all, it had been at least a week since Rachel had seen her husband. "You miss him a lot, don't you?"

Her sister nodded. "His schedule's really been awful. Ten days on, ten days off. I hated that he couldn't even get away for the memorial. I think they would have let him off if it hadn't been for that big fire."

"He's a good guy."

"They're hard to find," Rachel reiterated. "I guess that's why I thought you and Scotty—"

"Nice idea, but don't forget, I live in Texas."

"Okay. I won't try to push it anymore. I guess I was a little obvious."

"You think?"

"Plus, it's kind of nice just to have a guy around. This week has been pretty . . . hormone heavy."

Liv had to admit, Scott had played the part of emotional buffer more than once. "Poor guy. He probably feels like he walked into a Bette Davis movie."

The creaking and clumping of Mom's crutches heralded her approach. Rachel said, "Don't give her a hard time about last night. It was my idea. She just went along with it."

The sound of crutches came closer. Sudden realization seized Liv.

"My clothes!" She flew to her feet to snatch her staged evidence off the living room floor.

The last thing Scott expected to see when he pulled up to The Snowed Inn was Rachel's blue sedan. He didn't think he would have recognized Rachel's car until earlier this week, when he loaded the silver Christmas tree into the trunk.

That tree. With the color wheel he'd volunteered to help Liv hunt through the attic for. He'd forgotten about that when he left last night. He hadn't been thinking straight at all. No, last night he'd been too busy trying to make something happen when Liv obviously had too much else on her mind. When he just needed to grow up and take no for an answer.

He gave the steering wheel a brief, tight squeeze and got out of the truck. He had work to do, and he'd get it done. He just hadn't counted on running into a Tomblyn this morning.

It could be Rachel. It wouldn't be Faye. But his gut, and Murphy's Law, told him it was Liv in there.

He went inside and found Jake, who led the way to the problem: a leaky kitchen sink. Scott refrained from mentioning that the sink was one of the things he hadn't installed at the hotel. Something about Jake's wanting to give The Snowed Inn's business to more than one local repairman. Scott didn't buy it. He knew he wasn't one of Jake Wyndham's favorite people. Friendly and diplomatic as Jake was, most people would never notice. But Wyndham always maintained an extra layer of polite professionalism when he dealt with Scott.

As fate would have it, the kitchen wasn't empty. They walked in on Mandy and Liv, who appeared to be in the midst of some sort of cabinet reorganization project. The counter across the room from the sink was scattered with mugs, canisters, cinnamon sticks, and mysterious-looking bottles of what might be flavored syrups.

"Hey, ladies," Scott said.

Liv turned, looking startled, and banged the top of her head on the open cabinet door above her. "Ouch!"

Scott started toward her, but Mandy was already right next to Liv. She put a hand on Liv's arm. "Are you okay?"

"Fine," Liv said in the irritated tone of someone who'd just banged her head. She shut her eyes and rubbed her scalp.

"Sorry," Scott said. "I was trying *not* to startle you."

Liv opened her eyes, their expression still carrying a glimmer of annoyance. And Scott remembered the last time they'd locked eyes.

Apparently, Liv did, too. Her annoyed look dissipated into something like confusion. "Hi, Scott."

"Hi." He tried to will away the awkwardness. "Sorry about your head."

She made a face. "I'm okay. No real damage done." Rubbing her head again, she turned back toward the cabinet and picked up where she and Mandy had left off.

"Think left to right," she said. "That's how we read, so that's how our brains tend to work. So if you set up your *first* ingredients on the left, and just work your way down the line, you spend less time scrambling back and forth."

"So, coffee and cocoa on the left, sprinkles and cinnamon sticks on the right," Mandy said.

"Exactly. You'll get a system down in no time."

Jake showed him the problem and vanished back toward the lobby. Scott slid under the sink and moved the drip-catching bucket aside after making sure the water was shut off. He examined the pipes, working to the tune of the murmured conversation between the two women. Once he found the problem, he lingered under the sink, because he knew he couldn't get any further without a trip to Coffman's Hardware.

"Thanks," Mandy said. "I'm used to making one or two drinks at a time, so whenever we get more than that, it's a rush."

"Business is good, then?"

"Picking up."

"Everyone loves Mandy's hot chocolate." Jake came back in from the lobby. As Scott emerged from under the kitchen sink, Jake walked up behind Mandy and leaned over to kiss her cheek.

"Do you see this?" Mandy stepped backward, leaning easily into Jake as she gestured at the tidy cabinet shelves. "I owe you a cup, Liv."

"Thanks so much, but I'll have to take a rain check," Liv said. "I need to book that room and get back to my mom and sister."

Scott clambered to his feet, wishing he knew a less clumsy way to get up off a kitchen floor. He kept his eyes off Liv, wondering if she was watching him, or if he was imagining it again. "I found the problem," he told Jake. "But I'll need to pick up some parts. You've got a couple of options."

Jake wore the disconcerted look of a man who didn't relish making mechanical decisions. Scott knew the look well; he saw it on customers a lot. Jake shifted his glance to Mandy, who was still occupied with refining her cabinet shelves into a model of order. "Tell you what," Jake said. "Let me get Liv squared away first."

Curious about what was going on with Liv and a hotel room, Scott followed Jake and Liv out to the lobby.

"You're booking a room why?" he asked as Jake settled in behind the check-in counter and Liv took her place on the customers' side.

"Rachel's husband is coming for the weekend." Liv leaned her elbows on the varnished wood. "We've been sharing a double bed in our old room. But she thrashes

134

around a lot, and I found out the other night my mom's couch is an instrument of torture."

Scott frowned. "So you're booking yourself a room to keep from sleeping on the torture-couch?"

She looked at him as if he'd lost his mind. "No, the hotel room is for Brian and Rachel. This way I can stay in the double bed without breaking my back. And I thought a couple of romantic nights might make kind of a nice early Christmas present." She frowned. "Unless that seems selfish, with everything that's going on."

Selfish? "No. I think it's nice of you."

"We have five rooms open for Friday and Saturday," Jake said from behind the check-in computer monitor. "Not counting the bridal suite. It's a little pricier, and— oh, hey, it's actually booked," he noted with a smile. "Let's narrow it down a little. I've got three with a fire-place, two with a wood-burning stove. Which sounds better?"

Liv frowned and turned to Scott. "What do you think? Fireplace or wood-burning stove?" She blinked self-consciously, as if she suddenly remembered who she was talking to.

She'd be more self-conscious if she could read his thoughts. Unbidden, his mind conjured a picture of a room with Liv in it, and the way firelight would play on her already-fiery chestnut hair. He didn't dare think any further, because he felt his face reddening.

He forced his mind back to practical matters. After all, that was why she'd asked. Wasn't it?

"Probably the fireplace," he said. "The wood-burning stove is pretty, too, but once those get going, it can get *really* hot."

Did that sound suggestive to anyone besides him, or was his mind in the gutter?

And Jake stood by, hands on keyboard, hearing every word.

"Fireplace," Liv said to Jake, delivering Scott from his brief stint in purgatory.

"Okay, that leaves us with . . ." Jake turned the computer monitor toward Liv. Over her shoulder Scott saw listings for the remaining rooms, each with a photo insert showing its decorating scheme.

"That's really impressive," Liv said.

"Thanks. It's the same screen we use on our website, so out-of-towners can see what we have."

Scott knew they were talking businessperson to businessperson, but he still felt a stupid sort of envy as Liv admired Jake's professional handiwork.

After a few moments' contemplation, Liv said, "I think . . . 'White Christmas.'"

It was the room with the snowflake decorating scheme. Jake nodded, turned the monitor back his way, and started typing. "That's one of Mandy's favorites. Heck, they're *all* Mandy's favorites. She really enjoyed putting them together."

Liv's face settled into a smile as they finished making the arrangements. And once again, Scott felt Jake's watchful presence. Then, thankfully, the phone rang, and Jake picked it up.

As Liv turned from the counter, Scott asked, "So, are we still on for Tuesday?"

She may have stiffened. "Sure." She paused. "Unless that doesn't work for you."

She stood back slightly, and at first Scott thought she

was trying to physically distance herself. Then he realized she was trying to avoid tipping her head back to look up at him. He leaned against the counter of the front desk, the relaxed posture lowering his height by a couple of inches.

"No," he said, "I want to be there when the heater guy shows up. But if you'd rather go along to your mom's appointment, I could borrow a key. I mean, if you'd feel comfortable doing that."

The air between them seemed to stir with invisible atoms of unease. "No," Liv said. "I mean, I want to sort through the attic, and Tuesday's a great time to do it. I won't have to worry about Mom or Rachel trying to climb around like mountain goats."

As she referenced his comment from last night, she cracked a smile, and Scott gladly returned it. The awkwardness was still there, but maybe they were past the worst of it. "The heater guy gave me one of those great time windows," he said. "Between noon and four. When is your mom's appointment?"

"Two thirty."

Behind him, Scott heard Jake hanging up. Scott straightened from his leaning position, and Liv took another step back.

"I'd better get going," she said. "I told Mom and Rachel I was picking up donuts. I want the room to be a surprise."

Scott nodded. "See you Tuesday. I'll be there by noon."

As Liv walked to the door, his eyes dropped to her retreating shoes. Rose-patterned tennies again, but this time the roses were actually rose-colored, probably to go with the maroon sweater she wore. Scott's eyes lingered on the door as it closed behind her.

"Give her a break," Jake said. "Her grandmother just died."

Scott turned. "Give her a break? What does that mean?"

"I mean, I'm sure Liv has a lot to deal with. And you're looking at her like she's another Tiffany. Or Angie."

Was *that* why Jake was always so carefully polite to him? Really?

Scott leaned against the counter again, forcing a casualness he didn't feel. "I didn't know you were so interested in my social life. You didn't even live here when I was going out with Angie. What exactly are you getting at?"

Jake let out a slow breath, as if he was trying to get a handle on his usual good manners. "Never mind. Tell me about the sink."

But today, for some reason, Scott found he *did* mind. "No. Back up a minute. What makes you think—"

Mandy came in from the kitchen, two whipped-cream-topped mugs in hand, and Scott fell silent. She raised her eyebrows. "What is it?"

Suddenly Scott wished he'd just kept his cool.

Jake, looking shamefaced, gave the time-honored reply: "Nothing."

Mandy scrutinized them, clearly not buying it. "I brought you both a hot chocolate." Her tone was slightly disapproving, like a parent who'd walked in on a couple of eight-year-olds squabbling over a game of Monopoly.

"That's okay," Scott told her. "You can have mine. I was just heading out."

"Wait," Jake said. "First I need to know about the sink."

Scott heaved a sigh. He usually avoided criticizing other workmen, but today he found he just didn't have the patience. "Your problem," he said, trying and failing to keep the terseness out of his voice, "is the guy you hired didn't know better than to use copper pipes up here. So when we had that big freeze Sunday night, the pipes cracked. Now you need to decide—"

Mandy strode past him to the little coffee bar and set both drinks down. "Drink your hot chocolate. And, please, whatever's going on with you two, fix it." She turned, her eyes darting between them. "Really, I don't get it. The two nicest guys I know, and it always seems like you're one step away from butting heads."

Scott wouldn't have thought it was obvious to anyone else.

"We weren't . . ." Jake began, and ran out of steam under Mandy's skeptical stare.

"Sit. Drink. Please." She threw up her hands like an orchestra's maestro.

She vanished back into the kitchen before either of them came up with a response, and the two of them stood alone in the cheery lobby. Scott wasn't annoyed anymore. Just really uncomfortable.

"Okay." Jake passed a hand roughly through his hair. "That was embarrassing." The edge had gone out of his voice, returning them to their usual strained unease.

"Look, I'm going to go."

"Not so fast. Remember, I have to live with her." With

a rueful shake of his head, Jake made his way to the coffee bar. "And I think I owe you an apology. Come on. You don't want to pass up Mandy's hot chocolate, anyway. Trust me."

Scott eyed the exit longingly. "What happens if I bail instead?"

"I have no idea. This has never happened before."

Scott could argue that he didn't have time for this. Or he could drink the darned hot chocolate and satisfy Mandy, who usually didn't have a cross word for anyone. So he joined Jake, taking the high-backed stool one down from Jake's, leaving an empty seat between them.

Scott took an experimental sip of cocoa and no longer regretted sticking around. It was amazingly rich, and the perfect drinking temperature. "So," he said, after relishing his drink for a moment. "The pipes. You can either replace the copper with PVC pipe, which I recommend, or—"

"Done. Put in what we need."

"You don't want to know how much?"

"I trust you. Your prices were better than the other guy's anyway."

"That's because copper's more expensive. It didn't used to be, but now some people assume it's better just because it costs more." Either that, or the other guy had been looking for ways to jack up the price. But Scott held his tongue.

Instead, he asked, "So why hire somebody else?"

Jake took a deep drink and appeared to consider. "Maybe because I wanted to give another contractor a shot at some of our business—"

Scott had heard that one before.

Jake sighed. "Or maybe because you got on my nerves."

Now they were getting down to it. Did he really want to hear this? "Why?"

"Okay, I'll just say it. The first time I ever saw you, you were eyeballing my wife. I guess I've never forgotten that."

Scott tried to remember what Jake was talking about. Then it came back to him. A late summer evening a couple of years ago, out on the town square. Mandy Reese, with some guy he'd never seen before. He'd been staring, all right. Mandy was always pretty to look at. But that night, what had really drawn his eye was the way she was looking at the stranger in the polo shirt. "She wasn't your wife yet."

Jake shrugged. "I didn't say it was rational."

"You can't be serious. You *got* the girl. I haven't been able to pull that one off yet."

"Either that, or you've gotten a few too many." Jake's tone didn't have the earlier sharpness, but he grimaced at his own words. "Sorry. That didn't come out right. I was trying to be funny."

"It's not what it looks like."

"I know." At Scott's double take, Jake went on. "Angie works for us. She comes in nights to help Mandy with the coffee bar." Jake fiddled with his mug. "And she only says nice things about you."

Scott laughed. So that was how he knew about Angie. "So you were worried about me and Mandy?"

"I wouldn't say worried. But sometimes first impressions die hard. Dumb, I know."

"I don't think she even forgave me for nicknaming her 'Mandy Claus' until about two years ago," Scott said.

"Oh, yeah." Jake grinned. "There was that, too."

"Truce?" Scott stuck out his hand.

Jake took it.

Scott returned to his hot chocolate. "The fact is," he heard himself admit, "I've never seen her this happy. And I've known her since kindergarten."

Jake quirked an eyebrow. "Nice to hear. I just hope I'm not wearing her out with this hotel. When she married me, she ended up married to the business. And she's great at so much of it. She's a genius at decorating, people love her, and she makes amazing hot chocolate. But organization isn't her strong suit. And she knows she can't do everything herself, but she hates telling people what to do."

"Liv's good at that," Scott said before he thought. He remembered the way she'd fearlessly recruited the waitresses to make sandwiches, and the way she'd made sure they knew they were appreciated.

"Is she looking for a job?"

Scott wasn't entirely sure if Jake was kidding. "Wouldn't that be nice."

Jake raised an eyebrow again, but said nothing.

"What? You don't have to worry about Liv, either," Scott said. "She's only here for a few weeks. I couldn't do any damage if I tried."

That sounded dangerously close to self-pity, so he lifted his mug again.

"Mandy says you and Liv both graduated the same year she did," Jake said. "Is this the first time you've seen her since high school?"

"Just about. I must have seen her at Rachel's wedding, but . . ." He didn't remember much about that day. He'd been in the middle of a fight with Angie, who'd been one of Rachel's bridesmaids. And Liv, being Liv, had probably taken the next flight back to that business of hers in Texas.

"The thing is," Scott said slowly, "there are two kinds of people in Tall Pine. The kind who never want to leave, and the kind who can't wait to grow up and get out of town. I'm the first kind. Liv's the second."

Definitely veering into self-pity. He took another drink of the warming chocolate to shut himself up.

"There's a third kind," Jake said suddenly. "People who come here for the first time, and find out it's home." He frowned. "I sound like a greeting card." Jake tilted his mug forward and studied its remaining contents. "What's *in* this stuff, anyway?"

Scott took a whiff of his own nearly empty drink. He smelled only rich chocolate, and maybe some cinnamon. He did feel more mellow, but surely . . . "Mandy wouldn't do that."

He didn't think so, anyway. But this was easily the longest conversation he'd ever had with Jake.

Scott stepped down from the tall chair and found he was steady on his feet. And now that he was on his feet, he remembered he had work to do. "Okay. Time for me to go."

Jake stood, too. "We're good, then?"

Scott nodded. "We're good."

As he walked out to his truck, he felt perfectly fine. But just to be sure, before he climbed inside, he tipped his head back, extended his arms and touched the tip of his nose with each index finger. He was sober, all right.

And, as he'd always reluctantly suspected, Jake Wyndham was a decent guy.

Jake drained the last of his hot chocolate and carried the mugs to the kitchen.

Mandy's cocoa really was the best he'd ever tasted. The flavor might be a little different today—if anything, maybe even better than usual.

In the kitchen, he found her wiping down counters. Jake held up his empty mug. "Mandy, what was in this?"

Eyeing the mugs, she flushed. "You caught me."

Jake stared at her in mild alarm. "Are you serious? We're not licensed to serve alcohol."

Mandy raised her eyebrows. "Are *you* serious? I just meant, I put in some ground cloves this time."

He peered into his mug again and saw a few dark grains. But then, Mandy always put in some cinnamon.

"I've been playing with the recipe," she went on. "I didn't want to make it like a chai, exactly. Just a little richer. Too much?"

He frowned. "So there's really no alcohol in it?"

"Of course not. Why?"

Jake leaned against the counter. "Well, you told us to sit down and make up, and darned if we didn't."

Her blue eyes shimmered with amusement. "You made up with Scotty, so you thought I got you two liquored up?"

"It's hard to explain." He loaded the mugs into the dishwasher and gave her a wry grin. "But maybe you ought to lay off the cloves for now. And maybe . . . we ought to keep an eye on the people we serve hot chocolate to. If they're not getting along—I know it's crazy, but I think the cocoa might make a difference."

When you married a woman who'd seen Santa Claus, Jake had discovered, you learned to expect unexplained things. Like the first Christmas they were married. At the crack of dawn, he woke up and realized he'd forgotten all about Mandy's stocking. Pretty embarrassing, especially since her present to him the year before was a stocking she'd needlepointed herself. Nevertheless, that morning, her stocking had been filled with an orange to round out the toe, peppermints, chocolates, even a gingerbread man.

He didn't think she'd done it herself. He'd just never had the nerve to ask.

"Jake," Mandy said, "that's silly. I thought *I* was supposed to be the one with the vivid imagination."

"Sue me." He crossed the room and folded his arms around her, relishing the easy, warm way she fit against him. "After all, you're the one who got me believing things I never thought I'd believe in."

Chapter 13

Liv, Rachel, and Mom couldn't face the task of boxing up Nammy's clothing, so they asked Rachel's husband to do it.

The three of them took a quick look in the closet and dresser drawers of the master bedroom, and that was hard enough. Clothing was so personal. It wasn't as if any of them could really wear any of Nammy's old outfits, but nearly every article brought back a memory. Mom saved a crocheted scarf, and that was all any of them could manage before turning the job over to Brian.

While he worked, the three of them put their energy into the seldom-used guest room down the hall, where most of the items didn't hold any personal memories. They'd boxed up most of the room inside of half an hour when Brian appeared in the doorway.

"Done," he said, and Rachel went to him with a grateful hug.

If the chore was hard on Brian, he didn't show it, but it probably would have been hard to tell. Tall, sturdy, and blond, he'd been patient and uncomplaining these past couple of days—the textbook illustration for strong-and-silent. His support of Rachel was palpable, but Liv wondered if her sister ever got starved for dialogue.

One arm still around Rachel, Brian nodded at the new stack of boxes. "Want me to take those out to the living room?"

"All but the one in front of the closet." Rachel nodded toward an open box on the floor, still half-empty. Brian scooped up the other two and carried them toward the living room.

They emptied the closet in short order and had the last box ready a few minutes after Brian returned. They accompanied him out to the living room, where he added the box to the to-go pile. It had grown substantially in the last couple of days. Except for the barely touched living room with all its furniture, the house was looking less and less like Nammy's. It had to be done, but it hurt.

Faye eased into one of the living room armchairs, this time without any prodding from Liv or Rachel, and propped her foot on the ottoman in front of the seat. She was showing more fatigue today, and Liv was struck once again by the amount of gray hair her mom had picked up over the last few years.

Liv leaned against the arm of Mom's chair, not quite sitting on it, but close. "Tired?"

"A little."

Rachel perched on the other arm of Mom's chair. "You can have another painkiller, you know. Dr. Melendez said that's what they're for."

"Then I'd be tired *and* groggy."

Brian stood by, waiting for more orders. Liv thought

clearing Nammy's closet had probably been easier for him than it would have been for Scotty. Brian had known her, but as far as Liv knew, Nammy had never had a chance to feed him soup.

She missed Scott.

The thought came out of nowhere and hit her right in the solar plexus. She missed Scott, not just for the bazillion ways he'd helped them, but for his warm, steadying presence. The way he had of lightening the mood. The way he looked at her, his eyes turning serious at moments when she least expected it.

Yep, it was a good thing she had a break from him. She couldn't afford to get used to having him around. She'd see him Tuesday, when they'd get together to clear the attic.

That was still two days away.

Brian surveyed the living room. "Have you decided what to do with the furniture yet?"

"We're leaving that for last," Mom said. "There might be a couple of pieces I'll keep, and the girls are welcome to anything they want. After that, I think we'll start showing the house with the furniture in it. A lived-in look might be nice. And the buyers can decide what they want to keep."

"The boxes are piling up," Brian said. "Do you guys know anyone with a truck?"

"We gave him the weekend off," Liv said, too quickly to be nonchalant.

Monday saw Brian headed back down to San Diego for his next standby shift, thanking Liv for their two nights at The Snowed Inn. Sunday night, Brian and Rachel had shared the double bed in Mom's guest room, while Liv tangled herself up in a pretzel twist on the torture-couch.

And Tuesday, Liv went to Nammy's house on her own to wait for Scotty and the heater expert.

"Wow," Scott said when he stepped into the living room. "You guys have really been at it."

The living room still had all its furniture, but the stacks of boxes had grown monumentally. Liv suspected they'd need to weed more things out of the to-keep pile before it was over, but they'd cross that bridge when they got to it. Just beyond the living room, the kitchen was all but gutted, leaving nothing but the old Shaker table and the refrigerator. Nammy had never seen the need for a dishwasher.

"It's starting to echo," she said as they walked into the kitchen. The heels of her boots clattered on the floor.

"Boots?" Scotty said.

"They're comfortable," Liv said defensively. "And warm." And they had heels.

"Speaking of warm, any trouble with the heater this weekend?"

"Come to think of it, no. But it was warmer this weekend. We didn't need it much." She crossed the floor to the hallway and looked up at the recessed door, clearly framed, in the ceiling. "So, there's the door to the attic," she said. "How do we get up there?"

Scott went out to the garage. Moments later, he returned with a stepladder, grinning in satisfaction. "Right where I left it last time."

Liv's mom's house had a crawlspace, too; the door

leading up into it was a similar recess in the ceiling. As a little girl, she'd begged to see inside, and her father had finally caved in. He'd stood on the two-foot kitchen stepladder and pushed the rectangular slab that served as a door up into the crawlspace. Then he'd held Liv on his shoulders, and she'd poked her head up through the opening. She didn't remember what she'd expected—probably hidden treasure—but she'd been disappointed to see a small, dark area about three feet high. Her father's flashlight had revealed nothing but raw wooden beams, insulation, plenty of dust and, undoubtedly, spider webs. It hadn't been long before she asked him to set her down.

He'd offered Rachel a look, too, probably trying to avoid having to go through the same process again in the future. But for four-year-old Rachel, her big sister's disappointed and slightly repulsed reaction was apparently enough to end her curiosity.

Her family had never stored anything in the attic because her father said it was a firetrap. Nammy's attic must offer a little more space than that.

"Will we actually be able to fit up there?" Liv asked as Scotty climbed the ladder.

"You'll see." Scott pushed up at the trap door. "It's not exactly roomy, but—"

He shoved upward again. After several seconds of resistance, the door flung up into the ceiling, accompanied by crackling noises, a shower of dust and other unidentified particles.

Then it slammed back down. Liv jumped involuntarily.

"Oh, right." Apparently unperturbed by the dust that

now sprinkled his head and shoulders, Scott pushed the door up again. This time it didn't resist as much. He climbed the ladder ahead of her and held the trap door open. Liv started up after him. Near the top, she paused and waited as Scott, now on his knees in the attic, slid a box in front of the door to hold it in place.

"I forgot that," he said. "It's on hinges, and it won't stay up by itself. It goes up to ninety degrees and stops."

"Weird." Liv resumed her climb, accepting Scott's hand to bring her the rest of the way in as she stepped onto the floor of the dimly lit attic.

"Watch your head."

He said it just in time. Except for a neighbor kid's tree house, she'd never come so close to hitting her head on a ceiling before. She stood slowly, knees bent, as Scott's hand steadied her. The room was about five feet high.

"Thanks." Once she'd stopped flailing for balance, she let go of Scott's hand. "Who on earth makes a room *almost* tall enough to stand up in?"

"Maybe people were shorter before World War II."

"It's that old?"

"I'm not sure. That's what Nammy told me. She said it's one of the oldest houses in Tall Pine. I do know she and your grandfather weren't the first people who lived here."

Liv surveyed her dusty new world. They'd actually entered near the tallest part of the attic. The ceiling slanted downward, matching the angle of the roof outside. The lowest point was probably about three feet high. Near the top of another wall, a short, wide window let in the dim sunshine. Dust motes flittered aimlessly

151

in the air where the direct sun came in. And half a dozen boxes littered the aging wooden floor, away from the walls, probably to spare their contents the worst of the temperature extremes outside.

Stepping away from the trap door, Liv found a higher section of the ceiling. If she stayed right here and didn't move, she could actually stand up straight. Scotty wouldn't have that luxury.

She brushed her hands against her jeans, already feeling as if she were absorbing the dust. "So," she said, "let's get started."

Liv found her prime directive, the color wheel, in its original box from the manufacturer. She set it near the trap door. It would be the first thing down. What remained to be seen was whether any of Nammy's other stored items would be worth keeping.

So far, every box should have been labeled *Miscellaneous.*

"Another jar candle," Scott reported, holding up the fourth one.

"What flavor is this one?"

He squinted at the label. "Vanilla."

"I wonder why so many."

"They're all the same size, and they look like the same manufacturer. I'll bet these are the ones the kids from school sell door to door, along with magazine subscriptions and peanut brittle."

Liz made a face. "Definitely the most useful choice out of that group."

"What do you mean? I always buy the peanut brittle. I *love* peanut brittle."

"That takes care of my Christmas shopping for you, then."

Being with Scott, even in this tight space, was starting to feel almost normal. It looked like they'd put the discomfiture of last week behind them, and for that, Liv was grateful. She couldn't fight the urge to keep chattering, though. As if another uncomfortable moment was waiting behind the next silence.

"Dishes," Liv said. "Here's a whole set of dishes, still in the box they came in."

"She already *had* a set of dishes."

Liv studied the picture on the box. "Pretty pattern." But obviously, she'd never used them. "I wonder if she was starting to get a little of that hoarder gene."

"Doesn't sound like her."

"And the rest of the house didn't look like it." Except for those decorating supplies. Liv brushed the troublesome thought aside. Nammy had been eighty-three, after all, and if she'd had a couple of eccentricities near the end, they'd certainly been mild ones.

From down below, the doorbell rang. Scotty half rose and edged his way to the trap door. "That must be our guy. Want to come down with me?"

"Do you mind going ahead, and letting me know when he's ready to give me the results? I'll be more use up here for now."

While Scott was gone, Liv continued sorting. As she worked, she heard the heater click off; several minutes later, there was the familiar preliminary click, followed by the sound of the unit kicking back on again. The

153

process repeated a few more times while Scott was gone. As the heat rose into the attic, she started to wish she'd worn something other than a sweatshirt, or that she'd worn something lighter underneath so she could shed the warm layer. This was turning into one of those perverse December days in California when it felt more like spring than winter.

Half an hour later, Scott's head poked back up through the rectangular trap door. Somehow, Liv wasn't surprised by the news: "He can't find anything wrong, either."

"Just like a car. It won't act up in front of the repairman."

Liv followed Scott down the ladder. Down in the hallway, she met a khaki-shirted man with the name *Russ* stitched over his pocket.

"Congratulations," he said. "You've got me stumped. I couldn't get it *not* to come on."

"What do we do?" Liv asked.

"For right now, keep track of it. If it keeps acting up, do me a favor and write down the days and times. I'm going to talk to corporate and see if they'll offer a replacement if it keeps happening. I should have an answer by the end of the week." He held out a business card to her.

"Thanks." Liv took the business card and slipped it into the back pocket of her jeans.

When Russ-the-repairman left, they climbed back into the attic. Liv contemplated the mini-mound of boxes. They'd gotten about halfway through. She turned to Scott. "You know, you don't need to stay for

all of this, if you've got something else to work on—"
Why did she say *if*? Surely he had somewhere else to be.

Scott shook his head. "A bigger name on the other line? Nah. Besides, I don't want to find out tomorrow you took a spill when no one was around."

"What if I knock you down the ladder and we *both* take a spill?"

"Let's don't do that."

She was starting to give up arguing with him. And as the afternoon wore on, she didn't know if going through things with Scott was actually faster, but it was easier.

"Now, here's something you don't see every day." Scott held up a white ceramic cow's head, about the size of an orange, obviously designed to be mounted on a wall. Straight-faced, he said, "I hope I'm not treading on a sacred cow."

Liv grinned. "Believe it or not, I think that's for hanging hand towels. She did the whole bathroom in cows once."

"And then she came to her senses?" Scott produced a furry, round throw rug with black and white spots.

Liv remembered that rug. But seeing it through someone else's eyes, it looked a lot more ridiculous.

What got harder to ignore, the more comfortable she felt with Scott, was how much smaller the attic started to feel. And how much warmer. She wished, again, that she'd worn something lighter than a sweatshirt. Scott had shrugged out of his down vest some time back and rolled back the sleeves of his plaid flannel work shirt.

She turned to the box she'd just opened. "Fishing tackle box. Ever go fishing?"

"No. Too impatient. And I wouldn't know what to do with a fish if I caught one."

Liv thought of Nammy, griping good-naturedly about the chore of cleaning the trout her grandfather used to bring home after catching them at Prospect Lake. To Liv, cleaning fish was a mystery best left unexplored, but she did know how good fresh-caught trout could taste. She remembered her whole family coming over Saturday afternoons, if her grandfather had a big day fishing, and enjoying the bounty.

Her grandfather died when she was fourteen, a few years before her father. Those couldn't have been easy years for Nammy or her mom.

Moments later, she found a whole box of painting supplies—more mementos of her grandfather. The brushes, rollers, and pans all looked well used, but well cleaned, too. Liv fingered the long bristles of a paintbrush. It probably still had a lot of life left to it, unlike the user.

She realized that it was after her grandfather was gone that Nammy had started going to the Pine 'n' Dine regularly on Saturday afternoons, when there were no more weekend fish to fry. She wondered if the new ritual had been an effort to fill part of the hole her grandfather left behind. She wondered, twelve years later, how much her grandmother had still missed him. Things that hadn't occurred to her at the time.

"Hey." The familiar word from Scott called her attention up from the rough bristles under her fingers. There were those blue eyes again, seeing more than she wanted him to see, his head tilted slightly to peer down at her face. Another *are-you-okay* moment.

"Don't say it," Liv warned, smiling through slightly clenched teeth.

"I didn't." Returning her smile, Scott squeezed her arm gently.

It was an innocent gesture, and she knew it. So why did she feel flushed inside, as if a heater had suddenly flared up inside her stomach?

The heater. Of course. Maybe that explained some of it.

She edged back. "He left the heater on, didn't he?"

Scott lifted his hand carefully from her arm, his head cocked in a listening attitude, his eyes drifting past hers. "I can't hear for sure. But it feels that way."

"I'll go check," Liv said promptly, and scrambled for the ladder.

"Careful." Scott's voice followed her down.

Sure enough, the heat lessened as Liv descended. *Heat rises.* It was a law of nature. The fact that she'd been in a small, enclosed space, just a few feet away from Scotty, had nothing to do with it.

Liv switched off the thermostat in the hallway, leaned against the wall beside it, and took a few deep breaths. Scott was being his old self—friendly, funny, encouraging. If he'd gotten past their near miss the other night, so could she.

Taking time for one more deep breath, she clambered back up the ladder. Like a mountain goat.

Chapter 14

Scott added the last box to the stacks by the trap door, raising dust motes in the waning afternoon light. "I think that about does it."

Liv brushed at her jeans again and nodded. "Thanks. I really killed your afternoon."

At least she wasn't talking about offering him money anymore. "I'll catch up tomorrow. No problem."

They could just as easily have toted all the boxes downstairs to begin with, for Liv and her family to sort through at their leisure. Scott wondered if Liv realized that. He hadn't wanted to be the one to point it out.

Apparently he was a glutton for punishment. He'd been on his best behavior all afternoon, and Liv seemed content to put the other night behind them. Which was good, of course.

Somewhere over the course of the afternoon, she'd pulled her hair up behind her head into a careless knot, and the sleeves of her sweatshirt were pushed up to her elbows. All business. He had to admire the way she went about things—methodical and productive, without being too type-A about it. Once upon a time, he would have figured her for a major control freak, but she'd proven him wrong.

Scott perched on a box to keep from bending under the too-low ceiling. He'd spent the day stooping, sitting, or kneeling; odds were he'd have a couple of good kinks in his spine by tomorrow morning. And he was still sorry to see their project end.

An *absolute* glutton for punishment. He tried to focus, like Liv, on the business at hand.

"Now," he said, "to get these things downstairs. I figure I can go down and bring the kitchen table alongside the ladder. Then you push the boxes over to me while I stand on the ladder and—"

He heard Liv walk toward the far wall behind him, where the trap door stood propped open. "Duh. We didn't even think to check through *this* box."

Scott heard the slide of cardboard against the floor— then, before he could open his mouth, a loud slam.

He wheeled around, whacking his head on the ceiling.

Liv stood beside the closed trap door, next to the box that had served as a doorstop.

"You didn't." His words snapped out ahead of his brain. "Tell me you didn't just do that."

She stared at him, startled. Then her eyes went to the closed trap door as comprehension dawned. "Wait. You mean we're locked in?"

"I mean the handle's broken off. Yeah. We're trapped."

She stared at the rough-hewn door. Then she dropped to her knees, her fingertips digging frantically around the crevices at the door's edges. "Is there a way to pry it up?"

She looked one shade away from panic. But at least she was thinking in terms of action.

"Stop." Annoyance forgotten, he joined her by the trap door. "It's more than an inch thick. You'll rip up your fingernails."

She jerked her hands back and picked at a splinter in her fingertip. Tension came off her in waves. "*Damn* it."

Scott crouched next to her and reached for her injured hand. Without thinking, he spoke the forbidden words: "Are you okay?"

She pulled her hand back. "No," she said. "I'm not. I trapped us in here." Frustration swam in her eyes. "I can't *believe* I—"

"Hey, I'm the one who didn't tell you about the handle." And he should have fixed it in the first place. But the blame game wasn't a very productive hobby.

Liv sat back on her heels, staring at the door again. "Do we have anything up here we could use? A crowbar, a slim jim?"

"A fishing pole?" He couldn't help it. She knew the contents of this attic every bit as well as he did.

"Don't make fun." She raised her fingertips to her temples, rubbing that area in front of her jaw. "Never mind. Go ahead. This is my fault."

"Chill. It's not that bad."

"What are you talking about? You're mad, too."

"No, I *was* mad. You skyrocketed past me in about two seconds."

She closed her eyes and huffed out a long breath. Scott stared at her in fascination. She was wrapped *way* tighter than he was. She dug into her jeans pocket and fished out her cell phone. The small square screen illuminated.

"No bars," she muttered. "Of course."

"Okay," Scott said. "Let's go over what we've got here."

He rose from his crouched position, but of course there still wasn't room to stand up straight. He went to the nearest wall and sat on the floor with his back against it, legs in front of him to give the illusion of a little more space.

Her eyes opened to focus on him. "What are you doing?"

"Getting comfortable. We might be here a while. And I'm a little claustrophobic."

"What are you talking about? You've been up here all afternoon."

"Yeah, but we were busy." He couldn't resist adding, "And I knew I could get out."

"Oh." Liv surveyed his long legs as comprehension dawned. "Scott, I'm—"

"Say you're sorry again and I'll try to stuff you out through that little window up there. Come on. Let's hash this out." He extended his fingers. "Plan A. We go over what we've got in here, see if there's a way we can pry open the door. Plan B—"

"That little window?"

He shook his head. "Too high off the ground."

"Then on to Plan C." Liv frowned. "No cell phone

161

reception. Maybe we could break the little window and holler for the neighbors?"

Scott grinned. "A little drastic. And a little embarrassing. If they even heard us, which is doubtful." The homes on Nammy's street, in this older neighborhood, were spread farther apart. "Your mom and sister *are* coming back eventually, after all. They can open the door from the other side, or get someone to help."

"So, Plan D." Liv looked downcast. "We wait to be rescued."

"It's probably the most likely. What time will your mom and Rachel be back from that appointment?"

"With doctor's appointments, you never know. They could have waited an hour before they even saw him."

"Okay. Let's say, worst-case scenario, they get stuck there till the doctor's office closes. Five, five thirty?"

"Say five thirty."

"Okay, five thirty. It's about an hour and fifteen minutes back from Fontana—"

"Unless they hit traffic."

"All right. Hideous rush-hour traffic from Fontana all the way up to the mountains. And we know the weather's good. So add, what, an hour?"

"Okay."

"That puts us at—"

"Seven fifteen."

"They get home, they miss us, they come up here to check."

"Unless they think maybe we went out to eat."

"You're a real glass-is-half-full kind of gal, aren't you?"

She ran a hand through her hair silently.

Lacing his fingers together, Scott extended his arms

in front of him, taking comfort in the stretch, as he considered. "So. Here's our next move. While there's still daylight, we check through these boxes and figure out what we've got up here to sustain life until the rescue team arrives. And we'll take a shot at Plan A, too."

Without the proper tools, Scott didn't hold out a lot of hope for getting that door open. But he wouldn't be worth his salt as a handyman if he didn't give it a try. If nothing else, it would kill some time. And the very act of planning seemed to put Liv more at ease.

For the next hour, she impressed him.

Now that she was done kicking herself, Liv helped Scott sort through their resources with efficiency and logic. Her ideas for prying up the trap door were pretty creative, too. In her grandfather's box of painting supplies, she found a metal paint edger slim enough to fit into the crevice of the trap door opening. When they tried to pry the door up, however, the two-inch blade of the edger was just too short to give any useful leverage against the thick, heavy door.

Their last attempt was more far-fetched. Liv came up with the idea of stringing a fishing hook to a pole, pounding the hook into the wood of the trap door with a shoe, then trying to reel the door up. But when they tried it, the hook came up out of the door, bringing out chunks of wood along with it. The effort was worth it just for the visual of trying to fish open a trap door. Best of all, it made Liv laugh.

But now, just before five PM, it was getting dark. And, though Scott didn't want to bring it up, cold. Without

163

the sun hitting the roof, the temperature dropped rapidly. They had light, thanks to the fund-raiser candles, but the flames in the jars didn't provide more than the illusion of heat.

Sweatshirt sleeves pulled down, Liv hugged herself, rubbing her upper arms vigorously. "Too bad we can't build a campfire," she said with a wry smile.

She'd been a good sport, all right, once she recovered from her initial tailspin. Now, if he could keep her distracted from the cold. Because the more she rubbed her arms, the more he felt like shivering, too.

Scott held out a tin of cookies they'd unearthed from the boxes. "Pfeffernuss?"

Liv picked one out of the tin. "Hey, I sent her these."

"How long ago?"

"Last year. Or the year before." She squinted in thought. "Last year. So how'd they wind up in a box in the attic? Unless they're from some other year." She frowned at the cookie in her hand.

"I carried some boxes up for her last year after Christmas. They probably got mixed up with some of the other things."

Liv took a tentative bite and nodded. "Still edible." She finished the cookie, then began an elaborate process of dusting the powdered sugar from her fingers—first rubbing her fingers together, then rubbing her fingers on her jeans. Then, with the backs of her fingers, she tried to dust the sugar from the jeans themselves.

Liv was orderly and meticulous, but she wasn't *that* obsessive.

Scott had a fair idea why she was suddenly so fixated.

They were trapped alone together in a small, dark space. He'd thought about that, too. It was pretty hard not to.

Not in the cards, he reminded himself. But surely she knew him well enough to know he wouldn't try anything she didn't want to do.

Didn't she?

She shifted her weight from one foot to the other, rubbing her upper arms again, casting her eyes around as if searching the darkening nooks and crannies for small talk.

"Liv," he said gently. "Sit down."

"Moving around keeps me warmer."

Scott sighed, remembering the down vest he'd taken off before they came up here, now lying somewhere useless in the kitchen. He stood—as much as the low roof would allow—and searched through their reserve pile until he found the closest thing he could to a blanket: a musty white tablecloth.

"Here." He handed it to her. "Now, pick a spot and settle down. All that fidgeting is getting on my nerves."

He retreated, pointedly, a respectable distance away, where he sat back against the box of paint cans that had held the trap door open. The box provided a buffer from the cold of the outside wall. The attic ran half the length of the house; she was welcome to the rest of it, if it made her feel better. He folded his arms across his body as he sat, trying not to look *too* cold.

Okay, he wasn't above playing on her sympathy.

Liv held the tablecloth in front of her, looking guilty. "This isn't fair."

"No big deal. I'm bigger than you. More body heat."

If he remembered right, women were supposed to

have more body heat than men, but he wasn't going to bring that up.

Slowly, Liv crossed the room and sat next to him against the box, draping the tablecloth over them both like a blanket. She kept her shoulder a couple of inches away from his.

The tablecloth wasn't all that heavy, but it helped a little. The small amount of heat radiating from Liv—or his perception of her nearness—helped more.

Say something that doesn't have anything to do with body heat. Or . . .

Scott wasn't often at a loss for conversation, but suddenly his mind was a blank.

Liv drew her knees up close to her body, hugging them. "I'm really sorry about this."

"Want me to clobber you with a great big stick?"

"Sorry," she said again, then laughed.

Into the silence, she added, "I just felt stupid. I hate feeling stupid."

"There's nothing stupid about you, Liv. And it wasn't even your fault. I should have warned you about the door."

She hugged her knees harder, with a tremor that was visible.

He couldn't stand it. "You're shivering."

She rested her cheek against her knees, her head turned to face him. "And you're not?"

"That's my point. You know you're safe, right? I mean, I'm not going to grab you and—squeeze you to death or anything."

She contemplated him seriously, unblinking. "I know."

A bayberry candle flickered nearby on the floor, casting a dim light that left her features indistinct. What the heck was a bayberry, anyway?

He took a deep breath. "So, let's be real. You know we'll both be warmer if we're not sitting two inches apart."

She nodded slightly. Then she edged closer, until her arm rested against his. She shivered again, but then her warmth seeped in through his arm.

Yes, this was better. He just had to make sure it didn't feel *too* much better.

"So," he said. "How about those Dodgers?"

That set a tiny ripple of laughter through her. "I'll let you know in six months."

"Oh. Right."

Strangers on city buses had to sit this way all the time, shoulder to shoulder, he reminded himself. Liv sat motionless beside him, facing straight ahead.

"Okay, here's a real question," he said. "What's the story with you and all the shoes?"

"I don't think it's so weird. Women love shoes."

"Still. You're the queen of decluttering, right?"

Liv shrugged and sighed at the same time, two simple movements that put all his nerve endings on high alert. "Okay. I *always* loved shoes. They're like candy. But when I started learning to streamline things, I knew I had too many." She turned her head toward him. "Some women would say you can never have too many, you know."

"Right."

"So, I made a rule. I can keep as many shoes as I want as long as I wear them. There's no point having a closet full of shoes if you only really wear two or three pair. So, I make sure I use them. I enjoy them. That way they're not clutter. It's a little silly, but . . ." Another delicious shrug.

"But you found a way to make it logical."

She brought her head to rest on his shoulder, and Scott felt warmer still. He tried to think of porcupines. Gila monsters. The Wicked Witch of the West.

It didn't work too well. He was pretty sure the Wicked Witch didn't have soft hair that smelled like vanilla. Or maybe that was one of the candles.

"My turn," she said. "Serious question. How did you and Nammy get so close?"

"I told you about that. I started doing repairs here."

"Right. But when did she start feeding you and stuff?"

"I can't remember. I guess it just happened by degrees. Things like, one day I was working on her fridge. I made some joke about how mine was full of Budget Gourmet. I wasn't hinting, really."

"But you didn't turn down her homemade soup."

"I'm no freeloader, but I'm no fool either." He shifted. "Liv? My arm's starting to fall asleep."

It was almost true. In reality, his arm was getting stiff from the effort of trying to keep still next to her. Liv raised her head, allowing him to put his arm around her, then returned her head to his shoulder. More gingerly this time.

Keep talking. "So, every couple of weeks, she'd have

some kind of little job for me to do. With a house this old, there's always something that needs doing. And when I was done, out would come the cookies. Or the soup. Or the coffee. I think she kind of liked taking care of me, and I enjoyed it too. I liked her company."

"She adopted you," Liv said slowly. He heard something wistful in her voice.

"Maybe a little." He paused. "She really did talk about you a lot."

"Good." He felt a quiet breath go out of her. "I'm trying to stop beating myself up over it. It doesn't do any good. But I wish I'd been here more. I guess for some dumb reason I thought there'd always be time."

He heard the catch in her voice and gave her a short squeeze with his arm. *Keep talking.* "Why'd you stay away?"

"I'm not sure. Plane fares, I guess. And scheduling. When you're running a business, it's hard to get away."

"Right. But why'd you stay in Texas to begin with? Why not come home?"

"Well, when Terri and I got out of college, we were already there in Dallas. And for what we wanted to do—you said it yourself. Most people here aren't sure what a home organizer *is*. Even if they understood it, even if some people were interested, there are only so many closets in Tall Pine. And—"

Liv stopped. She hadn't meant to go on.

"And?" Scott prompted. His voice, low and deep, reverberated in her ear where it rested on his shoulder. Coaxing her to go on.

"I was afraid." She wished her voice didn't sound so

small in the dark. Somehow, this little chat in the attic was starting to feel like a game of Truth or Dare.

"Afraid?"

She sighed. "I guess it sounds conceited, but I felt like when I graduated high school, everybody expected me to do something big. And I wasn't sure I could do it here." She paused. "When you live in the same place all your life, people—expect things."

"I wouldn't know," Scott said, his voice laced with irony. "Nobody expects anything out of me."

"I don't know about that. I think people count on you. I know we sure have."

He shifted the conversation back to her. "So it was less scary to start out on your own, a thousand miles from home?"

"I know it sounds weird. But if I failed up here in Tall Pine . . ."

Forget Truth or Dare. This was starting to sound more like psychotherapy. She'd never put this into words before, was surprised to hear the words coming out of her mouth.

"I'd feel stupid," she confessed. "I told you, I *hate* feeling stupid. I'm supposed to be the smart girl, remember? That's why I got so frustrated when I trapped us up here. You know the guy who just broke up with me? That's what really got me. He got engaged to someone else right away. And I felt stupid."

Scott stirred, disturbing her comfortable position on his shoulder. "You know what?" he said. "For once, let's don't talk about the other guy. Not right now, anyway."

"Why not?"

He hesitated. "Trying to break precedent, I guess.

170

Same reason I haven't gone out with anyone since Tiffany and I broke up. By the time other people are making jokes about it, you kind of figure you're becoming your own cliché."

Another way to break precedent would be to let me talk about the other guy, then not put a move on me, Liv thought.

She didn't say it. Maybe because the longer they sat huddled together, the harder it was to remember that she didn't want him to make a move.

But he hadn't. Not since the other night, when he found out she was coming off of a breakup. In fact, he'd gone out of his way to be a gentleman. Especially now, with his arm around her and her head resting on his shoulder.

Probably he was trying to hold to an unspoken code of ethics. Or else she'd convinced him she wasn't interested. Or maybe she was just more resistible than she'd like to believe.

She huddled closer to Scott again, feeling the texture of his flannel shirt against her cheek. Feeling the firmness of his shoulder underneath. Wishing, suddenly, that she hadn't been so determined to push him away the other night. *Be careful what you wish for,* she thought.

Then again, she shouldn't be wishing for anything now, up here in the dark.

His other arm came up around her, and she held her breath. But no. He was just pulling the tablecloth up higher, past her shoulder, tucking it below her ear. Then he lowered his arm again.

Of all the dirty, rotten, respectable things to do.

"Thanks," she murmured.

Liv listened to the silence of the attic, punctuated only by the sound of their breathing, as the cold crept in around them. If anyone was going to make a move tonight, clearly, it was going to have to be her.

Not that she *had* to. But the longer they stayed quiet, the less she could think about anything else.

"Okay." Scott broke into her thoughts. "I spy, with my little eye, something—"

"Dark?" Liv interrupted.

"Well, in here, it'd have to be something dark. Unless it's something light, in which case it's a candle flame. Got to admit, it's a pretty lousy game right now."

Liv laughed a little, knowing he was trying to break the tension, grateful for the way he could make her laugh. And somehow, that made up her mind.

"Scott?" she said, knowing he'd turn his head.

She could thank him for being here, for making this past week so much easier than it would have been without him. Or she could just do what she wanted to do.

So, when Scott turned his head, she leaned toward him, hearing the sudden clamoring of her own heart, and it seemed the temperature of the air between them changed. She brushed his lips tentatively with hers, afraid he'd pull away, thinking, *This is how he felt the other night.* It was scary, going out on a limb. Heat shimmered through her as their lips connected, and she hung suspended, waiting to see if she was about to be humiliated. Whether she'd get back what she'd given him the other night.

Instead, his arms fit easily around her, as if he were catching her from a fall. He pulled her closer, his lips meeting hers, joining them together. So gentle, yet so

172

wonderfully solid. She wrapped her arms around his neck, and his arms folded more firmly around her, and now her heart pounded not from fear, but something else entirely. He deepened the kiss, and Liv forgot all about the cold. All about the attic. All about anything but the way it felt being in his arms and letting time stop.

In the back of her mind she wondered why on earth, after being kissed like this, any of those other women ever let him go. Except that she would, too. In a couple of weeks she'd go back to Texas . . .

He kissed her again, blotting out the meandering thought, blotting out any thoughts at all. She was only aware of his lips on hers, how very warm she felt, and the thrumming of her own heartbeat.

Then, distantly, another sound, almost like the rhythm of her heart. Only this sounded more like a steady click.

The source of the sound had just begun to register when Scott raised his lips from hers. In the dim candlelight, she saw him cock his head slightly, listening.

"The heater?" His voice was a husky whisper, although there was no danger of anyone else hearing.

"It can't be," Liv said.

A faint *whoosh* came from below, the sound she usually heard coming from the ceiling above her head. Air rushing through the vent above the kitchen.

Scott frowned. "I thought you said you turned the thermostat off."

"I did. I *know* I did. It's the whole reason I went downstairs." That, and the fact that the attic had felt excessively warm back then.

173

It felt pretty warm again now, and it didn't have a lot to do with the furnace kicking on below them. Not yet. Eventually the heat from the house would reach them. This was another kind of heat entirely.

Liv straightened, breaking the spell, at least enough for her to think rationally again. She and Scott exchanged a look, and she thought she saw a question in his eyes. Of course, it was hard to tell in this light.

She rearranged the tablecloth over them both again and resumed her former position, huddled against him, not daring to speak.

Chapter 15

The attic warmed, the heater clicked off, and a few minutes later, Faye and Rachel arrived. Scott heard the car outside, then the front door opening.

"Liv? Scotty?" Both women's voices called in bewilderment from below as they walked into the dark house.

When they got the attic door open, Scott came down the ladder ahead of Liv. He wanted to be below to catch her if she slipped or fell. Blinking in the unaccustomed light of the hallway, he couldn't yet decipher Faye or Rachel's facial expression. He felt like a mole emerging from underground, except he was climbing down instead of up.

"It's a long story," he said.

Ironically, Rachel had needed to climb partway up the ladder after all, pounding on the trap door with a broom handle until the door finally flung up to set them free. Rachel stepped aside as Scott descended the last few rungs. "How long were you two up there?"

"Um—" Unlike Liv, he didn't have the habit of digging out his cell phone, even to check the time. "What time is it now?"

"About six thirty," Rachel said.

Funny, how much could happen in a couple of hours. Ignoring her earlier question, Scott took Rachel's place at the bottom of the ladder and held it steady as he watched Liv's boots descend the rungs. Halfway down, the boots halted.

"The color wheel." Liv peered down at him, her eyes squinting, too. "Could we—"

After their long adventure, their original mission seemed secondary. Scott sighed and answered her calmly. "Climb back up. Then hand it down to me. Be careful."

When Liv disappeared into the attic, Scott remounted the ladder and waited until she handed him the brittle old cardboard box. It wasn't very heavy, but Scott took a couple of steps down before he handed it to Rachel, who set it on the nearest kitchen chair.

"Thanks," Rachel breathed.

You'd think that box contained the family jewels. As his vision readjusted to the light, Scott sent a questioning look past Rachel to Faye, who gave a tolerant smile and a barely perceptible shrug. Propped on her crutches, she seemed in good spirits, although it had to have been a long day for her.

Then Scott held the ladder again while Liv came down, blinking the way he'd been a few minutes ago.

"So, what happened?" Faye asked.

Liv began, "I—"

"I need to replace the handle on that trap door," Scott interrupted. "Once we got in, we couldn't get out. In my business, we call that painting yourself into a corner."

Liv spared him a grateful smile, brushing off her jeans yet again as if to put the whole horrible experience behind her. Then she went to hug her mom and sister. What else did he expect? An engagement announcement? Still, her brisk, cheerful air sent an unspoken message: What happened in the attic would stay in the attic.

You're the one who kissed me, *remember?*

He stood by and listened while Liv got the update on Faye's doctor appointment. In addition to the sprain, Faye had chipped her kneecap, which added to the swelling, which wasn't really anything to worry about. Keep the knee elevated, more hot and cold compresses . . .

As they started to leave, Faye asked, "What happened with the heater?"

At the reminder of the temperamental appliance, Scott and Liv turned to each other. Then they turned, as one, toward the thermostat in the hallway. In the process, Liv jostled into him, sending a ray of warmth up through his arm into the rest of him.

It didn't take two people to check a thermostat, but if he hadn't seen it for himself, he wouldn't have believed it.

"I *knew* I turned it off," Liv said.

Sure enough, the switch was set, indisputably, in the *off* position.

"What?" Faye and Rachel asked.

Liv's face flushed with color. "It's a long story."

Scott said his goodbyes and left the same way he'd arrived—separately. If Liv wanted to explain, he'd leave it up to her.

* * *

That night, Liv slipped out of the double bed, wrapped herself in her robe and furry slippers, and crept down the hall to the living room. She plugged in the color wheel and sat on the floor, watching the passing colors bathe the tree in light.

She hugged her knees. It couldn't be as cold on her mother's carpeted floor as it had been up in the attic. But it was definitely lonelier.

The tree, however, matched her memories at last. She and Rachel had sat at the foot of this tree so many times at Nammy's house, watching the colors change. Warm red. Frosty blue. Fiery orange. And a green that wasn't anything like a real pine tree. She'd have to give her mother that one. If you wanted a "real" tree, this wasn't it.

The adult in her knew it was corny. But the child in her still saw the beauty, the sparkle, the magic. She could see the tree the way it had looked to her back when ten days to Christmas seemed like a long time, the waiting nearly unbearable.

Liv did a mental count. It was twelve days to Christmas now, and it felt like no time at all. Two days after that, she'd fly home.

She rested her chin on her knees and remembered sitting this way just a few hours ago, a solid arm coming around her shoulders to make her feel, suddenly, a whole lot warmer.

No point, she told herself, and thought of Scott's eyes, blue and questioning. The way she'd dodged the questions with happy chatter when Mom and Rachel arrived. He'd gotten the message, all right. Shortly after they got home, he'd sent her a text: Do not. I repeat, do NOT try to move the boxes down from the attic. I'll get them next time you need a load picked up. Let me know when. S.

Not a word about those Dodgers, and it didn't sound like he'd be dropping by Nammy's house uninvited any time soon.

Footsteps shuffled on the carpet behind her. Rachel's voice whispered, "What are you doing up?"

"Couldn't sleep." Liv didn't turn around. "What's your excuse?"

"Haven't you noticed how often a pregnant woman has to get up and go to the bathroom?"

Liv chuckled in spite of her mood. Good thing Rachel hadn't been the one trapped in the attic.

Bare feet came up beside her, followed by a series of groans as Rachel lowered herself to sit on the floor next to Liv.

"You'll never be able to get back up, you know," Liv said.

"Tell me about it."

Liv wasn't sure if she wanted company or not. But Rachel sat in silence for several minutes, sharing the sight.

"Pretty, isn't it?" Rachel finally said, her voice just above a whisper.

Liv nodded without raising her chin from her knees. "Mom was happy to see it, too. She just couldn't admit it."

"Remember how we used to go to Nammy's on

Christmas morning?" Rachel asked. "We'd open our presents here first. Then we'd go over there."

"And we shook all the packages for weeks before, at both houses. You always wanted to peek."

"And you wouldn't let me," Rachel said.

"And there'd always be something extra under Nammy's tree. From Santa. A box that wasn't there before."

"Maybe she did that in case we did peek."

Liv smiled and did something she never would have done when they were ten and seven years old: she reached over and squeezed her sister's hand.

Rachel hadn't asked any questions about what happened between Liv and Scott tonight, although theories had to be running rampant in her head. Once upon a time, her present-peeking sister wouldn't have been capable of that kind of restraint. Maybe curiosity had brought Rachel down the hall to the living room.

But there was nothing to tell. Not really.

"Who gets the tree when we take it down?" Liv asked instead. "Or do we fight over it like we fought when we were kids?"

"No, it's yours," Rachel said. "You're the one who saved it."

"I'm also the one who put it in the to-go pile to begin with."

"Christmas trees don't hold a grudge. Also, Brian would probably hate it."

Liv wondered if Scott would like it. She should have invited him over to see it. If only she hadn't caved in to her impulse. Now things would just be strained between them again. Her eyes teared over.

180

The blurring of the colors in front of her just made the tree look more beautiful. She dropped her forehead to her knees.

"Hey," Rachel said. "I'm supposed to be the emotional one."

Liv didn't dare lift her head, didn't dare speak. *I don't know what to do.*

But she knew exactly what she was going to do. She'd finish up here, spend Christmas with her mom and sister, and go home to pick up where she'd left off. Starting anything with Scott just didn't make sense.

It was the right thing to do. She was sure of it. Why start something she couldn't finish? Something that would pull her back toward Tall Pine, when there was no way she could stay here? It wasn't even fair to Scotty.

Leaving Tall Pine would be hard enough as it was.

"Next time, leave me the key and I'll have the tree up and waiting when you get home," Scott told his parents.

He wrestled the noble fir into the stand, making sure the base of the trunk made it all the way to the bottom so it would take more water.

"What? And miss out on this?" His father adjusted the screws around the trunk of the tree for its preliminary position. "Okay. Let go."

Scott did, and the tree promptly listed forward and to the right.

Ray and Norma Leroux had been back from their cruise less than two days, and now they were determined to make up for lost time, getting their Christmas decorations in place. Scott was still included—or maybe it was drafted—in the annual ritual of setting the tree up, if only because, unlike his father, he could get through this part of the process without swearing.

"Next year, an artificial tree," his dad muttered.

Scott had been hearing that since high school. He'd believe it when he saw it. Until then, he didn't mind being included, with or without the swearing and muttering. And he was pleased to note that although he'd moved out nearly ten years ago, they still made it a point to choose a tree that was significantly taller than his six-foot-five. Even if it made the thing that much harder to get into the house.

"Did you put up your tree yet?" his mother asked.

"Yes, ma'am." Never mind that his tree was spindly, about five and a half feet tall and looked like someone's disreputable uncle. He'd gotten it last weekend, while Liv and her family worked on Nammy's house with Rachel's husband. Maybe that was why he'd picked out a tree Charlie Brown would be ashamed of. He hadn't been in the mood to fuss with it.

"What I don't understand," Scott said, "is why you want the tree back here in the family room, instead of the front window."

"This way we don't have to move all the furniture around," his mother said.

"Besides, it'll block our view of the tree house," his dad said.

Scott looked past the drawn-back curtains, through the window, to the remains of his first-ever carpentry project: a dilapidated tree house resting uncomfortably on the limbs of the weathered oak in the backyard.

"You really should take that down," his mother added gently.

It was an old discussion. During the winter, cold and snow kept him from getting around to it; summer was his busy season; in between, one distraction or another got in the way. Besides—

"Hey," he said, "it's a historical landmark. A Leroux original."

"It's the work of a ten-year-old." His father's eyes gleamed. There was affection behind the old harangue, as well as the unspoken comment: *a talented ten-year-old*.

"Like I said," Scott said lightly. "A piece of local history."

More history than they knew.

After the Christmas tree had been properly straightened, lit, and decorated, Scott went out to see his old handiwork in the gathering dusk. Not a bad piece of handiwork at the time, although it had always tilted about ten degrees to the south. But years of neglect and weather had turned it into a bit of a hazard as well as an eyesore. He ought to get out here, the next warm day, and dismantle it for useful firewood before any prowling neighborhood kids got too adventurous and sneaked in to explore. The rungs leading up the tree weren't as secure as they used to be, there'd be splinters everywhere, and who knew how well the floor would hold by now.

But oh, the memories.

In spite of the stiffening evening breeze, Scott tested the flat boards that served as rungs and made a tentative climb, high enough to rest his arms on the floor through the open doorway. As long as the rungs and the floor didn't both give out at the same time, he should be all right.

He breathed in the scent of damp wood—at least this time of year, any bugs that lived up here were dormant—and remembered secret club meetings with Dane and Ron when they were ten, eleven, twelve. Once puberty hit, the old hangout was forgotten, until it dawned on Scotty that the former boys' hangout would be the perfect make-out pad. He'd tried it once, with Michele Fitzsimmons, the literal girl next door. His clumsy attempt at a first kiss had ended with a shove that almost landed him flat on his back in his own backyard. So much for his bachelor's lair.

Women in high places, he thought. He'd fared better with Liv yesterday. At least, until it was time for her to escape.

He needed to accept that some things weren't meant to be.

When Scott arrived at Nammy's a few days later, Liv almost let Rachel answer the door. But that would be cowardly. And obvious. So she answered it. *As long as I'm not alone with him, I'll be fine.*

"Hi." She stepped back to let him in, her smile firmly in place.

He returned her smile with an equally fixed one of his own, one that looked so inconsistent with his usual easy grin. After just a few days without seeing him, it was ridiculous that he should seem so much more three-dimensional than she remembered.

Then his eyes went past her as he stepped inside. "Wow." His voice echoed.

They had been busy, and it showed.

By now the house was picked clean, except for the living room furniture they were leaving in place, the stacks of boxes, and the kitchen table in the room beyond. They'd even shrunk the to-keep pile down to a more manageable size.

"We're pretty much done," Liv admitted.

It *was* hard to admit. As difficult as the job had been, it was even more painful to see it end. After today, there wouldn't be much reason to come back here, unless they brought a real estate agent to make arrangements to list the house. Liv wished her mom would let her help with the process of putting the place up for sale. But Mom didn't see any point in doing that until the Christmas season was over, and Liv couldn't argue with her logic.

"You guys have done a great job." Scott's deep voice resonated as he walked through the nearly empty kitchen and into the hallway, the ladder still waiting under the trap door.

Liv hugged her arms against her ribs, feeling as hollow inside as the house was starting to feel. Eighty-three years on the planet, and soon the only evidence of Nammy would be the scattered mementos they'd kept. When Mom and Rachel greeted Scott as he passed through the kitchen, Liv heard that rare quaver in her mother's voice.

Mom really shouldn't be here anyway. With all the packing and sorting taken care of, there wasn't much left for her to do, and it was hard on her emotionally. Still, she was determined to see this through to the end.

Scott set up a system of handing the boxes down the ladder. He climbed the ladder, reaching up to get the boxes down from the attic floor; then he handed them down to Liv, standing at the base of the ladder. She set them on the kitchen table, pushed to the edge of the hallway so she wouldn't have to handle their weight for more than a moment. It took less than ten minutes. After that, he carted them to the truck.

When they got to the box of Liv's grandfather's painting supplies, Faye said, "Wait."

Scott turned to her, questioning. He hadn't looked directly at Liv since he first arrived. The effort of not looking at her was starting to give him a crick in his neck.

"We might be able to use those," Faye said.

Scott shifted the box in his arms. It wasn't very heavy, but it was cumbersome. "The to-keep pile, then?"

"I was thinking we could use them here." The way the words rushed out of Faye, coupled with her suddenly straight posture despite the crutches, made Scott see Liv in her.

Faye turned to indicate the end of the hallway, where the mystery cabinet stood, still filled with Nammy's never-completed home improvement projects.

"Do you think—" Faye went on with that odd mix of tentativeness and determination that was so much like her daughter. "I'd want to pay you. But the house really could use a facelift after all these years. It'd be easier to sell."

Her voice wavered faintly at the last words, and like

a flash, her two daughters were flanking her, ready to offer support.

Rachel said, "I think it's a good idea."

Liv said, "Mom, are you sure?"

She seemed to be trying to catch her mother's eye, and Scott could guess at her thoughts: *More Scotty Leroux in my life?*

Scott leaned against the displaced kitchen table, waiting for the three women to kick this around before he weighed in. Maybe the decision would be taken out of his hands. It wasn't typical for him to turn down a job. It also wasn't in his nature to say no to a friend or neighbor in need. This proposition combined the two, with Liv thrown into the mix.

Liv, who was looking steadfastly at her mother, not at him.

Faye's voice remained just a touch unsteady. "It would be nice to have the house done the way she wanted it," she said.

And Scott knew what this was really about, at least for Faye: she wasn't ready to let go. Closing up this house was like another funeral for her. But at some point, a person did have to let go.

"It's a nice idea." He kept his voice as gentle as he could, trying not to disturb the delicate equilibrium of three sets of female emotions. "But you do know that whoever moves here next might want something entirely different anyway."

"Yeah," Rachel said, linking her arm through her mother's. "But right now people who come to see the house would probably walk away calling it 'the one with the ducks in the living room.' It's probably a good idea to update it."

"I *love* the ducks," Liv protested.

Scott knew the answer to that one. "Actually, she wanted to keep the ducks as sort of a border across the top of the wall," he said. "It'd look nice."

Apparently he'd paid more attention to her decorating talk than he realized.

Faye nodded, her eyes shimmering. "That *would* be nice."

Scott swallowed hard.

He knew what shimmering eyes meant. They meant there was no way he could bring himself to say no. He had no doubt that a home makeover project loomed in his future. But first, they had to decide they were going ahead with it.

Scott shoved his hands awkwardly into his pockets. "Why don't the three of you talk it over and give me a call," he said. "If you want me to do the job, I'm in."

Chapter 16

"His eyes are lopsided," Rachel said in mild dismay.

Sitting next to Rachel at Mom's kitchen table, Liv leaned over to inspect the snowman cookie Rachel was decorating.

"One of the red hots is bigger than the other," Liv said. "That's the problem." Liv snatched the bigger of the snowman's two red-hot eyes off the cookie, leaving behind a smeared white dot of the icing Rachel had dabbed on to hold the red hot in place.

"Hey!" Rachel swatted Liv's hand and turned to their mother, who sat at the head of the table. "*Mom!*"

"I was *helping*," Liv said innocently.

"Girls," Mom said reflexively in the admonishing tone she'd used since Liv and Rachel were kids. Which they'd pretty much reverted to. Mom didn't miss a beat as she turned a wreath, with green sugar frosting and more red hots for berries, into a work of art.

This was what Christmas should be like. In the background, Dean Martin warbled on the living room stereo. And roughly two hundred wafer-thin sugar cookies sat in the center of the table in intimidating stacks, waiting to be decorated.

"Besides"—Mom set down her finished wreath cookie and glanced up at Rachel with a glint in her eye—"if one of them isn't perfect, you've got a dozen more tries to get it right."

Mom had warned them that baking the cookies from her time-honored recipe was the easy part. But Rachel had seized on the idea, and Liv had taken it up. The cookie project brought a welcome relief after the sobering sight of Nammy's nearly empty house this morning. Trouble was, it looked like they'd be up until the wee hours decorating the cookies.

Liv welcomed the chance to keep busy. Sitting here with Mom and Rachel, this could be any Christmas from her teens. In the face of something so normal, those moments with Scott in the dark attic felt far away. Like someone else's out-of-body experience.

Liv watched her sister carefully position another red hot on the snowman's face. At the rate Rachel was going, it might take till New Year's. "Maybe you should concentrate on one-eyed critters." Some of the animal shapes were done in profile; Liv looked over the stacks. "We've got camels, donkeys, Scottie dogs . . ."

She bit her tongue.

"That reminds me." Mom picked up another wreath and began applying the white frosting with a butter knife and a deft hand. "You can take some cookies over to Scotty when he starts on the house tomorrow."

Did Mom *really* not know? Or was she still trying to set Liv up?

Liv bit her tongue again and didn't comment until Mom left the table for a bathroom break.

She hissed to Rachel, "Can't you take the cookies instead?"

"I'm a married woman." Rachel dotted frosting into place for a camel's eye. Her mouth had a smug set. "I have my reputation to think of."

"Very funny."

"She wants me to take her Christmas shopping for *you* tomorrow, nimrod," Rachel whispered. "She's having a hard time coming up with ideas. She's not sure what you like anymore."

Ouch. "She doesn't have to get me anything."

"Yeah, right. How many times has Mom said that to *us*? You know that's not how it works."

"I know." And shopping ideas or not, neither of them wanted Mom trying to trundle herself into a car and navigate the sidewalks of Evergreen Lane alone on her crutches.

Avoiding Scott was silly. She could handle it. She was only here another week and a half. Resolutely, she seized her next cookie to decorate. A Scottie dog. They'd always been a favorite, decorated with long, chocolatey sprinkles that simulated a dog's shaggy coat.

What did Scottie dogs have to do with Christmas, anyway?

It felt strange to knock on Nammy's door when Nammy wouldn't be the one answering it. But Liv had her hands full. She had to do the knocking with her foot.

In addition to the big platter of Christmas cookies, she'd picked up a bag of fried chicken from the Pine 'n' Dine, since she was getting here around lunchtime. She wasn't sure which would be the bigger loss if she fumbled, the platter or the cookies on top of it. They'd taken until nearly three AM to complete.

Scott opened the door and looked down at her burden. "I was going to say *we don't want any*," he said. "But if that bag has what I think it has . . ."

His tone sounded nearly normal. Nearly. *See?* Liv told herself. *No problem.*

Scott took the bag of chicken with one hand and tried to relieve her of the cookie platter with the other. He seemed surprised when she wouldn't let go.

"Sorry." Liv kept the plastic-wrapped plate gripped in both hands. "If either of us drops these, I'll cry."

Scott stepped aside to let her pass by. She walked in and looked for a place to set the platter. An end table still stood at the end of the living room next to the doorway leading into the kitchen. Just beyond, the kitchen was already turning into a new type of chaos. The big stepladder had taken up residence near the dining room wall, tarps were spread on sections of the floor, and the room had a scent of wet paper and—was it glue? Wallpaper paste, she realized.

She set the cookies down. "So you're starting with the wallpaper?"

"I figured I'd tackle the ugliest job first. That way it's all downhill from there." Scotty bent to inspect the cookies through the clear plastic wrap. "You guys made these? They're too pretty to eat."

"The wreaths are really good. You get the sugar frosting and you get four red hots. And I like the chocolate-sprinkled ones: the donkeys, the teddy bears . . ."

He squinted at the array of cookies in front of him. "Scottie dogs? For Christmas?" He looked up, crooked smile in place, and her heart flip-flopped.

Liv took a step back. It wasn't a good idea to get *too* comfortable. "Don't ask me why. We've had all those cookie cutters since I was a little kid."

"Your grandmother's recipe?"

"I don't think so. She was more into store-bought pfeffernuss."

Scott gestured with the Pine 'n' Dine bag, still in his hand. "I don't suppose you threw in a drumstick for yourself?"

She fought the urge to edge toward the door. "No, I have to go. But there's something I wanted to cover first." She fished a folded sheet of paper out of her purse and tried not to sound too officious. "Mom thought it would be a good idea to get a rundown from you of what you'll be charging for this, so I made a list."

She held the sheet out to him awkwardly, meeting his eyes with an effort. She knew eyes couldn't really change color, but Scott's seemed to shift from their usual warm blue to a lighter shade of polar frost. He made no move to take the paper.

Liv took a deep breath. "Scott, you know you can't do this for nothing. So let's get an agreement up front. We're worried about you short-changing yourself, not the other way around."

He still didn't take the paper from her hand. "This doesn't sound like your mother."

She hesitated. "She agreed it was a good idea."

That is, if you counted *I guess so* and *if you really think we need to.*

Scott leaned against the frame of the kitchen doorway, his stare unyielding.

Liv fumbled for language he'd understand: a joke. "I think her exact words were, 'I don't want that dirty rotten snake in the grass to bilk us for everything we've got.'"

That helped. Small crinkles appeared at the corners of his eyes, and some of the tension in Liv's stomach eased.

"Money between friends is always awkward," she said. "And you've done so much for us already, without asking for anything. I thought it would be a good idea to . . ."

Now she was rambling. But maybe Scott knew what she meant, because his eyes softened.

"All right," he said. "I'll look it over. But fair warning: I reserve the right to make deductions for fried chicken and free cookies. Can I get it back to you tomorrow?"

"Deal." Liv stepped back. "But if you don't give it back by tomorrow, *we* reserve the right to lock you out of this house."

"And how are you going to pull that off? Hire me to change the locks to keep me out?"

She grinned and took another step toward the door. Something was going on, because while her head was telling her feet to leave, another part of her kept pulling in the other direction. Heaven help her, she didn't want to go. "Thanks, Scott."

As she forced herself to turn away, a thud sounded from the kitchen.

Scott turned toward the noise, and Liv joined him in the jumble of chaos that used to be her grandmother's dining area. At the foot of the ladder, several feet from where Scott had been standing, was an overturned bucket. It had neatly missed the tarp, and thick goo was slowly spreading over the floor's aging linoleum.

Reaching the bucket before Liv, Scott righted it and set it on the floor underneath the ladder. Liv grabbed a stray rag, dropped to the floor, and tried to mop up the mess. The rag promptly stuck to the goo, which was already stuck to the floor.

"I think that's a lost cause," Scott said. "It's wallpaper paste. Good thing we're replacing the linoleum anyway."

Liv pulled up at the rag, trying to end its marriage to the floor. It brought up a thick stretch of paste along with it. "Hot water might help."

When he didn't answer, she looked up to find him grinning with amusement. "You're like a dog with a bone," he said. "Don't worry about it. Remember, the flooring's a goner anyway."

"But in the meantime, if you step here by accident, you could end up attached to the floor."

Scott bent and took the rag from her. "I'll cover it up with newspaper."

Liv gave up and stood. "Why did it fall, anyway?"

Scott shrugged. "Gravity?"

Spontaneous gravity, then. Because neither of them had been anywhere near the ladder.

Robbed of her last purpose for being here, Liv surveyed the nearly unrecognizable dining area. The living room, still untouched, retained Nammy's personality. This room, stripped of Nammy's belongings, had turned into a construction zone. Only the long Shaker table remained, and Scott had pushed it into the cooking area, away from all the tarps.

The old wallpaper was down, which explained the wet-paper smell Liv had noticed when she entered the house. In its place, Scott had covered the wall with sheets of some sort of plain white backing. It reminded her of primer on a car. Rolls of the new wallpaper were propped against the adjoining wall. Stripped of the old wallpaper, the plaster showed remnants of the glue that had held it in place. For how many decades?

Getting used to the idea that this was no longer Nammy's home—well, she probably still wasn't there yet. Getting used to the idea that this would become someone else's home—that was a thought she hadn't fully gotten around to.

Liv went to the wall and fingered the edges of the wallpaper backing, joined neatly against each other. She knew there were stages of grief. But she wondered when all the new adjustments would stop coming along and taking her by surprise. When she got back to Dallas, she supposed.

"That's the backing," Scott explained, as if he thought she was trying to fathom the paper's purpose. "It's thicker and smoother. It makes it easier for the new wallpaper to stick, and there won't be the irregularities you'd have from the surface of the wall."

She nodded.

"It's also a lot easier to hang than the wallpaper," he went on. "It's so thick it almost slides into place. The actual wallpaper is thinner, and it's a lot less forgiving. Getting that to hang without wrinkling or tearing is the toughest part of the job."

She raised her eyebrows. "How do you manage that all by yourself?"

He responded with the usual lopsided grin. "Very, very carefully."

The sensible thing, she supposed, would have been to just have him repaint. A little late to suggest it now. Plus, that wasn't what her mother had in mind.

Liv eyed the new wallpaper. It didn't look like Nammy's taste, but it was cute. "I like the apples," she said. "I hope it's worth it."

"I'll make it work."

"Thanks." *And we'll pay you for your trouble. Like it or not.*

She started to leave again, something like *good luck* trying to form on her lips. Instead, she turned back, and what came out of her mouth was, "Could you use any help?"

His smile wavered. "What, seriously?"

"Mom and Rachel are off doing super-secret Christmas shopping." Liv made herself shrug. "If you could walk me through what to do, it looks like you could use another pair of hands."

After all, helping with Nammy's old house served

more purpose than waiting at home for Mom and Rachel.

Scott's smile faded almost completely, and he regarded her seriously, as if he were sizing her up as a deckhand for a long sea voyage.

"It might help the job go faster," she heard herself say.

"Okay." Scott's grin tipped back up. "But I'm deducting it off your bill. If you're any good."

Scott honestly hadn't been looking forward to wallpapering the dining area by himself. He really should have recruited a friend in exchange for a share of the take. He certainly hadn't planned on Liv volunteering.

But here she was, an hour and a half later, sharing both the fruits and the exasperation of their efforts.

"I'm *wearing* it again." Carefully, she peeled the delicate paper away when it fell back onto her, trying to entangle itself in her hair. She didn't have her functional ponytail today; of course, she hadn't come here expecting to work with glue.

He should be shot for taking advantage of her offer. Her willingness to pitch in. But most of all, for the way her presence lightened his heart as much as his workload.

Masochist.

She'd made it very clear, with everything she *hadn't* said, that she didn't want those kisses in the attic to follow them downstairs. Scott was doing his best to honor that unspoken agreement. At times it was easy, because they worked together smoothly. But even that felt so natural, so right, that at times it felt only natural to . . .

Well, it was a good thing he was stationed on top of the ladder, sending the wallpaper down for Liv to secure before it got away.

Scott started down the rungs in case she needed his help, but Liv managed to peel herself free and set the paper where it was meant to go, carefully smoothing it into place with the wallpaper brush. It was a good job for a detail-oriented person, and Liv was definitely that.

One more roll, and they'd be done with the wall that separated the dining area and the living room. That left the adjoining wall that ran from the corner to the place where the kitchen cabinets began.

Liv pulled her cell phone out of her pocket, checking either for messages or for the time. She eyed the wall, then looked up at Scott, who maintained his distance from his perch at the top of the ladder.

"It's four o'clock. Want to finish this wall?" she asked, and something in his chest loosened.

"We should have just enough daylight to get it done," he said. "Once we lose the natural light from outside, things aren't as clear. Too much guesswork."

Liv nodded and set her cell phone down on the table he'd shoved into the middle of the room. "Let's do it."

The light in her hazel eyes made his heart jump. Like him, she got gratification from a job that reaped visible results. Or maybe, if he flattered himself, she was actually having a good time.

"*Rats!*" she said a few minutes later, when the paper threatened to tear in her hands under the weight of the glue.

No point in reading too much into her enthusiasm, he reminded himself.

* * *

Liv slid into the Pine 'n' Dine booth across from her mother. It was late afternoon on Saturday, when Nammy would have been stopping by for pie and coffee. She was sure that thought had occurred to Mom, too, when she suggested they come in here.

"Here you go, ladies." Sherry slid menus in front of them and grinned at Mom. "Down to one crutch, I see?"

"I'm giving it a shot." Mom smiled. "The other one's in the backseat, just in case."

Sherry scooted away, leaving them a few minutes to decide. She'd given them a corner booth by the window. Liv didn't ask, but she strongly suspected this was Nammy's usual spot. It was a prime location for people watching, with a view of Evergreen Lane's sidewalks in the graying afternoon. The little white Christmas lights that wound around the street's lampposts stood out against the muted background.

"I think we might get more snow tonight," Liv said.

Mom nodded. "We could use it."

However, even without the snow to entice tourists, the diner was three-quarters full, and most of them looked like out-of-towners. Of course, Liv wouldn't know a lot of the locals by now.

Until this afternoon, she hadn't been alone with her mother for any length of time. Today she was getting her turn escorting Mom on her Christmas shopping, this time for Rachel. They'd spent most of the afternoon chattering like magpies as they shopped, punctuated by companionable silences. Sitting across the table from her mom now, it was the first time Liv felt

200

awkward, as if there was a sudden need to hunt for small talk.

"So," Mom said, "you two finished the wallpapering this morning?"

Maybe because she knew *that* question was coming. Up to now, Mom had been more restrained than Rachel when it came to questions about Scotty.

"Uh-huh." Wishing she already had a cup of coffee to fiddle with, Liv picked up her menu again and pretended to give it a closer look. "I didn't get the estimate sheet back from him yet, though. He wants to deduct for the time I spent helping. But how he ever would have gotten wallpaper hung alone is beyond me. It's hard enough with two people."

She tilted her head to adjust the crick in her neck, and this time she wasn't faking. It did provide an excuse to avoid Mom's gaze, though.

"Asking him to put it in writing was probably a little bit much," Mom said. "The ballpark figure he gave me was fine."

"I was just trying to get things laid out ahead of time." She repeated what she'd said to Scott yesterday: "Money between friends is always awkward."

The word *friends* hung in the air, and Liv heard her mom's unspoken question loud and clear.

But they *were* friends, and nothing more. Scott hadn't made a move since that evening in the attic, and Liv had been the one to start that. He'd picked up her signals, and he respected them. Participating in the work on the house not only helped Scott, it also helped increase the chance that the job could be done before Liv had to leave after Christmas. She didn't want to leave Mom any more loose ends to deal with than necessary.

And if the time she spent around Scott was increasingly pleasant, leaving her increasingly reluctant to leave—well, she just had to deal with that on her own.

Liv added, with what she knew was forced casualness, "I told him I'd go by tomorrow afternoon after church to see how far he's gotten with the painting."

Mom studied her with gray-blue eyes that had been able to see through Liv all her life. "You know, there's nothing wrong with—"

Sherry appeared as if summoned by Liv's silent prayer. "Are you two ready to order?"

Liv looked at her mother. "What kind of pie?"

"Boysenberry. Always." Mom had come along with Nammy on a fair share of her weekly expeditions, especially after Liv's father died.

Liv took a deep breath and turned to Sherry. "Two slices of boysenberry pie. And two coffees."

Chapter 17

"Dusty rose." Liv watched her paint roller leave behind three feet of sky blue, covering the muted pink that had been there a moment before. "My grandfather must have been a patient man. I can't think of many men who'd sleep in a pink room."

Scott's voice came from her left. "Maybe she changed it after your grandfather died?"

"No, it's been that color since I was a kid."

After the adventure of hanging wallpaper, painting the master bedroom was a breeze by comparison. Liv just had to try to forget that this was the one room in Nammy's home she'd rarely been inside. Located at the back of the house, it was Nammy's inner sanctum, and she and Rachel hadn't had any reason to come in here, except when they sneaked in to smell Nammy's collection of vintage perfume bottles. Now it held only a four-poster bed, a dresser, and two night tables, all pushed to the middle of the room and protected with a tarp for good measure.

Oh, and standing in here, a few feet away from Scott, she also had to forget that it was a *bedroom*.

Liv swept her paint roller over the wall again, leaving a fresh trail of blue. "Maybe that was their compromise for the ducks in the living room. The dusty rose for the birds."

"For the birds," he echoed, and she turned to see him quirking a grin at her. Her heart lurched, then skipped.

That happened every now and then, catching her off guard, when he said or did something that was somehow quintessentially Scott. And every time it did, it got harder for Liv to kid herself about why she'd gotten so involved with this renovation project.

Back at the house, Mom and Rachel were putting together a small package for their uncle Bob in Minnesota. Along with the Christmas gifts they'd picked up, they were sending him some of the framed photos from Nammy's belongings. Liv supposed she could have helped with that, but unlike sorting through Nammy's house, it hadn't really seemed like a three-person job.

So here she was, painting a bedroom with Scott.

What had they just been talking about?

Oh, right. The birds. Ducks. The wallpaper.

"Do you think it makes sense to leave the duck border?" she asked. She kept her eyes fixed on the wall in front of her. "I mean, whoever moves in here will probably want to change it, anyway."

Scott sighed. "I think it'll look good, actually. But it won't make that much difference to whoever buys the house."

Liv silently continued rolling paint onto the wall. With her grandfather's old paint roller. Everything she did on this visit was steeped in nostalgia, one way or another.

The only reason to leave the ducks was for her family, and they wouldn't be the ones to see it. This was supposed to be about getting the house ready to show. Complying with Nammy's wishes was an added bonus, and it made sense to use the materials she'd made available. Whatever upgrades they made to the house now, the time was coming when they'd have to let it go. Soon.

Her grandfather had been gone a dozen years longer than her grandmother, and one strip of wallpaper was a silly thing to be concerned about.

When she didn't answer, he said, "You're quiet, Tomblyn."

His tone was light, but the warm resonance of his voice held the beginnings of concern. As if he was ready to catch her and steady her. Again.

"Still here," she said. She was *not* going to start pouring out her heart. Even if all her old memories seemed to be coming loose, at random moments. This morning she'd caught herself singing a sappy old song Nammy had taught her, one Liv hadn't thought about in years. "Want me to start another chorus of 'All I Want for Christmas Is My Two Front Teeth'?"

"Don't even say it. I finally got it out of my head half an hour ago."

She thought she'd successfully changed the subject until he added, "Maybe whoever moves in here will be a big duck lover, and that border will seal the deal."

Liv smiled in spite of herself, but she kept her reaction between herself and the wall. Scott was like medicine for her. Dangerous medicine, best taken in moderation. It occurred to her, again, that it wasn't hard to see why a woman with a broken heart would fall for him. What wasn't so clear was what he got in the bargain.

"Okay," Liv said. "We'll leave the ducks. Kind of like initials in a tree trunk."

"Spoken like a true romantic."

Liv watched more blue appear under her roller, admiring the instant result. It was so easy to make a difference with this type of work. No wonder Scott liked it.

She turned to sneak a glance in his direction. He was working his way across the top half of the wall adjoining hers, standing on just the bottom rung of the ladder to reach. He wasn't looking at her. Good.

The heater had come on this morning without a hitch. The same way it had yesterday, and the day before. By tacit agreement, neither Scott nor Liv commented on its mysterious recovery, any more than they mentioned the heater's strange behavior the night they were trapped in the attic. Or Liv's own out-of-character behavior that night. And Scott showed every sign of being sincere about trying to get away from his penchant for lovelorn women.

That was good, too.

Scott stepped back from his touch-up job around the edges of the doorjamb and sized up the freshly painted bedroom. Liv had left over an hour ago, and he'd broken his own credo, working past sunset to get the room finished. But he wanted to be ready to move on to the next phase of the project tomorrow. They were halfway home.

Wallpapering the kitchen had been the biggest task. With the master bedroom done, that left painting the living room and putting fresh tile in the kitchen and the bathroom. He liked leaving floors for last. Scott remembered his dad's advice, one of the first things he'd ever learned about do-it-yourself projects: *Do everything from the top down. Always. Period. Don't argue.*

The wallpaper-paste spill the other day certainly made a good case for his father's method.

Scott took the last couple of brushes to the kitchen sink to rinse. Liv had rinsed the rest of the brushes and rollers when she left an hour ago. One nice thing about working with Liv: she liked leaving everything clean and ready to go for the next day.

Okay, there were a lot of nice things about working with Liv. What wasn't clear was why she was working with him. Probably she wanted to help hurry the project along; she'd implied it would be nice if it could be done before Christmas. Because two days after Christmas, she'd be gone.

No point in wondering about Liv's motives, any more than she saw any point in talking about What Happened In The Attic. A job was a job, and if this one was more pleasant than most, that just meant it would be a little tougher when it ended. No big deal.

If he could just convince himself of that.

Scott finished rinsing the brush and set it alongside the other brushes Liv had lain—neatly, of course—on the counter to dry. New tile for the counter might have been a nice idea, too, but it hadn't made it onto Olivia's shopping list.

As Scott picked up the dish towel hanging by the sink to dry his hands, something clattered to the kitchen floor. He recognized the shiny red case of Liv's cell phone.

He bent and scooped it up, grateful that the phone hadn't come apart when it hit the floor. Thumbing a key at random, he saw the screen light up to display the time. No reception bars, of course. Liv still muttered about that sometimes, but she'd started to learn that up here, her phone was more often a glorified, less convenient, more expensive wristwatch.

She probably wouldn't like being without it overnight, though.

He eyed the time on the screen: 6:40. He'd drop it off at Liv's mom's house on his way home. Maybe he'd see if she'd eaten dinner yet.

The house looked dim when Scott pulled up, but Rachel's car sat in the driveway. Some sort of light was playing against the curtains at the front of the house. Maybe they were all inside with the lights out, watching a movie.

Well, it wasn't like he'd be interrupting brain surgery, he thought, annoyed with himself for being so tentative.

Then Liv answered the door, and any trace of irritation melted.

She still wore the sweatshirt she'd been painting in,

its white now accented with fresh splotches of blue. Her hair was gathered in the same loose ponytail she'd worn at the house, numerous strands escaping by now. And she was in her stocking feet, although the raised threshold gave back some of the height she would have lost.

She looked rumpled and inviting, and his voice caught in his throat as he held up her phone. "You forgot something," he said.

"Oh!" Liv patted down her jeans pockets as if she expected, somehow, to find her phone there instead of in his hand. "I can't believe I didn't notice."

"Yeah, well . . ." He fumbled for something clever to say. "Paint fumes. They go to your head after a while."

Her face lit in an unguarded grin as she took the phone from him. He saw that the living room behind her wasn't completely dark. A lamp on an end table provided some illumination for the gift wrap and boxes that were spread out on the living room carpet. The rest of the light came from—

Scott peered in to the right and saw the silver tree they'd put up last week, the light from the color wheel now washing over it.

"Oh, hey," he said. "So that's what it looks like."

"That's right. You haven't seen it." Liv stood back to let him in, although he hadn't been hinting for an invitation. Not consciously, anyway. Scott walked in, and she closed the door to shut out the chilly night.

Scott stepped closer for a better look at the tree. It was a simple enough trick, the way the silver metal of the artificial needles mirrored the changing colors. Still, he'd never seen anything quite like it.

"I know it's corny," Liv said. "I think maybe you have to see it when you're a kid to really . . ."

As he gazed at the tree, watching the colors change, it took him a second to realize Liv had trailed off. "No," he said, "I wouldn't say that."

The play of colored lights had a sort of fascination to it, like watching the waves of the ocean. Scott watched the shiny branches go from a frosty, pale blue to a warm, fiery orange . . .

When the tree was new, no doubt it had seemed modern, state-of-the-art. Now it was old-fashioned in a different kind of way, with a charm that was hard to describe. Maybe because the colored lights had passed over it enough times for the tree to witness its own set of memories.

That sounded weird. Scott settled for, "I like it."

From the television set in the next room, he heard Desi Arnaz's distinctive laugh. Darned if they weren't watching *I Love Lucy*, something that was probably already in reruns the first time the tree was set up. He grinned at the unintentional time warp as he caught Liv's eye. She smiled back.

"Welcome to 1959," he said.

His hand started for the small of her back in a reflex that felt as natural as breathing, just to put his arm around her, nothing more. He stopped himself, remembering the unwritten set of rules that had sprung up between them. But not touching her didn't keep him from feeling close to her.

He returned his gaze to the tree, now an unlikely shade of red, and for some reason he thought of a red bandanna handkerchief.

210

"Even my grandfather used to make fun of it," Liv said. "He said the red made it look like a fire truck."

The blue returned, and suddenly Scott was thinking of blue denim. Overalls.

He frowned. "He wore overalls a lot, didn't he?"

"That's right." He felt her eyes on him. "Did Nammy tell you that?"

"She must have mentioned it." It made sense. He was a house painter, after all.

Orange washed over the tree again, and Scott pictured two red-haired girls, sitting on the floor in front of the tree. Then it was green, like the Grinch who stole Christmas. Red again . . .

Scott pinched his nose, trying to clear his vision. He didn't say anything this time. But he was pretty sure Liv had had a red-checked flannel bathrobe when she was little. That Rachel had one like it, but in blue. And that their grandfather used to carry those old red bandanna handkerchiefs.

He looked at Liv, who was contemplating the tree with a gentle smile of her own. "I'm glad you like it," she said. "And I'm *really* glad you went back in and got it that day. It's always been special. One of those childhood things."

She turned to look up at him, shorter now than usual in her stocking feet. Her eyes were soft, probably under the spell of nostalgia, and something inside Scott said, *now.* He wanted to reach for her, to kiss her.

Liv's cell phone chirped. She checked the screen, and Scott saw that softness fade away as her brow furrowed.

"What is it?" he asked.

She lowered herself to the couch, still frowning. "I don't know yet. It's from Terri. She wants to know if I got her voice mail."

"Terri?"

"My business partner."

Scott waited and watched as she entered codes into her phone and listened, one finger in the ear that didn't have the phone held up to it. *I Love Lucy* still sounded in the background, but he felt the emotional climate in the living room shift as the furrows across Liv's forehead deepened.

Then she slammed the cell phone, facedown, onto the coffee table in front of her. Scott flinched. Liv rose, her body rigid.

"You do know that's not how you hang up that kind of phone, right?" Scott kept his tone mild.

Something like a stifled scream escaped through her clenched teeth. She paced the short distance to the living room wall, then wheeled, obviously aware she had nowhere to go. Cuddly-living-room Liv was gone, replaced by five-foot-eight of barely contained fury.

No way would he make the mistake, at this moment, of asking her if she was okay.

Instead, he asked, "What's wrong?"

"I can't even speak English." Liv closed her eyes and rubbed her jaw below her temples. Scott hadn't seen her do that in days. "The guy I broke up with? Kevin? He was our silent partner. He was the one who convinced us to open a storefront for the business. *He* was the one who was supposed to put up his share of the rent at the beginning of the month, and Terri's been trying all this time to reach him. She didn't tell me."

Her eyes opened. They locked with his. Her fury wasn't directed at him, thank God, but he was the only other person around. He felt the force of it.

"She finally reached him," Scott offered.

"And he's bailing. Of *course*." She took a deep breath, teeth still clenched, fingertips still at her temples. And with that deep breath, he saw her pull it all in, condensing her anger and frustration into a white-hot knot.

If all that concentrated wrath was ever released, he could see it knocking out the power of a major city. But when she spoke, her voice was quiet.

"We'll be okay this month," she said. "But it's going to wipe out most of our reserves. She didn't want to tell me, with everything that's going on. And I'm the one who got us into this. I feel so *stupid*."

"You're not stupid. He's a jerk."

"So why did I ever trust him?" Liv lowered her hands from her temples, and just for a moment, her eyes glistened. "I feel like hitting something."

Then she blinked hard.

"I want a margarita," she said savagely.

From Liv, those sounded like fighting words. Scott studied her.

"I know of something better," he said.

Chapter 18

The small white blur of a ball rushed out at her, and Liv swung the bat. Her hands buzzed with the impact as the bat connected. But, once again, the baseball spun straight upward and thumped ineffectually to the ground behind her.

Another ball came flying. She swung hard, and this time she stirred up a *whoosh* of air, but missed the ball completely.

"Whose idea was this?" She was only half joking.

"Yours." Scott stood on the other side of the chain-link fence surrounding the town recreation center's batting cages. "You said you wanted to hit something."

"Hit something," she repeated, swinging again. "Not chip it."

This was her second round of pitches fired from the weird automatic cannon several yards in front of her. She was still having trouble connecting with the ball at all. A lot of foul tips and, so far, about three grounders. But when she connected at all, man, did it hurt. The ball was hard and it was moving fast. Fifteen minutes in, her hands, arms, and shoulders were complaining loudly.

"It takes practice," Scott said. "That's the name of the game."

Did anything faze this man? He'd weathered her embarrassing tirade back at the house without even blinking. Now he had her outside, as the temperature dropped into the thirties, playing baseball. Or trying to, anyway. Her loose jacket flapped around her with every swing, and the sponge-filled helmet she was required to wear made her feel like Atom Ant.

The sadistic machine stopped humming, and Liv lowered the bat.

"My arms hurt," she said, rubbing her shoulders.

"Good," Scott said. "Now maybe you're ready to focus some of that energy. Make it count."

Opening the gate, he walked into the hypothetical batter's box and stood alongside her. Scott pointed beyond the fenced area, clear to the horizon at the neighboring mountain peak darkly silhouetted in the distance. "Aim right there," he said. "Try to hit it all the way to Mount Douglas."

He stepped away and loaded more tokens into the coin slot mounted next to the gate. Liv eyed the mountain as the light on the ball-firing machine blinked to life again.

"Mount Douglas, or Kevin's face," he added, exiting the cage again. "Take your pick."

A laugh of surprise blew out of her, and she missed the first pitch altogether. But half an hour ago, she wouldn't have bet she could laugh at anything tonight.

She swung again and missed. "How do I keep an eye on the ball and the mountain at the same time?"

"Okay, I gave you bad advice. *Aim* for Mount Douglas. But keep your eye on the *ball.*"

A few swings later, Liv hit another grounder. Then another. It still hurt, but it was starting to feel good, too.

"Try to get *under* the ball a little more when you swing," Scott said. "Sort of scoop it up. That's how you'll get the ball in the air."

He seemed to know a lot about this. "Did you coach Little League or something?"

"Something like that."

She made a few more tries as she tried the new swinging technique, missing the ball entirely. Then, suddenly, she hit the ball and it sailed straight out, level with her waist. It didn't land until it collided with the tentlike structure that held the cannon, somewhere beyond where the pitcher's mound would have been.

"That, madam, is a line drive."

Liv felt a surge of satisfaction. She wanted more. By the end of the round of balls, she was hitting about half of them. Two more were line drives. Probably that was as good as it would get. She *really* wanted to hit a fly ball, but she'd kept Scott watching her for half an hour as it was. All on his dime—or his tokens, at any rate—and of course, he'd refused to take any of her money when she offered.

Reluctantly, she stepped back from the painted home plate on the concrete. "You want to hit a few?"

"Nah. It's my night off. But I'd like to see you hit at least one home run before we go. I'm pretty sure you've got one in you."

Crossing her arms in front of her, she rubbed her upper arms and shoulders. She rotated one arm, then the other. Her muscles protested.

"Is that you loosening up?" A spark of challenge lit in his eyes. "Or is that you *giving* up?"

She knew darned well what he was doing. A little reverse psychology, trying to tick her off and get her motivated. But at this point, she was as ticked off at the ball as she was at Scott or even Kevin.

In fact, she'd forgotten about the mess with Kevin for a few minutes.

Liv lifted her chin, accepting Scott's challenge. "I'm game."

"Okay." He opened the gate again and walked toward her. Her stomach dropped, not sure if she was ready for whatever he hand in mind.

But when he reached her, he turned her around, giving a brisk, loose massage to her neck and shoulders, shaking her arms to loosen them.

"All right," he said. "Now, before we start the next round of balls, step up to the plate again."

Liv did. He followed, still standing behind her.

"Hold your bat."

She did. Then he put his arms around her, his hands holding hers over the bat, directing her to reposition her fingers higher up the neck of the bat. She felt the warmth of his body against her back. This could turn into funny business pretty quick, but so far he seemed to be playing it aboveboard. And when had Scott ever not been on the level?

Even so, her heart was speeding up.

"Widen your stance," he said, a suggestive line if ever

there was one. Liv set her feet farther apart, bending her knees, trying to ignore the touch of his hands over hers. And the way her palms were sweating.

"Work with me here," he said, his voice near her ear. "Concentrate." Slowly, he guided her arms back, then forward into that scooping-swinging motion. Back and forth. It was a little like dancing. "Feel that?"

Oh, she was feeling it, all right. Scott stopped swinging, and she closed her eyes, grateful that her back was turned to him. *Baseball*, she reminded herself, letting her breath out in a slow, silent sigh.

"Now, put your weight behind it," he said. "All the way back, then swing and follow through."

He guided her through the motion several more times. Liv tried to follow suit, ignoring the little sparks that stirred up inside her.

She really wanted to hit that ball, she reminded herself.

Scott let go and stood back. "Let me see your swing again. Remember, keep your weight with it."

Standing alone, feeling self-conscious, Liv pantomimed a few more swings until she felt slightly less ridiculous. She could do this. She was nothing if not a good student.

"Okay," Scott said. "This is the last round. You've got twenty tries. You're going to nail that ball."

A clink of tokens, and the machine revved to life. Liv watched the blinking light and tried to keep her mind on baseball.

The ball fired out, and she swung. And swung. And swung.

A tip. Another tip. A line drive. Her arms and

shoulders ached in protest, but so far she'd connected with every pitch.

"Eye on the ball," Scott reminded her after her third tip in a row.

Liv took a deep breath, kept her eye on the ball, and swung hard. Another line drive. Silence from Scott.

She didn't know how many balls she had left, but she knew it was less than half. When the next one flew out, she put all her weight into the swing, right where she wanted it, and somehow she knew it was right before she connected with the ball. Then she felt the solid impact of wood against ball that set her shoulders screaming. And sent the ball sailing.

Up. And up.

She stared at the ball against the night sky, and for a moment it seemed to climb straight for Mount Douglas in a beautiful arc before it hit the rope mesh that hung overhead. It sank like a wounded bird, landing far at the back of the enclosure.

"Keep going," Scott said. "Here comes your next one."

She'd barely cranked her arms back when the ball fired out, and she kept swinging, but it didn't matter much now.

Three more line drives, in a row, solidly connecting with the ball every time. And then the light on the machine went out.

Everything after her lone fly ball had been anticlimactic, but it was enough. Liv lowered the bat and shook her arms out as she met Scott's eyes. She couldn't keep a triumphant smile off her face. She stayed where she was, beside the imaginary home plate, relishing the moment. Outside the batting cage, reality waited, and she didn't want to think about that right now.

Scott gave her a nod of satisfaction as he came back into the cage with her. "Atta girl," he said. "I knew you could do it."

Liv's heart skittered. Under the bright outdoor floodlights, suddenly the scene felt unreal, like something out of a movie.

Not sure what to say, she held the bat out to him. "That did it for me," she said. "Want to hit a few now?"

He shook his head. "No, I'm good."

"You sure?" She dangled the bat loosely, letting it swing like the pendulum of a clock. "What, are you chicken?" she teased.

It didn't get the reaction she expected. Scott inclined his head and stared at her.

"Chicken?" he echoed.

She'd sparked something, hit some sort of nerve, and she wasn't sure what it was.

Not until he sauntered purposefully toward Liv, blue eyes never leaving hers as he stopped before her and pulled the silly batting helmet off her head. He tossed it carelessly to the ground a few feet away, his gaze still unwavering.

"Which one of us is chicken?" he said softly.

The moment still felt surreal, like a movie. Or a dream. Maybe that was what kept Liv pinned in place, watching it all in slow motion.

But no dream had ever felt like this.

Hands on her shoulders, he bent to kiss her, and Liv never thought about pulling away as his lips pressed over hers, warm and sure. Purposeful. Like someone

220

who knew exactly what he wanted. And Liv knew she'd been wanting the same thing all along, ever since that moment earlier tonight in front of the silver tree, and all during the past week as they worked side by side.

When they'd kissed in the attic, he'd let her take the lead. This was different. Liv stood on tiptoe to meet his kiss head-on, clasping her arms around his neck to hold on. Scott brought one arm down to encircle her waist, closing more of the space between them, steadying her.

Maybe it really was a dream, because when he released her and eased her back down until she stood squarely on her feet, it was hard to open her eyes.

Liv kept her hands clasped behind his neck, because for some reason, her legs didn't seem to be working right. They trembled, and she didn't think she'd been on tiptoe that long.

"What was that?" she murmured.

"A good idea?" He brushed a strand of hair back from her face, and dimly she remembered she was wearing the same ponytail she'd started the day with. It had to be a mess by now, especially after the baseball helmet. She brought her hands to her hair, trying not to wobble as she disengaged herself from Scott.

"Want to get some dinner?" he said. "And maybe that margarita?"

Earth to Liv. Earth to Liv.

What had she been thinking? Surely, it was the longest she could remember going *without* thinking. And she sure couldn't blame it on spring fever.

"I'm sorry." She stepped back and saw Scott's eyes go dim in an instant. "I can't. I've got to—"

"Liv, don't do this. Not again."

"I'm only going to be here one more week—"

"Then what are you so afraid of?"

He'd asked her that before. Maybe she owed him an honest answer. If only she knew what that answer was. All she knew was that, standing this close to Scott, thinking about how lost she'd been a few minutes ago, she felt something close to panic.

"I don't know. I'm afraid I won't want to leave. It's going to be hard enough as it is."

"Maybe you don't have to."

And under the warm weight of his eyes, she felt her near panic turn to terror.

"I *have* to," she said. "I have a business. I have a partner. I have commitments."

That word *commitment* hung in the air, and in a moment of inspiration, she seized on it.

"What about *you*?" she challenged. "Maybe you *like* the fact that I have to be gone in a week. Maybe that's why you keep going after these transitional girls. You like things with a built-in exit."

He looked as if she'd slapped him in the face. Had she hit on a truth?

Scott's eyes shuttered and his hand went into his jeans pocket for his car keys.

"You win," he said. "I'll take you home."

Half an hour later, Joe Velosa frowned quizzically at Scott from behind the counter at the recreation center. "Scotty," he said. "You're back."

"Yep." Scott handed him a twenty to make change for the token machine.

"We close in fifteen minutes," Joe said.

"That's okay. It won't take long."

Scott passed once again through the recreation center's arcade to the batting cages outside, popped in his tokens and stood ready with his bat.

And one after another, with a swing that was second nature, he scooped those balls toward the now black sky. There was barely time to watch each ball hit the mesh at the back of the cages before the next pitch came, but that wasn't the point. The point was hitting them, one after another, feeling the sure, solid connection of bat against ball.

She didn't remember.

He'd been Tall Pine High's star hitter, with a pretty decent throwing arm in the bargain. His coach had urged Scott to try out for the minor leagues, but he hadn't been interested. Playing against Mount Douglas—and kidnapping their goose—was as competitive as he got. He knew the professional sports world was intense, maybe even cutthroat. The idea of leaving Tall Pine, traveling across the country to compete, hadn't interested him on anything but a fantasy level. He just liked hitting the ball.

He wasn't that competitive. Which, he supposed, was why Liv was in Dallas, and he was still in Tall Pine.

He sent every one of the machine-pitched balls soaring, wishing he could at least get the satisfaction of wearing his muscles out. The way he felt right now, he'd need another couple of hours to do that.

Coming here to the cages was usually a good way to

vent his frustrations, if he had any. Mostly he just enjoyed keeping his swing in shape. Liv probably wouldn't understand that.

And that remark of hers about the other women he'd dated—

The light on the machine went out, and Scott reloaded the tokens quickly, before time ran out and the place shut down.

Liv's comment bothered him so much he should probably think about it, but it felt wrong. All wrong. The other breakups had left him scuffed and bruised, but not mortally wounded. This was something else. It wasn't even over, had never even really started, and he felt like hell.

Scott would finish the job on Nammy's house. Liv's mother would pay him with a check he didn't even want. Then Liv would get on a plane, and that would be that.

Two intense kissing sessions. Not even one date. And Liv Tomblyn was breaking his heart.

Chapter 19

Liv woke up feeling as if she'd been run over by a whole convoy of buses. When she opened her eyes, the room looked faintly gray. What was it, five in the morning?

Propping herself up on her elbow, she checked the digital clock on the night table on the far side of the bed. Usually she had to look over Rachel's head to see the time. Today, only a pile of squashed pillows rested between Liv and the clock. It read eight forty-five.

That startled her into sitting fully upright. It was two hours later in Dallas. Terri would be waiting to hear from her. And Liv didn't know what to say.

She'd sent Terri a quick text on the way to the batting cages: Got your message. I'm sorry for the mess. My brain is processing. I'll call you tomorrow and we'll figure things out.

In Liv's world, "processing" now apparently meant hitting one fly ball, kissing Scotty Leroux, and running for the hills. Again.

Liv scrubbed her fingers over her sandy eyes and willed herself to concentrate. Things were supposed to look clearer in the morning. But all she could see was the same thing she'd seen, on and off, all night long while she tossed: Scott's eyes under the artificial lights at the batting cages, with their changing expressions of warmth, teasing—and, finally, blue frost.

It hurt, all the way down to the pit of her stomach. She kept coming back for a taste of something she knew she couldn't have. It just wasn't possible.

Melt into Scott's arms, for a little while. Stop being strong, for just a moment. But then, the inevitable tearing-away process when she pulled away to stand up straight again. It wasn't good for either one of them.

She wiped at her eyes again, alarmed because this time they felt wet instead of gritty.

This wouldn't do. Where was her cell phone?

The bedroom doorknob turned. Liv jumped at the sound, her heart racing as if she'd gotten caught naked in Dillards' display window.

"Hey, Rip van Winkle." Rachel came in, obscenely perky, in an oversized blue sweater and navy leggings. For the first time since Liv's arrival in Tall Pine, Rachel was fully dressed while Liv was still in bed. "I came in to see if you died."

"Just woke up." Liv turned her head away as she slid out of bed, hoping her red eyes hadn't registered with her relentlessly chipper sister. She spotted the red metal glint of her cell phone on the floor next to the old dresser that served as Liv's nightstand. She picked it up. The battery was still half full. But no new messages.

"You were restless last night," Rachel said. "It was like sleeping on board the *SS Poseidon*."

"Welcome to my world." Liv knew she'd been tossing,

but she was surprised her sister knew it, as much as Rachel had been snoring.

"I know something that'll make you feel better."

"A Christmas cookie?"

Rachel didn't answer. Liv turned to see her sister pulling back the curtains of the bedroom window. Watery daylight filtered into the room.

Liv joined Rachel at the window and beheld a world of soft gray and white.

That was why it looked like five AM in here. It had snowed overnight, and it was still trying, pale flakes drifting lazily to rest on the juniper hedges in front of the window.

"I didn't want you to miss it," Rachel said.

Liv drank in the sight of the white coating that covered the back lawn. The first snowfall since Nammy's memorial. To most people in Tall Pine, snow meant an increase in tourist traffic. To a few, it meant a commuter's nightmare. To local kids—and adults who hadn't outgrown it—it meant beauty and wonder.

Liv found she hadn't outgrown it.

"I want to hear it." Liv lifted the window sash, letting in a cold blast of air that her T-shirt nightie was no match for. She listened to the whisper of snow falling on snow.

Nothing like this in Dallas, is there? Scott's words from a couple of weeks ago echoed in her mind. She steeled herself. Then her teeth started to chatter.

"Okay, that's enough." She closed the window. "Before we die of frostbite."

"I was thinking maybe we could take a walk in it."

Liv looked at Rachel and saw two people: the little

227

girl she'd once been, and the pregnant grown woman who stood before her now. A grown woman who might have a hunch that the snow was just what Liv needed. Liv hadn't said much to Mom and Rachel when she got home from the batting cages, declining a cup of hot chocolate and heading straight to bed.

Maybe the kid in Rachel just wanted to go out in the snow, or maybe the adult in her wanted to give Liv a chance to talk. Maybe the teenager, somewhere in between, was waiting for a chance to pounce with questions before she exploded.

It didn't matter. Liv loved them all.

She cracked a smile. "Give me twenty minutes. First I've got a phone call to make."

"I'm sorry," Terri said. "I should have told you before. I've been trying to reach Kevin since the first, and when I finally got hold of him . . ."

"He weaseled out," Liv finished for her. "I don't know why you're apologizing to me. I'm the one he suckered into this whole storefront thing in the first place."

"It hasn't exactly paid for itself." Terri had left that unsaid the entire time they'd had the lease. The physical location had brought an increase in business, to be sure, but not enough to compensate for the increase in overhead. *Give it time,* Kevin had said. *You have to take the long view.* Worm.

Sitting on the bed, legal pad propped up on her knees, Liv pressed the fingertips of one hand above her jaw, willing the pressure to help take away some of the tension. Her sketchy night of sleep wasn't helping her concentrate. So far the legal pad was blank except for aimless black scribbles.

"What we need to do," Liv said slowly, through the ache in her jaw, "is figure out where we go from here. Whether it makes more sense to keep the lease till it runs out, or walk away from it now. Have you asked what it would cost to get out of the lease?"

"No, I didn't want to talk to the landlord until I talked to you." Terri paused, and Liv heard the weight of something unsaid on the other end of the line. "There's something else."

Liv tried for dry humor. "What? If a tornado hit the building, our troubles could be over."

"Nothing like that." It wasn't like Terri to stall, or to be indirect. "That event planner we did the home office for last month? She offered me a job."

Terri wasn't telling her this because the client had paid her a nice compliment. Liv gulped. "It must be a pretty good offer?"

"The money's decent," Terri said. "And it's a regular paycheck. I wouldn't be thinking about it, except now—"

Liv nodded, though Terri couldn't see her. "The variable income thing is tough. I know. We've made it work for five years, but . . ."

Terri didn't elaborate. "I said I'd think about it. I don't want to leave you in the lurch. But since we need to rethink, I guess I thought I'd throw it out there. See how you felt. In case you might be ready for a change . . ."

With one hand, Liv pressed her temple as hard as

she could. With the other hand, it was all she could do to hold on to the phone. "Let's both think about it," she said, her mouth dry.

"It's just one option," Terri agreed hastily.

She'd worked with Terri for five years, been friends in college for the four years before that. Terri wasn't a weasel-worm like Kevin. And if Liv demanded that she stick it out, at least for the duration of the lease, she was pretty sure Terri would do it.

What Liv *should* do was let her go with no argument. But she wasn't ready to say the words just yet. Her mind was too much of an avalanche to make a permanent decision.

The part of her brain that was so good at sorting, sifting, and deciding hadn't been much use to her since she'd been in Tall Pine.

"Let's talk again in a few days," Liv finally said. "Give ourselves some time to chew it over some more. And Terri?"

"What?"

"Thanks for taking this all on this month. I picked a heck of a time to leave, and I had no idea what a hassle I was leaving you with."

"Honey, it was your *grandmother*. It was what you needed to do."

When Liv hung up, one decision was already made. She wouldn't force Terri to stick around. She had to let her go, with her blessing.

She grabbed Rachel's pillow, hugged it to her, and pulled her knees to her chest. Eyes closed, face scrunched into the pillow, she made herself breathe slowly and deeply.

Everything was falling apart. This wasn't a batting-cages moment. This was a curl-up-and-eat-chocolate moment.

By now Scott was at Nammy's house, starting the day's work, undoubtedly not surprised that she hadn't shown up. It was five days till Christmas. At the moment she could think of only two options.

Pull the covers back over her head. Or go out there, grab some toast, and take a walk in the snow with her sister.

Scott didn't make it to Olivia Neuenschwander's house until nearly ten o'clock, stopping along the way to shovel the front walkways of a few of the older people in town. Millie Bond. Stan and Emma Fratelli. His uncle, Winston Frazier, although Scott knew Winston would be insulted if he caught him.

Thankfully, the unexpected snow hadn't resulted in any more frozen pipes. Otherwise his voice mail would have been going crazy.

No, it was less than a week before Christmas, and for most people, home repairs could wait unless they were an emergency. The perfect time frame to finish up on Nammy's house. And he knew he'd be doing it alone.

He sighed as the chilly living room greeted him. He flipped the thermostat up to a hardy sixty-two degrees and set up shop in the living room. By the time he'd pushed the furniture to the center of the living room and put down the drop cloth, he'd warmed up a bit. But it was still probably about forty degrees in here. And he hadn't heard the heater click on.

Scott sighed and went into the belly of the beast: the garage, where the heater lived. He switched the unit off, waited for a ten count, then flipped it back on.

He went back inside and set up the ladder. *Work from the top down, always. Period. Don't argue.*

The heater still didn't click on.

Back to the garage. The behemoth sat stone cold. Scott switched it off and counted off a full sixty seconds. Then, just to be sure, he counted off sixty more. Then he switched the heater back on.

And waited for the click that didn't come.

Up to now, his Captain Obvious method had always worked. Not today.

He stared at the heater with his arms crossed over his chest. "Are you serious?"

It wasn't the first time he'd spoken to an inanimate object. But it was the first time he'd halfway hoped to get an answer.

The heater had behaved perfectly for the past few days. While he and Liv were working amicably together on the house. The correlation was hard to ignore, much as he wanted to.

"What do you want from me?" he demanded.

But of course, the heater couldn't answer him. Neither could the house. And any other explanation was even more ridiculous. It was time to stop fooling around.

Liv had the business card from the heater rep, but he had the manufacturer's number in the call log of his cell phone. And if Faye Tomblyn wanted to sell this house, it needed to be taken care of.

He got into his truck and headed to the corner in front of Coffman's Hardware.

Liv and Rachel walked side by side in the gray quiet. The snow was too fresh and soft to make much noise under their feet, and Liv almost hated to break up the pure, smooth whiteness as they walked down the street. The scattered snowflakes, the mist from their breath, and the cold air brought Liv a kind of Zen feeling, at least for moments at a time. Every few steps brought back a thought of Scott, or the business, or Terri, but a deep breath was enough to shrivel the inside of her nōse and shock her back to the present moment.

"Is it hard to go back to San Diego?" Liv asked suddenly, surprised by the sound of her own voice.

"It was at first," Rachel admitted. "But it's home now. It's where Brian's job is. And I always know I'll be back here before too long. I'll probably come up here less, once the baby's born."

"Maybe Mom will make a few trips to San Diego."

"Oh, she's planning on it." Rachel laughed. "She's always telling me how fast babies grow. She doesn't want to miss it."

Before Liv went out in the snow with Rachel, Mom had handed her an English muffin with a tomato slice on top. Another favorite of Nammy's, from her childhood back in Minnesota, if Liv remembered right. And prepared rather capably, as Mom rounded the kitchen on just one crutch. Gray hair or no gray hair, she was definitely on the mend.

Up at the end of the street, three kids scurried in their yard, gathering up material for a snowman. Their bright hats and scarves stood out against the monochrome landscape. It reminded Liv of a Christmas card.

"You're lucky," she told Rachel.

"Why?"

"If it wasn't for your delicate condition, I'd be looking for a chance to belt you with a snowball."

Rachel's gray eyes glimmered. "You wouldn't dare."

The street took an uphill slant, and Liv felt a little out of breath, working against both the incline and the fresh snow. She ought to get more exercise. She paused as they reached the next corner. "One more block, or turn back around?"

Rachel didn't answer right away.

Liv turned and saw Rachel had stopped a few steps back, bending to rest her hands on her knees. *Better turn back*, she thought. She rejoined her sister, who remained stooped, catching her breath.

"Rachel! Are you okay?" She rested a hand on her sister's shoulder.

To her relief, Rachel straightened. "That was weird." She wrapped an arm loosely across her rounded stomach.

"What?"

She looked at Liv, her eyes wide. "I don't *think* it was a contraction. But my stomach felt really tight for a second."

"You're kidding." Liv looked at their footprints, leading back to Mom's house. It seemed a lot farther than she remembered.

"I'm all right now," Rachel said.

"We'd better get back anyway." Liv elected not to add the words *just in case.*

They'd traveled most of the first block back before Rachel paused again, one hand over her stomach, the other on Liv's arm.

"Again?" Liv didn't know much about pregnancy, but if these were contractions, they seemed awfully close together. She reached into her jeans pocket for her cell phone to check the time—and maybe call 911—but it wasn't there. She tried her coat pocket, too. Not there, either. She turned to Rachel. "Did you bring your phone?"

Rachel shook her head. "Nine-Mississippi, ten-Mississippi, eleven-Mississippi . . ."

She stopped counting at thirty-three-Mississippi. Liv asked, "What does that mean?"

"I'm not sure. I just figured it was a good idea to know how long they are. I know how far apart is important."

Her mouth dry, Liv put a hand on Rachel's arm to start her forward. They started walking again. As they rounded a bend, Liv saw the hunter-green trim of Mom's house through the thinning snowflakes, still more than a block away. "Do you really think it's labor?"

"I'm not sure." This time there was a faint edge of panic in Rachel's voice. "But I didn't really plan on having a little snow-baby."

"Hold that thought," Liv said, putting her hand over Rachel's where it still rested on her arm. "We'll get you back to Mom's and figure out where to go from there."

Chapter 20

"I think he came to the house on the twelfth or the thirteenth," Scott told the heater company operator who was trying to field his call. "His name wasn't Butch . . . maybe Bruce?"

A keyboard clicked faintly on the other end of the line. "That would be Russ," she said. "On the thirteenth."

At least he'd been warm on the date.

Scott waited while they chased Russ down from whatever end of the earth he was at. Russ remembered the service call immediately. He listened to Scott's account: from a week of perfect performance to stone-cold dead.

"Oh, and the night you came over, the heater came on when the thermostat was off," Scott remembered to add belatedly.

"You must have the possessed model," Russ joked, but this was one time Scott didn't feel like laughing.

The verdict might not be far off, Scott supposed, given the erratic symptoms and the fact that the heater hadn't acted up for the repairman. Although the unit was out of warranty, the corporate office was willing to replace the heater at half the wholesale price. That still meant several hundred dollars.

Scott couldn't very well fold the price of the heater into the cost of the remodeling project. Before he could tell the heater rep to proceed, he'd have to call Liv's family and run it by them. They might want to put the brakes on the tile or the paint.

Liv's number was programmed into his cell phone. So was Faye's landline.

He'd try Faye first.

"Do you smoke?" the urgent care doctor asked.

Rachel looked at him as if he were insane. He amended, "Or did you before you were pregnant?"

"No and no."

"Any history of drug use?"

"*No.*"

Liv could only imagine how testy Rachel would be if she actually were in labor. Then again, a lot of the questions the doctor was asking were pretty embarrassing.

It didn't help that the doctor—the intern, probably—was Max Azaria. He'd graduated from Tall Pine High the year before Liv. Rachel would have been a freshman then, so she wouldn't remember him as well. But still.

"Sorry. It's all on the form." Dr. Max folded his arms around the clipboard and sat down on the rolling stool alongside Rachel's knees. He'd grown a beard somewhere in the intervening years, and while it made him look more mature, it didn't make Liv inclined to take him more seriously. The beard didn't seem very clinical. And she still remembered clobbering him in debate.

Liv and Mom were seated in uncomfortable metal folding chairs by the head of the bed. Rachel sat propped up at a forty-five-degree angle, her belly connected by little adhesive electrodes to a monitor that looked a lot like a lie detector machine from the movies. The nurses had hooked her up minutes after she arrived, but in the half hour they'd spent waiting for the doctor, she'd only had one contraction, and Rachel admitted it was the weakest one so far.

"The good news is, I'm pretty sure this is a false alarm," Max said. At Rachel's indignant look, he smiled. Liv couldn't remember her sister looking so irritable. "You've probably heard of Braxton Hicks contractions?"

"In Lamaze class." Rachel looked suddenly sheepish.

"They're like rehearsal contractions," the doctor went on. "It's your body's way of preparing for labor, and it's perfectly normal. All women have them, but they're not always noticeable. Certain factors can make them more pronounced, like dehydration—you mentioned you hadn't had much to drink this morning besides coffee. By the way, I assume that was decaf?"

Rachel reddened. The doctor nodded as if in satisfaction.

"Caffeine could be a factor," he said. "Another possible factor is sudden activity. You mentioned you were out walking when they started."

Now it was Liv's turn to feel shamefaced. "It's my fault."

Three faces—Rachel's, Mom's, and Max's—all turned

to stare at her. Rachel was the one who spoke. "What makes you say that? I'm the one who wanted to go for a walk."

"I should have thought. It wasn't a good idea."

"Actually, walking during pregnancy is a very good idea," Dr. Max put in. "And if you started having contractions when you weren't being active, getting up and moving around can actually make Braxton Hicks contractions stop."

"So, what should she be doing?" Mom asked. "Resting or moving around?"

"Before I answer that, I want to do a quick exam," the doctor said. "It sounds like Braxton Hicks, but there are a couple of things that make Rachel a candidate for premature labor. Emotional upsets, like your grandmother passing away recently. And you might be a little underweight. Your chart shows you at 122 now. How much did you weigh before you were pregnant?"

"About 105, I think."

Under other circumstances, Liv would have glared at her sister. But Rachel always had been a skinny, delicate thing.

The doctor frowned and peered at the chart. "And you're five-three," he confirmed. "If you two ladies could give us a few minutes, I'll bring a nurse in and check Rachel over. But I still have a feeling my prescription is going to be a little caution. And maybe a few donuts."

As Liv and her mother rose to wait in the hallway, Max turned to Liv. "By the way, how's the furniture business?"

"Home organizing." Liv smiled weakly. "It's fine. Thanks."

She stepped into the hallway with Mom, where they found another two metal chairs, just as uncomfortable as the ones in the urgent care examining room. Liv took her mother's hand, no longer sure who was comforting whom.

"She'll be fine." It was Mom who spoke.

Liv didn't argue. She certainly didn't want to worry her mother, and Max had seemed fairly sure they weren't dealing with anything serious. But Rachel wasn't *his* sister.

Or daughter. Liv stole a look at her mother, the single crutch propped beside her on the wall almost like an afterthought. Mom had come a long way, and she sounded more confident than Liv felt. But it was in a mother's nature to worry.

"Did you have any kind of trouble when you were pregnant with us?" Liv asked.

To her surprise, Mom chuckled. "When didn't I? You were nearly two weeks overdue. And I had twenty-four-hour morning sickness with Rachel. She's had a really smooth pregnancy. Maybe she was due for a bump in the road. But she's a lot tougher than she looks."

"I still have a hard time believing she's married with her own house. Let alone having her own baby."

"It takes getting used to." Liv heard the unspoken sigh in her mother's voice. "But you'll never stop being my kids."

Liv leaned her head on her mother's shoulder, silently pretending she was a kid again for just a moment. Funny how, as Mom's knee recovered, the urge to lean on her—literally—came right back. No wonder Rachel came back up here so often, especially with Brian's schedule.

And Liv lived so far away. The specter of regret hovered over her again. She'd gained more independence, gained a livelihood, but she'd lost a lot in the bargain.

At the thought of her livelihood, unease crept in. She had to find a way to keep it going. But now wasn't the time to be thinking about her own problems. Instead, she raised her head. Time to be a grown-up again.

"We should call Brian," she said.

"We will." Mom's fingers squeezed hers. "First let's see what the doctor says. We'll be able to tell Brian more after that."

Liv's cell phone jangled in her pocket.

"Hello?" Liv's voice, over Scott's cell phone, sounded hushed and hollow.

"Hi, Liv, it's me." Her phone display had probably already told her that. At least she'd picked up.

"Hi, Scott. What's up?"

He frowned. "You sound funny."

"Sorry. I'm at the hospital—"

"The hospital?" He cut her off involuntarily.

"Everything's okay. Rachel started having some contractions and we brought her in to check her out."

Contractions didn't sound okay to him. "Rachel's having contractions and you didn't call me?"

He felt stupid as soon as he said it. Of course they wouldn't call him for something like that. He wasn't family. And the problem didn't call for a truck, a hammer, or a screwdriver.

"They're probably rehearsal contractions." Liv spoke patiently. "The doctor's just double-checking to make sure it isn't premature labor. She's still got about six weeks before she's due."

Scott found himself nodding, even though he knew that didn't work on the phone. He wasn't sure how premature six weeks was, but it sounded too early. "Tell her to take it easy."

"I will. Thanks." There was a softness in Liv's voice, and a trace of something else he'd heard once or twice in Faye's voice. A faint shakiness.

Without thinking, he asked the forbidden question. "Are *you* okay?"

"I'm fine."

"No, you're not." That was the macho part of him talking. That part of him that wanted to be the one who could fix it.

A long silence. He waited.

"I'm fine," she repeated. "What were you calling about?"

He'd almost forgotten. Now didn't seem like a good time. "Nothing important."

"What?" she persisted.

He fumbled. "The tile," he said. "It's the blue patterned tile in the bathroom, the red brick tile in the dining room, right?"

She sounded baffled. "Of course." Because the other way around would clash like a nightmare. Not to mention the fact that Nammy had only bought about one-third as much of the blue patterned tile for the much smaller bathroom.

Just get off the phone. Instead, he asked, "Did you talk to Terri?"

"Yeah." Her voice sounded fainter, not like Liv at all.

"How'd it go?"

"I—we've got a lot to figure out. Usually I can break down all the pros and cons. I'm just a little muddled lately. It'll be okay."

Another area where he wouldn't be much use. But he thought of someone who probably would. Before he knew what he was doing, he said, "I know who you ought to talk to."

He gave her Jake Wyndham's number. And after they hung up, he dug into his wallet for his one and only credit card. He hadn't touched plastic since the first year after he'd moved out of his parents' house. Fortunately, it hadn't taken that long to pay off a year's worth of pizza and CDs, but he'd learned his lesson. Right now, though, he didn't see another choice.

It had to be taken care of, and Liv and her family would never notice that the heater in the garage had less dust on it.

Max's examination didn't rule out preterm labor, since he said it sometimes stopped on its own. On his instructions, they took Rachel home, propped her feet up next to Mom's, and made sure her diet included plenty of water and nothing with caffeine in it. It was getting hard to keep Mom seated, but Liv insisted on waiting on the two of them for the rest of the day. It gave her something to do when she wasn't at her laptop, poring over the business's facts and figures.

The next morning, she sat next to Jake Wyndham at a round table in the Man Cave at the hotel, trying to read his mind as he studied the columns on her laptop screen. Fortunately, the history of the home organizing business was already laid out cleanly. It was the future that was a big question mark.

Jake frowned and nodded, and Liv tried to interpret the two conflicting signals. "You have an orderly mind," he said.

"Sometimes." Liv tried to relax in the admittedly comfortable chair. But she couldn't keep from wrapping her arms across her stomach, as if to contain the turmoil that was going on inside it.

Jake nodded again, pushing back slightly from the table. "Okay. So, you're trying to weigh all your options."

Liv unfolded her arms and reached for the yellow legal pad on the table in front of her. She waited.

"You could try to stay the course, at least for the duration of the lease. Of course, that's easier to do if you can get Terri to stay on board."

Liv remembered Terri's voice on the phone, the tone she'd tried so hard to keep out of her voice. Maybe the entrepreneurial life had been wearing on Terri already, and Liv had been too wrapped up to notice it. She shook her head.

"Don't rule anything out yet. Remember, we're talking options. Get them all in front of you first. Now, Kevin. Have you tried to contact him?"

"Yes. Strangely enough, he didn't pick up."

"Did you ever have an agreement down on paper?"

"An informal one, between us. His name isn't on the lease."

Jake showed neither surprise nor judgment. "Kevin, we can go over pretty quickly, and I think I know what the outcome is there. You could try playing nice and getting him to come through, and it sounds like Terri's been working that option for a while now. You could try threatening legal action. It probably wouldn't work, but it wouldn't cost anything to try. You could try actually pursuing legal action, but that involves time, energy, and money." He cocked an eyebrow. "I'm supposed to be impartial here, but frankly, that's the one option I wouldn't recommend. It would probably be . . . a waste of resources."

Liv felt her face color with a mixture of anger and embarrassment. What came out of her mouth was, "I feel so stupid."

"Don't." Jake shook his head emphatically, tapping a pen on her laptop screen. "This is not a stupid person. You trusted someone to do what he said he'd do. In this case it was a mistake. You didn't know that. If there's one thing I've learned in the business world, it's that people will surprise you. But sometimes they'll surprise you for the better."

"The storefront was a bad idea." She'd sensed it at the time. And for some reason, Kevin had gotten her to turn a blind eye to those misgivings.

Jake regarded her screen again. "It did increase your business," he noted. "But it also shrank your profits. Still. You had profits. Give yourself credit where it's due." He turned back to her. "So, in terms of options. We're down to one woman, a business, and a lease.

You say you and Terri haven't asked the landlord yet about getting out of the lease?"

"Not yet." Liv put her free hand over her flip-flopping stomach.

"I'd say that's what you need to do next. You don't know until you ask, and asking isn't the same thing as signing your name in blood. So, compare the options of continuing on your own, with or without the lease. You don't have any liabilities other than your month-to-month expenses, which is a big advantage. I doubt you'd have any trouble qualifying for a small business loan, if you need it. But that's a pretty large commitment, and you should give it some serious thought first. You could also try subletting for the duration of the lease, although there's always the chance your tenant might not be a reliable payer."

In other words, don't sublet to Kevin, she thought.

Jake paused. "There is one more option."

"What's that?" Liv looked up from her scrawling.

"You could cut your losses." Jake said the words quietly.

Liv felt the color drain from her face.

"I know that's hard to hear," Jake said. "But remember, we're talking about *all* the options."

"Failure isn't an option," she said reflexively.

"*Failure* isn't the right word," Jake said. "Any business venture is a risk, and it can turn on a dime. Economies change. Circumstances change. New competitors can spring up. There might not be enough demand for a product, or consumers might not have enough disposable cash if it's not an essential. In your case, you're going from a three-way partnership to a one-woman

246

operation. You're dealing with a lot of circumstances beyond your control."

Liv slowed her breathing, aware that both of her arms had wrapped across her stomach again. Too bad she hadn't taken that Lamaze class along with Rachel.

"Remember, I'm not *telling* you to do anything," Jake said. "Just exploring the possibilities. You might be able to sell off the name, and I see you were smart enough to maintain a mailing list of previous clients. Depending on the size of your obligation to the landlord, you might clear enough to buy you out of the lease."

Liv jotted the word *Sell* on the legal pad, reminding herself that it was just an ugly four-letter word. Even so, she fought the urge to scratch it out. There wasn't much writing on the pad as it was. Jake was nothing if not succinct.

She stared down at the word. Her personal empire. Everything she'd accomplished in five years. The business her grandmother had praised, that everyone in town congratulated her on, even if they didn't exactly know what it was.

The thought of giving up set an ugly little coil of panic tightening in her stomach.

She looked up at Jake, trying to school her features into a neutral expression. But his frank, steady gaze seemed to see through it.

"Remember, I'm not telling you to quit," he said. Still, Liv winced inwardly at the word. "I'm just laying out options. And before you even think about beating yourself up, look at this." He nodded at her laptop screen again. "You've done a lot of things right. You and Terri started this up right out of college, and you turned it into a profitable business. You know the odds against that as well as I do. If we had more time, I'd tell you about the coffee cart I tried to start up when I was in college." He shook his head ruefully.

Liv gave a weak smile. "I've taken up enough of your time as it is. Thanks"—she started to rise—"for not pulling any punches."

Jake quickly stood. "Don't give it a thought."

Liv closed her laptop and slipped it into its case. Facts were always simpler through someone else's eyes. Jake had definitely helped with that. If nothing else, talking to him had given her a clearer idea what she *didn't* want. She turned to go, trying to keep her back straight and her shoulders square.

As Jake walked her out into the lobby, Liv noticed a light hum of activity. Several groups of people sat scattered over the small tables and soft chairs, chatting over their cups. Liv remembered how quiet the inn had been when she'd visited the first week of December.

"It looks like business is up," she said.

"It is. In fact, we're full up through the end of the year. We added on a little extra help in the afternoons and evenings."

They came to the front desk, and Mandy came around from behind the counter, dressed in a white sweater with blue snowflakes. "You're going? I still owe you a cup of hot chocolate."

"Maybe another rain check," Liv said, although she knew the odds of her getting back here in the remaining days before Christmas weren't good.

"Okay." Mandy's tone told her she was dubious. "But

the offer stands. I hope you make it back before you leave. Bring your mom and Rachel, too, if you want."

"Thanks," Liv said, and meant it. "You too, Jake. I owe you a lot more than a cup of cocoa."

"Forget it." Jake put his arm around Mandy. "I'm no expert. Just a sounding board. You have to do what's right for you, and that, I can't tell you. But if you ever wanted to do a chart called Liv's Career Options, come back and see me. Remember, those organization skills can come in handy a lot of places. If you lived up here, I'd hire you in a heartbeat."

Liv felt her stomach do a full-on somersault. She shook her head. "I have to make it work."

Jake nodded without surprise. "It sounded that way when we were talking. But don't be afraid to sleep on it first. Good luck."

"And merry Christmas." Mandy slipped out from underneath Jake's arm to give her a hug. Liv had barely known Mandy in school, and she'd just met Jake, but she'd miss these two.

"Merry Christmas." Ignoring the lump in her throat, Liv pulled back and looked from Mandy to Jake. "I think this goes without saying. But just to be sure— don't tell anyone about this."

"Of course not," Jake said.

"Mom and Rachel think I'm Christmas shopping," she confessed.

Mandy frowned. "You haven't told your family?"

"No."

Jake cocked his head. "But you told me."

Liv couldn't explain. "The kindness of strangers?"

"You're not a stranger. You're Mandy's classmate," he said, as if that made sense of everything.

Liv said her goodbyes and hurried out to the privacy of her car, anxiety knotting tighter in her stomach. Before she started the engine, she sat for several minutes in the driver's seat, drawing in gulps of air.

What *was* she afraid of?

Losing her business? Partly.

Worrying her mom and sister? Maybe.

Failing in front of everyone in Tall Pine? Definitely.

Being in love with Scotty?

No, she realized. Because somewhere along the line, without ever consciously thinking about it, that had become a given.

She just couldn't *do* anything about it.

She gripped the steering wheel and fiercely bit her lip. She had to leave Tall Pine. Had to leave *him*. Staying here because her business folded—it just wasn't an option.

She closed her eyes and willed the slamming beat of her heart to slow. Several deep breaths later, she started the car.

Sucker.

Scott knelt on the bathroom floor at Olivia Neuenschwander's house, laying pretty blue-patterned tile and cursing himself for an idiot.

Sucker wasn't exactly fair. Liv hadn't knowingly backed him into ponying up his own cash for half a heater. In fact, she'd gone to great lengths to try to make sure he was fairly paid.

Russ-from-the-heater-company had changed out the heater this morning. Scott would have installed it himself, except that he didn't want to leave any room for doubt. If anything went wrong this time, it wouldn't be because of anything *he* did.

And he wondered if it would make a darned bit of difference anyway. Because when he'd returned to the house yesterday after scheduling the installation, the heater was humming happily, allowing him to get the painting done in the living room. Scott had shut the heater off when he left and resolved not to say anything to Russ when he arrived.

This went beyond an "intermittent" problem. This was more of a "convenient" problem. It fell outside anything in Scott's years of experience, and when he was tired and discouraged—the way he was now—he doubted there was a mechanical solution.

Because, at moments like this, he doubted there was a mechanical cause.

Scott sat back on his heels, viewing the results of his work. The tiles came toward him in a neat diagonal arrangement: start at the far corner, work toward the door. Even cutting the tile to fit it around the fixtures was child's play by now. And, he noted with some satisfaction, he would end up with about three tiles left over. Even though he hadn't taken Nammy's project ideas very seriously, in his mind he'd successfully eyeballed the size of the bathroom with just a little to spare. They might make nice walkway stones, or garden ornaments.

For whoever lived here next. The thought gave him a pang that he tried to brush away.

Today, the bathroom tile. Tomorrow, the kitchen.

The next day, if everything stayed on track, he'd have Liv and her family come down for a walk-through to check over his handiwork. Right on schedule, two days before Christmas.

Right on schedule. That ought to make Liv happy. As if he knew anything about making Liv happy.

She'd been right, of course. What point was there in pursuing anything together when he'd known all along she was leaving? And in his own way, he'd pursued her head-on. The girl with the ultimate built-in exit. A plane for Dallas.

And even now, given half a chance, he'd take her in his arms again. He knew Liv wasn't going to let *that* happen.

She'd texted him this afternoon—not called, texted—to thank him for referring her to Jake, and to let him know Rachel was doing fine, enjoying being waited on under the doctor's instructions to take it easy. Brian would be back in town by Christmas Eve, and he'd take her home the day after Christmas.

Brian would take care of Rachel. Until then, Liv would take care of Rachel and Faye. As for Scott? He was taking care of a haunted heater. On his own dime.

Sucker.

He knelt forward and got back to work.

Chapter 21

"It's not like I can't drive," Rachel protested again.

Liv kept her grip on the car keys as the three of them walked up to the car. "We're not taking any chances," she insisted. "One contraction and you could be driving all over the road. With Mom and me in the car."

"But I haven't had a contraction since—"

"Hush." Liv held open the back door for Rachel. It was the door behind the driver's side, because the front passenger seat was already pushed back as far as it could go for Mom and her crutch. After all these years, Mom had first dibs on the coveted "shotgun" seat Liv and Rachel always used to bicker over.

Liv's desire to drive didn't really have much to do with concern over untimely contractions from Rachel. They were meeting Scott at Nammy's house to look over the work he'd completed, and Liv needed something else to focus on, even if it was only the road.

* * *

"It's amazing," Mom said.

Liv stayed close to her mother in the center of Nammy's kitchen, struck by the difference some wallpaper and tile could make. She'd been here for the wallpaper, of course, but not the tile, made to resemble the bricks of a hearth.

"I love the reds," Rachel said, echoing Liv's thoughts. The apples on the wallpaper, together with the deeper red of the simulated brick, gave the room a warm, fresh feel. It wasn't quite the same house anymore, but Nammy's guiding hand still showed in the new touches. Nammy had always loved color.

Scott stood by the doorway to the hall, waiting to lead them onward to the bathroom and the master bedroom. He wasn't dressed for construction work today; he wore the blue sweater that brought out the color of his eyes. Liv didn't trust herself to meet them.

He was doing what he often did, Liv noted, standing back while the hens talked among themselves. If Mom or Rachel noticed that Scott was uncharacteristically quiet today, they didn't show it.

Liv's eyes fell on the scarred Shaker table, and she thought of all those fish-fry dinners. "One of us ought to keep the kitchen table," she said.

"Not too likely anyone else would want it." Leaning on her crutch, Mom clomped over to the table and ran a hand over the rough surface. Liv knew her mother understood how she felt.

Rachel, too, eyed the table wistfully. "Which one of us has room for it? Mom just bought a new dinette set a year or two ago. Brian could rent a U-Haul, but we've got a built-in breakfast nook."

"You could buy a plane ticket for it," Scott said. It was a typical Scotty Leroux joke, but Liv thought she heard an edge of sarcasm underneath it. Her eyes darted over to give him a sharp look—it would be the first time she'd looked directly at him since they walked in—but he was staring at the table.

"It'd take two airplane seats." Rachel chuckled. "And think of the complaining if someone was trying to watch the in-flight movie."

Liv quietly wrapped her arms across her stomach. By now all her tension seemed to have shifted completely from her jaw to its new prime location. And this morning she'd found poor Rachel on the torture-couch, complaining about another night of tossing aboard the *Poseidon*.

The table really should stay in the family, but Liv couldn't offer a solution. So she shut her mouth.

"Come on, ladies." Scott's voice returned to its normal congenial tone. "Let me show you the rest."

Liv trailed behind as they walked through the empty house. The lingering smell of fresh paint reminded her of apartment hunting. Vacant apartments felt like a blank sheet to her, empty of memories of the last occupants, waiting for the personality of a new tenant to place a fresh stamp. This house had a lot more character than that. But had changed enough that it felt as if it was ready and waiting for the next lives to move into it. She supposed they should be proud of that. And maybe it should make it a little easier to let go. Maybe that was what Mom had in mind when she suggested this unlikely project.

Thinking of her mother, Liv quickened her steps to

catch up. This might be hitting Mom harder than she was showing.

The bathroom was tiny, but the old-fashioned blue pattern transformed it and complemented the bedroom, just across the hall. The bedroom . . . Liv found she couldn't go in the bedroom. She stood in the doorway, smelling the fresh paint and admiring the airy, sky-blue walls.

Thankfully, no one said a word about keeping the bed.

Liv was no real estate appraiser, but she was sure Scott's work had added several thousand dollars to the price of the home. All with materials Nammy had stored up. "It's like she was looking ahead," she murmured.

"It's beautiful," Mom said as they passed down the hallway again. "You did a wonderful job, Scotty."

"Scott."

"Really?" Leaning on her crutch, Mom was digging into the pocket of her purse. She pulled out her check, already filled out, and frowned at the writing on it.

"Don't worry. The bank knows me." Liv saw the wry curl at the side of Scott's mouth. "But I still don't feel right about taking—"

"Don't do this." Liv stepped in, took the check from her mother, and held it out to Scott. "Remember, we had a deal. We wouldn't *let* you do all this work if you didn't let us pay you for it. After all, we deprived you of a week's worth of your livelihood."

"Oh, I got some sidewalks shoveled." Scott didn't move to take the check as Liv held it between them.

She met his eyes. That was probably what he was waiting for—for her to look him in the eye.

She remembered the laughing look in those eyes the

day he'd picked her up at the airport, and the way she'd wondered if the joke was on her. When she met them now, he was smiling at her, half-defiant, as if he were going to milk this awkward moment for all it was worth. But his eyes were tinged with sadness, and she knew she'd put it there.

She wondered if he could read her eyes.

Refusing to back down, she rattled the check in front of him. "Take it." She kept her voice steady and mustered a smile of her own. "Before I clunk you with a great big stick."

He took the check, and for a moment they were both holding it. Liv realized it was the last connection between them, and to her alarm, she felt her eyes blur as she let it go.

She knew Scott had to have seen, but she turned away, so that Mom and Rachel wouldn't see her face. Now she had to find her voice.

"Thanks," she said to the empty corner that used to hold one of Nammy's artificial ferns. "For everything." She blinked hard and turned back toward Mom and Rachel without meeting their eyes. "Ready to go, guys?"

Her mom and sister both stopped to give Scott a hug before they left. Liv waited by the door, then led the way out. Mom and Rachel followed close behind, as if afraid they suspected she might be the one to tip over this time. And wouldn't that be perfect? Take a spill in the driveway, and they could all spend Christmas with their feet propped up while Brian waited on them.

Nearing the car, she patted the pockets of her jeans. Nothing there but her nearly useless cell phone. "Do you have the keys?" she asked Rachel.

"No, nimrod. You drove."

Of course she had. And she'd been carrying her purse, for a change, trying to get back in the habit. The car keys must be in there.

She heaved a sigh and opened the front passenger door for her mom while Rachel climbed into the backseat. She hadn't been thinking clearly when they walked in. She'd probably tossed her purse on the loveseat when they walked into the house, an old habit from sometime in her teen years.

"Be right back," she said, as if it was nothing.

She watched her feet make their way back up the front sidewalk. She'd worn her boots today. She'd been in Tall Pine long enough that her shoes were starting to repeat a second or third time.

Liv stepped inside, and there was her purse, on the loveseat right by the door, where she always used to fling it as soon as she walked in. She scooped it up, heard Rachel's keys rattle inside, and shouldered the purse as Scott walked in from the kitchen.

"Forgot my purse," she explained.

"So I see." He stopped near the doorway leading in from the kitchen. The length of the room and a sea of *awkward* stood between them.

As she fought back yet another apology, Scott asked, "Just as well you came back. I forgot, I still have my key."

He dug it out of his jeans and held it out. Taking a deep breath, she crossed the room, and he met her on the braided rag rug. They really shouldn't leave that behind either, Liv thought.

She took the key from him the way he'd taken the

check a few minutes ago. It felt like it should have been one more opportunity; instead, it was just one more severed connection.

"Has the heater acted up any more?" she asked.

"Not lately." He shifted his weight to one side; it brought him a little closer to her height. "How are things working out with Terri and the business?"

"I talked to the landlord. She's being really decent about it. She's looking for a new tenant, so we'll probably just owe for the time it's vacant." Her mouth lumbered ahead of her brain. "Terri's taking a job with one of our clients."

"Oh." His face wore that unreadable expression that was so unlike him. "So it's just you now."

She nodded, wondering why she'd said so much. "Fine" would have been sufficient.

"Maybe the universe is trying to tell you something," he said.

"Yes." Her jaw set, and she could feel it ache. "Maybe the universe is telling me not to give up. If I close down now, it's—humiliating. It's admitting defeat."

"That doesn't sound like a reason."

"Maybe not to you, it doesn't." She groped for a better explanation. "I have to fix it."

He raised his eyebrows. "Trying to use words I'll understand?"

"It's how I feel."

He studied her seriously. "You get all misty eyed about Tall Pine. In theory. But moving back home just doesn't really appeal to you, does it?"

Oh, but it did. And hand in hand with the thought came that sense of panic.

"It's not that." She tried to put her finger on it, to explain to Scott what she had trouble explaining to herself. "It's not that Tall Pine isn't good enough. I'm afraid . . . I wouldn't be good enough."

He looked at her, uncomprehending. A little of that chilly look dropped.

"People expect things," she stumbled on. "They've got this idea of who I am. If I fall on my face in Dallas, it's one thing. If I fail up here, in front of everyone who's known me all my life—it's different. 'Most likely to succeed,' remember?"

"I don't see you failing at anything."

"*We* could fail," she whispered.

There it was. She'd said it. And suddenly her vague panic blossomed into sheer, blinding, mind-numbing terror.

"Wow," Scott said. "That was fast. We haven't even started, and already we're failing?" A series of emotions passed across his face, too quickly for her to read them. Except for the last one. Disillusionment. "And your biggest concern there is that we fail in *front* of everybody?"

Liv groped for a response. She couldn't find one.

"I get it," Scott said. "If I fail, nobody's surprised. They're used to it. If *you* fail, you're another serial dater victim. And," he finished for her, "you feel stupid."

And I get hurt. Somehow she knew that losing Scotty wouldn't feel anything like losing with Kevin. Losing with the one who'd been so warm, supportive, undemanding.

Someone who'd been there when she needed him, time and time again, even in these few short weeks.

Someone who was looking at her right now with eyes that had turned to blue flint.

"Go." His voice sounded hollow. "Just—go."

She backed away, her heart jackhammering. She couldn't think of anything to say, any way to make this right.

Liv backed up again, but there wasn't far to go. The door was right behind her. She reached for the knob.

She'd failed anyway.

Chapter 22

Liv positioned the next two feet of green wire along the edge of the eaves and fired the staple gun again. The paint on the big colored lightbulbs was flaking off, but her mom's house was going to be lit up for Christmas if it killed her.

And it just might.

She almost had it down to a science. By leaning far enough to each side, she could get in three staples' worth of Christmas lights before she had to clamber down and shift the ladder over again. The middle staple was the easy one. Now, stretching to the right, she clenched her teeth, said a silent prayer, and stapled down another two-foot section of wire.

Below, she heard the front door open.

"Would you get down from there?" Rachel called as Liv gripped the ladder, fighting for a more stable position. "You're making Mom a nervous wreck."

"*You're* supposed to be off your feet," Liv retorted.

"Then come inside and sit with us." Rachel wrapped her arms around her coat. "We've seen enough of urgent care lately."

"I know what I'm doing. I saw Dad do this a million times." Some of their father's old, rusted staples still poked out of the wood, a testament to his use of the crude method. Had anyone else hung Christmas lights on this house since Dad passed away?

She wouldn't know. She hadn't been home for Christmas.

"Liv." Rachel's voice took on a rare, *cut-through-the-crap* tone. "Christmas is only two nights away. We don't need lights."

Liv knew that. But *she* needed something to do. And she was more comfortable teetering up here, seven feet out of her sister's reach, than she was climbing down and dodging questions.

"I'm almost done with the front of the house," she said. "Just let me finish this strand."

And maybe the one after that, if this string didn't wrap far enough around the front of the house.

She stayed on her perch, like a treed cat, until Rachel finally shrugged and went inside.

By the time Liv went in, the afternoon light was fading. But inside, she found not a lecture, not an interrogation, but the enticing scent of her mom's grilled cheese sandwiches.

"How come you're not sitting down like you're supposed to?" Liv gave her mother a hug in front of the stove.

"I'm getting a system." Releasing Liv and leaning on her crutch, Mom turned a sandwich with her free hand.

"And by the time you get it down, you won't need the crutches anymore." Liv went to the cabinets to gather plates.

"That's about the size of it."

They all sat at her mother's dining table. The old Shaker table would look nice in here, but Liv knew Mom had spent several hundred bucks on the new tile-topped table. Liv decided not to reopen that discussion.

"Thanks for hanging the lights," Mom said. She didn't complain about being a nervous wreck, but Liv knew what her sister had said was true.

"Did you put them on a timer?" Rachel asked.

"No, I didn't stop to figure that out yet. I could—"

"We'll just plug them in after dinner," Rachel said quickly.

They continued eating in silence. It was as normal and as strained a moment as Liv could recall from her visit so far. So many things hung, unsaid, in the air. Nammy's absence. The fact that Rachel would be leaving the day after Christmas, and Liv, the day after that. The question of what the heck was going on with Liv and Scotty. Mom and Rachel *had* to know something was up, and the very fact that they weren't asking only seemed to underscore it.

After dinner, they stood outside in the growing cold to admire the fruit of Liv's labor. Several of the colored bulbs were burned out, but no one mentioned that.

"We need one more good snow," Mom said instead. Only a few patches still remained in the shady areas of the front yard, and under the eaves themselves.

"I'll tell you what *I* need," Rachel said. "I'd really like to get out for a little while. I've been sitting for two days, except for Nammy's house this morning. We could get a cup of coffee at the Pine 'n' Dine."

"You girls go ahead," Mom said. "But Rachel, you'd better take it easy."

"You're not supposed to have coffee," Liv said.

"Decaf, then." Rachel's eyes brightened. "Or better yet. They've got spiced cider at The Snowed Inn."

Bowing to the inevitable, Liv agreed. After all, they owed her a hot chocolate.

"It's my mom's recipe." Mandy slid a pedestal mug in front of Liv, topped with whipped cream and festive red sprinkles. "I've just played with it a little over the years."

"Thanks." Liv scooped off a little of the whipped cream with her finger before she thought, then quickly popped it into her mouth. So much for table manners.

She hadn't expected to be back at The Snowed Inn, but she was glad they'd come. Two nights before Christmas, the place felt like an absolute pinnacle of holiday cheer with its soft white lights, warm pine scent, and glowing fireplaces. Christmas music played in the background at the perfect volume—enough to be audible, but not too loud for conversation. Liv was glad, too, to see that most of the tables in the little lobby were filled. In fact, it was crowded enough that she and Rachel sat in high-backed stools at the counter of the coffee bar near the ordering window.

Mandy set Rachel's hot cider in front of her. "No chocolate for you?"

"Cocoa has caffeine in it." Rachel nodded pointedly at Liv. "*Somebody* had to remind me of that."

Mandy grinned. "That's cruel and unusual. But I'm sure the baby will thank you. Someday." She rested one arm on each of their shoulders. "I'm glad you two came. Let me know if you need anything."

With that, Mandy vanished in the direction of the kitchen.

Liv spooned up a little more whipped cream, then took her first sip of cocoa. Its richness took her by surprise. "Wow. I guess I forgot what it could taste like when it doesn't come out of a packet."

Resting her elbows on the counter, Rachel sipped her cider with obvious relish before she turned to Liv. "So."

So. This was where Liv got to pay for all the tact Rachel had stored up over the past couple of weeks.

She tried to cut her sister off at the pass. "So. How about those Dodgers?"

Rachel gave her a nod as if to say, *Nice try.* "You want to talk about it?"

It occurred to Liv, belatedly, that hot chocolate might not be the best thing for her tense stomach.

"Not really."

"Where do you get that?" Rachel asked. "You've always been so private. Whenever I had boy trouble, I always came whining to you and Mom."

"Probably Dad's side of the family. He had that strong, silent thing going. Kind of like Brian." She raised her eyebrows at her sister.

"Thank you, Dr. Freud."

Liv took another sip, and her stomach relaxed a little. Not the effect she'd expected from something so sweet, as knotted up as she was these days.

"*Boy* trouble," she mused. "Not exactly the word I'd use for Scott."

"What's up with you two? Seriously."

Liv sipped her drink and took a deep breath. Was she really going to go there?

Might as well. Rachel wasn't giving up easily. And after all, Scotty was just the tip of the iceberg. Granted, six-foot-five made for a pretty big chunk of ice.

"It's pretty much what it looks like," Liv admitted. "I started something I shouldn't have started. I can't stay in Tall Pine, so . . ." She took a sip and shook her head.

There was no point in going into the rest of it—the breakup with Kevin, the resulting mess with the business. Mom and Rachel had never even heard of Kevin. Just as well, the way that relationship ended up. She *was* a private type, she supposed. She didn't like having people see her fail. Not even her own family.

And wouldn't Dr. Freud have had a field day with *that*.

Mandy peered around the corner, but Jake's hand on her shoulder gently pulled her back.

"You can't fix everything," he said.

"She's so sad," she said. "If we could just get Scotty down here—"

"We don't know that's what it's about."

"Don't you think?" She'd heard a fair amount about Liv's business troubles the other day. But to Mandy, the expression on Liv's face said *heart trouble*.

"Maybe," Jake said. "But maybe that's all the more reason to stay out of it. There's a difference between helping people feel a little better and getting involved in their personal lives."

Mandy sighed, the image of Liv's faintly furrowed brow playing in her mind's eye.

Her mother always used to say there wasn't anything a cup of hot cocoa couldn't make a little bit better. And over the course of the Christmas season, she and Jake had done too much observing to deny that her cocoa had a mellowing effect on people. A squabbling older couple, a mother and daughter at odds with each other after a rough meeting with a wedding planner . . . without flat-out eavesdropping, it was still easy to see the difference after a cup of hot chocolate. They also noticed the cocoa didn't seem to have quite the same effect if it was served by Jake, or any of the other staffers.

Getting Scotty down here to serve him a big cup of cocoa . . . maybe that did cross the line into meddling.

"I guess you're right," she said reluctantly.

"Things work out the way they're meant to work out," Jake said. "Try to force them, and it always backfires. Besides, what if Liv and Scott got together and she ended up beating him with a rolling pin? You'd have no one to blame but yourself."

Scott pushed the church door open for his parents, then held it for half a dozen other arrivals for the Christmas Eve service. They found seats near the middle of the church. At least this time his mom and dad were here, so he wouldn't have to join his uncle Winston and Dave Radner in the lonely bachelors' row.

"Presents tonight or tomorrow morning?" His father picked up on the mini-debate that had started in the car. His mom was a traditionalist; his dad was the kind who'd peek at presents if you didn't watch him.

"Tomorrow," Scott said. The fact was, he didn't want to spend Christmas morning with time on his hands.

"You just want the waffles," his mom said.

Any other year, that would have been true. This year, he hadn't even thought of it—a sure sign his mind was elsewhere. His mother's homemade Christmas-morning waffles were an institution, starting sometime after Scott's early childhood.

He smiled at her. "Frozen is okay, if it's easier."

Norma did a double take and held her hand to his forehead, as if to check for fever.

Flute music started as a few more attendees trickled in, and for the first time, Scott felt the spirit of the evening seep into him. Hearing Linda Washington's annual overture of "O Come, O Come, Emmanuel" made the trip worthwhile.

Still, his eyes wandered over the half-filled seats. He found himself wishing he'd sat closer to the back. His height, and concern for anyone who might sit directly behind him, would have been a good enough excuse for that. But it didn't look as though Liv and her family were coming, unless they'd sat down behind him. The last he heard, Rachel's husband hadn't been expected to arrive until today; most likely they'd decided to stay home.

He probably wouldn't see Liv again before she left, and probably that was for the best. He didn't need any more rounds of masochism. But he wished he hadn't left things the way he had with her. What was wrong with wishing her the best?

Aside from the fact that "the best" obviously didn't include him.

The overhead lights dimmed, and a somber-looking ten-year-old stepped forward, awkward and silent, to light the two sets of candelabra at the front of the church. Christmas, with all its small-town imperfections, had come to Tall Pine.

The next morning, when Scott opened the front door of his apartment, he found a reindeer-decorated canister waiting on the doormat. He scooped it up and carried it inside.

An envelope was taped to the side. Scott opened it to find a Norman Rockwell Christmas card with a note inside. It was short and sweet:

> *Thanks for everything. I'm sorry for all the hassle.*
> *Merry Christmas,*
> *Liv*

Scott opened the canister. It was filled with peanut brittle.

Not the prepackaged peanut brittle he'd mentioned that day in the attic, the kind local kids sold door-to-door. Scott picked up a piece and took a bite. This peanut brittle was light and fresh, probably from that little candy shop on Evergreen Lane.

He wondered when she'd bought it. *Let's see. Probably somewhere between the kiss in the attic and the kiss at the batting cages*, he guessed. She'd obviously delivered it sometime after he got home last night. She hadn't knocked on the door, leaving him to wonder just what it meant.

He supposed it could be a peace offering. But it felt more like a goodbye.

Chapter 23

"Drive safe." Liv gave Rachel one more hard hug in their mother's driveway, not far from the spot where they'd collided just a few weeks ago.

Goodbyes were always the pits. This one was hitting Liv hard. Rachel was still the same Rachel, but they'd gotten to know each other better this time around, no longer separated by grades in school.

No, just little things like marriage. And motherhood.

Rachel stuffed herself behind the wheel of her little blue car, and Brian immediately followed suit in his own hatchback. Liv wondered if they'd be in one of those family vans the next time she saw them.

Next time. How long would that be?

Liv leaned into Brian's car and gave him a quick one-armed hug. "I'll take good care of her," he said.

"I know you will."

San Diego was only a three-hour drive, and the chance of Rachel giving birth on the way there seemed pretty minute, but she didn't blame Brian for looking a little nervous. As they drove off, his vehicle kept a snug distance behind Rachel's. Liv closed her eyes, proud she hadn't cried, and sent up a quick, wordless prayer. When she opened her eyes again, the little mountain road was empty. She wished she could be there when Rachel opened her suitcase and found the blue-flowered tennies Liv had slipped inside. Rachel had always been a shoe size smaller than Liv. But thanks to the pregnancy, they ought to fit her now.

Inside the house, Liv rejoined Mom, who had busied herself at the kitchen sink. Propped matter-of-factly on her crutch, she stood washing breakfast dishes. Liv fought off the urge to lecture her about being on her feet. She knew why her mother was washing dishes. Mom hated goodbyes worse than anyone, which was why she hadn't followed Rachel and Brian out to the driveway. Liv suspected that was a big part of the reason her mother couldn't stand airports.

"It feels quiet, doesn't it?" Liv said.

Mom nodded, not looking away from the sink.

Ordinarily, Rachel was up here every month or so. That was a lot of comings and goings, and a lot of goodbyes. Maybe those smaller goodbyes weren't as hard. But this visit had been different—a longer, more emotional one. And the next time Mom saw Rachel, her youngest daughter would probably be a new mother.

And Liv knew the specter of her own departure, tomorrow morning, hung over her mother. Liv wondered if it would have been easier if she and Rachel had both left at the same time. Before the scare with the contractions, the plan had called for Rachel to drop Liv off at the airport as she and Brian headed back. But the possibility of early labor had everyone uneasy, so they'd left a day early.

"You know," Liv ventured, "you do have a dishwasher."

Mom didn't turn around. "I didn't want to risk it with these dishes. I'm not sure how old they are."

Of course. They'd used Nammy's old Currier and Ives dish set for a final, Christmas-style family meal. The plates and cups might be worth money, or they might not. But they'd been Nammy's, and now, that made them irreplaceable.

Liv joined Mom by the sink. "I'll help."

She pulled a dish towel from the drawer next to the kitchen sink and started fishing plates from the brutally hot rinse water in the right-hand side of the kitchen sink. These dishes ought to be sterile, all right.

After a few minutes of working silently side by side, Mom spoke. "Thanks."

"No problem."

"I mean, for everything. I don't think I've thanked you and Rachel enough. It's a weird feeling to have your own kids start taking care of you."

"You did it for Nammy for years."

"Nammy never needed much help." With soapy hands, Mom drew another mug out of the sink and examined the horse-drawn sleigh as if it were the Mona Lisa. "She was always busy. Always planning."

"I guess all the tile and paint she bought proves that."

Mom swiped her dish rag through the mug and handed it to Liv. "Sometimes I wonder just what she had in mind there."

Liv nodded, wondering again—as Scott must have wondered—how much time Nammy had figured she had left. She'd been in good health until the end, but still. When had she really expected to make those home improvements?

"Well, at least all those things went to good use." Liv dipped the mug in the scalding water and dried it conscientiously.

Mom said, "Did you and Scotty have a good time working on the house together?"

"Scott," Liv corrected without thinking. Then wished she hadn't.

"He's special, isn't he?"

So, Mom wasn't as preoccupied as she seemed.

Liv should have known. Of course her mother knew Scott was weighing on her mind. If she'd ever thought otherwise, Liv had been kidding herself. This woman had changed her diapers, put up with slamming bedroom doors, and nursed Liv through her first broken heart.

"Nammy sure thought he was," Liv said. After a silence, she admitted, "She was right."

Liv fished the last plate out of the hot water. Suddenly she wished there were a *lot* more dishes. She dried it slowly and looked for a change of subject. Casting her eyes around the room, she stopped at Mom's new, tile-topped dining table. "Isn't it funny how women gravitate to the kitchen table? For men, it's usually the living room. Where the TV is."

Once again, Mom steered the conversation onto the wrong track. "I can still ask Scott to save Nammy's old farmhouse table," she said. "I know you can't take it home right away, but I could keep it until you need it."

Liv shook her head. She couldn't ask Scott for anything. Not now. "Where would you even put it?"

"I could find room in the garage. Too bad I don't have an attic—"

The word *attic* sent Liv over the edge. Her hands went to her face to cover huge, hot tears. She still held the dish towel clenched in one fist, but nothing could hide the fact that she was breaking down, bawling, in front of her mother's kitchen sink.

"Oh, honey."

Liv heard the crutch clatter to the floor and felt Mom's arms around her, with the familiar feel of her mother's old red poinsettia sweater and her indefinable scent that reminded Liv vaguely of apples.

"Honey," Mom said, "I'm sorry. I didn't mean to—"

"I know." Liv shook her head against her mom's shoulder, grabbed her around the waist and held on, partly to steady herself, partly to make sure her mother didn't tip over.

"Don't fall," she said into Mom's sweater. "You need to sit down."

Somehow, without falling down or picking up the crutch, the two of them made it to the kitchen table. Mom scooted her kitchen chair next to Liv's and sat beside her, her arms around her.

"Easy," Mom said, stroking Liv's shoulder as her sobs slowed. "I haven't seen you cry like this since—"

She stopped, but they both knew the rest. Since Dad died. Liv, Rachel, and Mom had all taken turns during those days, one of them crumbling while the other two held her up. And then Liv had stopped. Because it wasn't doing any good. Because she shouldn't be leaning on her mother when Mom had to be hurting far worse.

Crying didn't do any good. So she stopped again

now, sagging against her mother's shoulder, so limp that she felt Mom lean over to peer into her face as if to make sure she hadn't passed out.

"I'm sorry," Liv said. "I'm okay."

"No, you're not."

"I will be." Liv straightened and blotted her eyes with the dish towel. She'd violated one of her prime commandments of adult daughter-hood: *Don't worry Mom.*

"Do you want to talk about it?" her mother asked gently.

Liv shook her head. "I need to pack for tomorrow." But she didn't get up. Instead, she wiped her eyes again, fighting the urge to hide her blotchy face.

"You've got a lot of your father in you, you know."

Liv lowered the dish towel and regarded Mom questioningly.

"When he was upset about something he always looked for something to do. I thought it was a man thing, but maybe it's in the genes on his side of the family. Like the way you got us all to paint the living room the summer after he died."

No need to point out the way Mom had busied herself with the dishes this morning.

Liv sniffed. "Hey, it looks good, doesn't it?"

"It does. It always reminds me of what you girls did for me."

"It wasn't much." And it had been the least Liv could do. Rachel had been there so many more times for Mom ever since, for big things and small things. Liv didn't know how she could ever make up for everything she'd missed. Yet her mom had never asked her to.

And here she was, with just a few hours left to her visit, talking about going off to pack.

Liv gave her mom one more squeeze and eased back in her chair, red eyes and all. "Let's get some of those dishes dirty again. I'll pour us some eggnog."

And then it was the night after Christmas.

Tonight Liv had the double bed all to herself. But she wasn't in bed. Instead, she sat alone on her mother's living room floor, at the foot of the silver tree, while the color wheel turned.

Red, blue, orange, green.

Sometimes when Liv sat under the tree, she just gazed at the wash of the colors. Sometimes she made a game of spotting favorite ornaments. Tonight she found herself spotting the bare patches. She and Rachel had chosen their share of the ornaments to take home, plucking them from the branches like fruit, so the tree was unevenly decorated.

Orange, green, red, blue.

Other than the light from the color wheel, the room was dark. It was Liv's favorite way to watch the colors play over the tree. But she'd let the fire in the fireplace dwindle when Mom went to bed, so it was cold down here on the floor. She hugged her knees close to her and rested her chin on them. It was only incidental that the position felt so much like curling up into a ball.

She was going back to Dallas tomorrow. She'd already packed. Her business and a load of decisions waited for her.

When she came back to Tall Pine a few weeks ago,

she was pretty sure she'd referred to Dallas as "home." After this visit, after tasting everything she'd left behind, she wondered if Dallas would ever feel like home again.

A voice in her brain said, *Stay.*

Another voice answered back, just as quickly: *Impossible.*

The argument had been going on in the back of her mind all day. There was no doubt she had a big piece of Tall Pine in her heart, with its evergreen scent, its kind people, and its maddening cell phone reception. Her mom was here. Mom, who had to be missing Nammy more than she ever showed. What would it be like living near her family, and why had she never considered it before?

She'd be close enough to see Rachel's baby when it was born, to watch a niece or nephew grow up.

And there was Scott.

In spite of everything else, would she have even thought of staying if it hadn't been for him? She thought of the chilly frost in Scott's blue eyes the last time she saw him. At this point, would he even be glad if she stayed?

Her heart said *yes.* But her heart had been wrong before. Recently. If she and Scott tried and failed . . .

She had a problem to fix, a business to save. She'd be running away from that. And she'd be admitting, to everyone in town, that this supposed empire she'd built had been a house of straw.

Impossible.

She'd made her decision. She had her commitments.

She had her plane ticket. An eight-hundred-dollar plane ticket.

And she'd already packed.

Driving up the street, Scott slowed the truck in front of Liv's mother's house. He'd tried to tell himself he just felt like going out for a drive to look at Christmas lights. *Liar.*

He slowed the truck, but he didn't stop.

The eaves were strung with Christmas lights—when in the heck had that happened?—and the porch light was on, small-town style. But the windows were almost completely dark. Except for the front living room window, which glowed dimly through the sheer curtains: red, blue, orange, and green.

That would be the color wheel, painting lights over that silly, kitschy silver tree. The only thing Scott had seen that was capable of making Liv crumble to mush.

Odds were she was in the living room with that tree right now. Just a few yards away. All he needed to do was walk up to the front door and knock. Surely the peanut brittle had been an olive branch. But if Liv opened the door, Scott had no idea what he'd say. Probably the wrong thing. His recent record wasn't too impressive. With every effort, it seemed, he gave her another chance to tell him no.

You could only drive so slowly without stopping, so the rear of the truck was already passing the bushes that bordered the neighbor's yard. Up ahead, the road continued on a slight incline, winding its way toward more homes, the real estate prices going up with the elevation. Like most of the residential roads in Tall Pine, it eventually dead-ended.

Scott continued a few houses farther up the road, far enough that the lights and sounds of his truck would be out of range of the Tomblyn house, before he turned around. He pulled into a driveway to execute a three-point turn, noticing for the first time a nice display of white lights and animatronic grazing reindeer.

Driving back downward, he saw that most of the homes were decorated, and he hadn't even noticed. He really had tunnel vision these days.

He slowed in front of Liv's house again and considered calling from his cell phone. That, he decided, officially entered creepy-stalker territory.

So he kept going until he reached his old standby, Coffman's Hardware. Tools and supplies, nuts and bolts. It was nice to think there was someplace where things could be fixed.

Liv's cell phone rang in her pocket. It had become such an infrequent sound that she jumped. What now? Another curveball from Terri?

Wriggling on the living room floor, she worked the phone free and glanced at the caller ID.

"Scotty?" She reverted to his old nickname without thinking.

"Yeah, me. I wanted to say thanks for the peanut brittle."

Her hand tightened around the phone. "You're welcome."

A pause. "And I'm sorry about the other day. I never

281

should have tried to tell you what you should do. It wasn't my place."

Liv hugged her free arm tight around her knees.

He asked, "Are you taking the tree with you?"

"I—" The words froze in her throat as she stared at the silver tree. Somehow she hadn't thought of that. If she was keeping the tree, she should have boxed it up tonight. She still had time to do it. Boxing up a Christmas tree alone at midnight—what an exercise in depression that would be.

"I left it up for my mom," she lied. "It's too soon after Christmas to take it down."

Mom would be thrilled about that, what with her healing knee and her well-known love for the tinsel branches and all their static shocks. Liv tried to think of someone she could enlist to help her mom take the tree down, but the only person she could think of was Scotty.

And, she realized, she was leaving her mother with two hundred feet of last-minute Christmas lights hanging on the house. So much left unfinished.

Scott's voice jarred her out of her thoughts. "Do you have a ride to the airport tomorrow?"

"I've got one of those airport shuttles picking me up."

"From Ontario to Tall Pine?" he scoffed. "That'll cost a fortune." He paused. "I can give you a lift. If you want."

"You don't have to do that."

"Don't be silly." This time she heard real warmth in his voice. "You know I'll take you."

And suddenly, Liv's throat felt huge. It ached.

That ache should tell her a ride from Scott was probably a really, really bad idea.

She reminded herself again of her eight-hundred-dollar plane ticket. That ought to keep her anchored to reality.

"Liv?" Scott prompted.

"You're not going to try to get me to change my mind, are you?" Her voice sounded muffled and unfamiliar to her own ears.

A short bark of laughter bruised her ego. "Try to change *your* mind? I'd like to see the guy who could pull that off."

She clutched her hand around the phone. Ego or no ego, she'd miss that laugh.

"Besides," he went on, less brusquely, "Texas needs tidy closets. Right?"

"Right." Liv pushed the words out. "Okay. If you're sure."

"I'm sure."

If he'd been driving his truck backward, this could pretty much pass for a rewind of his trip down the freeway with Liv at the beginning of the month.

Sitting beside him, staring out the windshield, Liv was silent and distracted. Scott would have given just about anything to make her smile, but he seemed to be out of material.

"I'll give your mom a call in a couple of days," he offered. "She'll need a hand getting decorations down."

It got her eyes off the road, at any rate. "You don't have to do that."

"I'm going to add that to the list of forbidden phrases," he said.

He stopped himself from pointing out that Faye had paid him more than he'd billed her as it was. That kind of discussion would just send Liv's gaze back out the windshield. Instead, he asked, "Who the heck hung those Christmas lights, anyway?"

That brought a sheepish smile. "Me. I got a little— restless."

He ached to squeeze her hand, but resolutely kept both hands on the wheel.

When they got to the airport, Liv tried to talk him into dropping her off at the passenger unloading area without parking. As if he'd leave her alone to struggle with her bags. Or tip some stranger to do it. She fell silent again, enduring the lines and the crowds as he went with her through the process of scanning her ticket and checking her bags. When her red suitcases disappeared behind the counter, she turned to face him with a small smile, as if she'd shed some weight.

She wore a forest-green sweater, and it brought out the most amazing flecks of color in her hazel eyes. As if pulled by a magnet, Scott felt his hand reach up to touch her cheek. He'd promised not to say anything. But maybe he could say it without words.

"Thanks." Liv took a step back, slipping away from his touch just as his fingers grazed her cheek. "I'd better find my gate."

She turned, and he went with her. Scott had to admit to himself that, deep down, he'd hoped bringing her here would give her one more chance to change her mind. But she'd handed over the bags without a blink. If there'd been a window of opportunity, it was over now.

He should have said something. Maybe he'd finally hit his limit on getting turned down. He walked her to the passenger gate, winding them through the post-holiday throng with a sinking heart.

He *should* have said something.

But when had he ever been able to talk a female into anything?

When had he ever, sincerely, tried?

They reached the check-in line with the metal detector for people and the conveyor belt for their belongings. She could fly back, he told himself. She *would* be back, to see her mother, and probably a lot sooner this time. The pull of family ties had definitely strengthened for her on this trip. Maybe he'd been some small part of that. He didn't know. The idea made him feel a little better, at least.

She'd be back someday, but it wouldn't be the same. They'd exchange friendly smiles and keep a safe distance. Heck, maybe he'd even be married by then.

Conversation stopped again until it was Liv's turn in line. She loaded her coat, purse, and shoes onto the conveyor belt and turned to him. "This is where I leave you," she said, her tone a little too bright.

She hugged him. And Scott felt a quick surge of hope. Because her arms wound tight around his neck, which wasn't easy, because she had to reach up pretty far to do it. She'd worn tennies today.

And he was fairly sure she was trembling. Or maybe it was him.

"Thanks for everything," she said, close to his ear. "You were really patient. You put up with a lot. You deserve someone really special."

The last words stung, but he had an answer ready. "That's what they all say."

Because most of them had.

Chalk up another one, he thought as she turned away, except this one had never really gotten off the ground. Maybe that was why this one hurt so much. But he knew it was more than that. So much more that when she stepped toward the metal detector, he took a step to follow her.

The steel-barred frame of the metal detector yawned before Liv.

Don't look back, she thought.

She was following her shoes through that metal detector and getting on that plane alone. And she hated it.

She was a fraud and a coward. Stupidly, at the last minute, she'd started to hope Scott would say something. When she'd made it clear, every chance she could, that there was no chance she was staying. Now, at the last minute, she'd thought he might try to change her mind. She thought he even wanted to.

It was like a breath-holding contest.

An eight-hundred-dollar breath-holding contest. And she'd lost.

Time to put that ticket to use. She held her head high, squared her shoulders, and started through the metal detector as a voice inside her screamed, *NO.*

As instinctively as a drowning victim flailing in the water, she reached her hand backward.

Scott's hand was there. It clasped hers firmly.

He yanked her back through to his side, bumping her into someone behind her. She didn't see who it was, because he pulled her into his arms.

"My purse—my shoes—"

Her words were muffled in his sweater; his arms had already wrapped around her tight. She felt him pull her away from the line, his solid form the only consistent thing as travelers bumped and shuffled past them.

"Don't go." Under her ear, she felt his voice vibrate in his chest. "I know I'm not supposed to say it. But don't go."

She lifted her face from the rough knit of his sweater. "I wanted you to say it," she choked out. "But I couldn't say I wanted you to say—"

"Hush," he whispered, and kissed her.

Standing on tiptoe, in her stocking feet, Liv held on tight and kissed him back.

She wasn't pulling away this time, Scott realized. And gradually, dimly, he became aware again of the hum of voices around them. They were standing in the middle of an airport. They should probably do something about that.

Reluctantly, Scott broke the kiss and gazed down at her. Liv's eyes were shining, her cheeks flushed. With his thumb, he caught the beginning of a stray tear under her eyelashes.

"You're sure about this?" he said softly. "Your purse and shoes, we can get. Your suitcases might already be on the plane."

"We'll figure it out," she whispered, her voice still shaky. "Just take me home."

"Home," he said. "I like the sound of that."

Liv melted against him. And, once again, Scott Leroux held a crying female in his arms.

But this time, he planned to hold on to her for the rest of his life.

Epilogue

"That one's Mom's." Liv plucked the sequined bluebird gently from Scott's hand.

"I remember."

Liv wrapped the bird in tissue and gingerly laid it in the canister of ornaments her mother was keeping.

It was January first. Time to put the silver tree away, but it wouldn't stay in the box as long this time. It would go up again next year. And if all their plans worked out, they'd be putting it up together, in Nammy's old house. The house they'd worked together to turn into a home.

"Ow!" Scott said. "I got another shock."

"That's the price you pay for beauty."

When all the decorations were down, Scott made one more trip around the tree, checking over the branches before they started to pull them off.

"Scott, I already looked. We got them all."

"That's what you think. Any tree I've ever decorated, there's always at least one ornament that gets left over." Scott circled to the back of the tree. "Aha!"

He stepped from behind the tree, brandishing a flat golden bell and wearing an *I-told-you-so* grin.

Liv frowned. "I already put away the bell." She remembered putting it in the canister of ornaments she and Scott wanted to keep. And Nammy's engraved bell hadn't been in back; it had hung on a prominent place at the front of the tree.

Scott studied the decoration with a frown of his own, then handed it to her. "I don't remember this one. Did you hang it?"

Liv shook her head as she examined the ornament. It was another flat, gold-plated bell, just like the one Nammy had gotten engraved for her first Christmas with Liv's grandfather so many years ago. The one she'd ordered from the cereal they didn't make anymore. But this bell was new and shiny. And there was one other difference.

"The engraving space is blank," Liv said.

Scott came up, put his arm around her shoulder, and looked at the pristine bell for a moment in silence.

"Well," he said, "I guess that space is for our names." Scott turned her to face him and smiled into her eyes. "All we need now is the date."

Mandy's Hot Chocolate for Two

½ cup sweetened condensed milk
3½ cups hot water
⅓ cup semisweet chocolate chips
1 teaspoon vanilla extract
¾ teaspoon cinnamon
⅛ teaspoon ground cloves (scant)

In a medium saucepan, stir sweetened condensed milk into hot water and heat together over low flame. When mixture is hot—but not boiling!—add chocolate chips and stir continuously until chips are melted. Add vanilla, cinnamon, and ground cloves and stir over low heat until well blended. (If mixture is too rich for your taste, add a small amount of whole milk.)

May be topped with whipped cream and your choice of cookie décor sprinkles, crushed candy cane, cinnamon, chocolate shavings, chocolate sauce, or caramel sauce.

Add your own special touch of Christmas magic . . . and you never know what may happen!

Please turn the page for an exciting peek at
Sierra Donovan's next
Evergreen Lane romance,

DO NOT OPEN 'TIL CHRISTMAS,

coming in October 2017 wherever
print and eBooks are sold!

"Just once, couldn't somebody kill someone?"

Bret Radner bit out the words as soon as he hit the period at the end of his latest story for the *Tall Pine Gazette*. The headline read: EVERGREEN LANE SHOPS PREDICT SUCCESSFUL CHRISTMAS SEASON.

Shocker.

"I'll get right on it." Bret's fellow reporter, Chuck Nolan, didn't even glance up from his own computer screen. "Who've you got in mind for the lucky victim?"

Bret released a long, slow sigh. Chuck had heard it all before. And there wasn't really anyone in Tall Pine he was *that* annoyed with.

"Okay," Bret said. "A tourist."

Chuck battered out a few words on his keyboard with his oddly efficient hunt-and-peck method. He was in his early forties, and somehow Chuck had never learned to type. "And how about the murderer? I'm not doing your dirty work for you."

"Another tourist. How's that? Two really *rude* tourists."

Bret returned his attention to the story on his screen, running the cursor down the text to proofread it once more before he sent it to his editor's in-box. Holding back another sigh, Bret reached for the writing pad that contained the notes from his interview with the head of the local water district.

"Radner." His editor, Frank McCrea, stood in the doorway of his glass-walled office, twenty feet from Bret's desk. "I need to see you for a minute."

A summons to the editor's office at four o'clock was pretty unusual. Too quick to have anything to do with the story Bret had just sent over. And if it was a reaction to his mini-rant, that would be a first.

Only one way to find out. Bret followed McCrea into the editor's inner sanctum, aware of Chuck's curious stare behind him. He sat in one of the straight-backed chairs facing McCrea's massive oak desk. Massive, but scarred with age, like just about everything in the *Gazette*'s offices. At thirty, Bret sometimes suspected he was the youngest thing in the newsroom. Including the coffee machine.

"What's up?" Bret asked.

McCrea—middle-aged, graying, and broadening around the middle—took his seat in the larger, cushioned chair across from Bret. "I've got a curveball for you."

Bret's brows lifted. Ordinarily, he loved curveballs.

McCrea continued, "I had a call last week from our corporate office in St. Louis. The editor at their paper in Chicago stepped down about six months ago, and the associate editor they promoted is making a hash of things. They asked me to step in and do some damage control until they find somebody permanent."

Bret blinked, trying not to show signs of whiplash. After all, it was logical enough. McCrea had headed up the Chicago paper before he moved his family to Tall Pine a decade or so ago. If he'd been looking for peace and quiet, he'd certainly gotten what he was after. What Bret had never understood was how McCrea had ever found Tall Pine. Tucked away in the mountains some two hours from Los Angeles, it was barely on the map.

But any good newspaper story led with the most pertinent point of the article, and Bret had the feeling his commander-in-chief had buried his lead.

McCrea moved quickly to correct that. "I'm putting you in charge."

That, too, was logical. McCrea had hired Bret when he came home from college, and Bret had spent the last seven years living and breathing the job, such as it was. When McCrea took vacation time, it was Bret who filled in. Although he couldn't recall McCrea taking as much as a full week off at any one time.

"Okay." Bret couldn't hold back a half-smile. "Sure you don't want to trade and send me to Chicago?"

"Were you listening? I'm going there to clean up the mess from another guy with years of experience in a major metropolitan area." Bret flinched at that. McCrea pretended not to notice. "You'll have your hands full here, I guarantee. The Christmas season is coming up next month, so you'll have to work smart, with the holidays to schedule around. I know you're not big on Christmas—"

"It's not my favorite thing, no," Bret responded automatically. McCrea knew that better than most. And he'd remember why, better than most.

297

"—but on the upside, as I said, this will keep you busy. It's no secret you'd like more of a challenge."

Bret inclined his head. "You think?"

"Trust me. There's more to running this place on an ongoing basis than you realize. We get by okay on two full-time reporters plus me. But you're going to need to delegate. I know your work ethic, and if you don't watch out, you could end up trying to write the whole paper by yourself. By the time you figured out you were in over your head, you wouldn't have time to look for someone else. So I hired one of our freelancers to fill in while I'm gone."

"A freelancer?" Bret kept his features still.

Generally, freelance reporters were amateurs. They worked from home, usually as a sideline to another job. Their skills left a lot to be desired, and they didn't tend to last long. More trouble than they were worth, in Bret's opinion.

"I know what you're thinking. But this one's consistent. She's been working with us for nearly two years. Chloe Davenport."

The byline rang a bell, but barely. Freelancers were entrusted with less timely articles, the kind that even Bret tended to skip over. Church bake sales, prize-winning pickles, interviews with this year's valedictorian. McCrea added, "She was in the office yesterday."

Bret remembered glimpsing the back of a blond female head through McCrea's glass walls. "I thought it was one of your daughters coming in for lunch money."

McCrea shook his head. "Chloe graduated college a couple of years ago. You've probably met her. She's a waitress at the Pine 'n' Dine."

Bret frowned. He didn't know of any blond waitresses at the local diner. Unless . . . A faint image surfaced in his mind.

"She works nights most of the time," McCrea added.

The picture snapped into focus. Bret didn't usually go to the Pine 'n' Dine in the evening. But a couple of months ago, he'd stopped in to write up his notes on a town council meeting before he came back to the paper to file the story. A petite, blue-eyed blonde had waited on him. She looked like a china doll, for heaven's sake.

He dredged his memory further. She'd made some sort of joke . . .

Whatever it was, it wasn't important right now. But he wondered if McCrea was suffering from a touch of middle-aged crazy. His editor was a family man, ethical to the core, and Bret didn't think he'd ever dream of cheating on his wife. But that didn't mean a pretty face couldn't cloud his thinking.

"Are you sure about this?" Bret picked his words with care. "She's awfully young."

"Older than you were."

Hard to get around that one. Bret flicked a brief smile. "Yeah, but I was a prodigy."

"Then you should have no trouble getting a newbie up to speed." McCrea leaned back in his chair. "Unless you're not up to it. I could always put Chuck in charge."

It was a transparent bluff, and both of them knew it. Chuck was a great guy and a good worker, but organization wasn't his strong suit.

"Hey, they say print journalism is a dying field," Bret deadpanned. "No point in rushing the process."

"It's a yes, then?"

"I didn't know it was a question. But sure. I'm your guy."

"Glad that's settled. I'm leaving this weekend. You take over Monday."

Monday? "You're telling me this on two days' notice?"

"Didn't want to listen to your griping any longer than that." McCrea sat forward again, resting his arms comfortably on his desk. "Now get out."

Most of their talks in McCrea's office ended that way.

"Fine." Bret stood. "But you're going to freeze your butt off in Chicago."

He walked back out, his head spinning. A lot had changed in ten minutes, but he'd be lying if he said he wasn't salivating just a little bit. He loved a challenge, and he was overdue for one. Now McCrea had given him the keys to the kingdom.

And a freelancer to babysit.

Chloe Davenport pushed through the door from the reception area to the newsroom Monday morning, brand-new briefcase in hand, trying not to feel like a kid on the first day of school.

It was only her third time inside the *Tall Pine Gazette* offices. All of her other contact had been by phone or e-mail. Just like school, it was a roomful of desks. Instead of thirty small ones, a half dozen big ones stood lined up in two rows. And at the back of the room, the mystical, glass-walled editor's office.

The editor's office was empty, and only one of the desks was occupied. Behind it sat a brown-haired man, probably about forty, rifling through disorderly stacks of paper on top of his desk.

"Good morning," she said.

He looked up, startled, although Chloe hadn't exactly tiptoed in. "Hi." The man gave her a puzzled but not unfriendly smile. She was a few minutes early, but he didn't look as if he'd been expecting her.

She smiled back and put out her hand. "I'm Chloe Davenport." As he rose to shake her hand, his puzzled expression didn't clear, so she added, "I'm looking for Bret Radner?"

The man looked distractedly over his shoulder. "He's around here somewhere." He turned back to her. "Sorry. I'm Chuck Nolan. I'm on my way to an interview at the school district office." He sifted through his papers again until he fished out what he'd apparently been searching for: a blank notepad. "You must be the freelancer?"

Good. They did know she was coming. "Right. Well, not a freelancer anymore. I'm here full time, at least until Mr. McCrea gets back. He said to come in at nine. I guess I'm a little—"

A door opened at the far side of the room, and a trim, dark-haired man burst through it, wearing glasses with thin black wire frames, a cell phone in one hand, a cordless phone handset pressed to his ear. As he spoke into the phone, his calm tone belied his rapid stride. "There's been a delay. We'll have your photographer out there shortly." He hit a button to disconnect the call, then punched a few keys on the handset. "Jen?" His tone was more brisk. "We still haven't heard from Ned? Okay, thanks."

He lowered the phone to his side, eyes closed as if in thought. Or as if willing someone to spontaneously combust. "Who dedicates a plaque at eight thirty on a Monday morning?" he said to no one in particular.

She recognized him.

She could only hope and pray he wouldn't recognize her. Chloe glanced at the pleasant, laid-back Chuck. *Why couldn't it have been the other one?*

Bret Radner had been one of her customers at the Pine 'n' Dine a few months ago. She'd noticed him because he was one of those men who looked good in glasses, which she liked. And he'd been typing away at a laptop, which intrigued her. Especially since the Pine 'n' Dine didn't have Wi-Fi, so he was probably writing something.

But he hadn't looked up from his laptop since he ordered. Not once.

Curiosity warring with frustration, she approached his table when his cup reached the half-full mark. "Would you like more coffee?"

"Please." Not taking his eyes from his screen, he unerringly maneuvered his cup under the spout of her coffeepot.

A little demon prodded her. "Excuse me."

She had to wait several seconds before he seemed to realize she wasn't going to go away. Finally he raised his head and met her eyes with a dark-eyed stare behind the black wire rims.

Now that his gaze was fixed on her, unblinking and waiting, she started to regret her gumption. But the little demon spurred her on.

"Thanks." She tried not to stammer. "We're required

to see all of our customers' faces at least once. That way, in case you turn out to be the Unabomber or something, I can give a good description."

His stare sharpened, and she knew she'd had it. *No tip for you, baby. You'll be lucky if he doesn't complain to the owner.*

"They caught the Unabomber in 1996," he said. "You're way behind on your current events."

Then his lips twitched in a faint smile. "Thanks for the coffee," he said, and returned to his laptop.

It all made sense now. The laptop, the writing, and especially the crack about current events. No wonder he'd known the year of the Unabomber's capture off the top of his head.

Great. He probably thought she really believed the fugitive was still at large, over twenty years later.

Maybe he wouldn't place her. Maybe she looked different enough without her uniform. She'd pulled her blond hair into a bun this morning, an effort both to look professional and to tame her uncooperative waves. Unfortunately, she realized, that was pretty similar to the way she had to wear it when she waited tables.

Right now, Chloe wasn't sure if Bret noticed she was standing here or not. He was speaking to Chuck. "Ned's missing in action. I'm going to have to steal the photographer for your nine o'clock. Can you shoot it on your phone?"

Chuck shrugged. "Sure." He nodded toward Chloe. "Uh, Bret? Miss Davenport is here."

Sharp dark eyes fell on her from behind his glasses, and Chloe's stomach did a twist. Maybe he remembered and maybe he didn't, but he looked as if he'd just found an overdue bill underneath his refrigerator.

Resolutely, she put on her best smile and put out her hand. "I'm Chloe Davenport."

He accepted her hand, his smile tight. "The freelancer."

She held his stare and kept her smile. "Not anymore."

"Right." He released her hand. "You're early."

Early was generally a good thing. Clearly, not today. "A little."

"I'm putting out a few fires this morning. I'll need about an hour to get my feet under me. Hold on."

He thumbed out a number on his cell phone.

"Winston? Bret." His voice returned to the brisk-but-polite tone he'd used with the receptionist. "I need to move our ten o'clock. Can we bump it up to eleven?" He nodded. "Great. See you then."

She only knew of one Winston in Tall Pine—Winston Frazier, the oldest member of the town council—but she couldn't imagine anyone speaking to him in that brusque tone. He was a regular at the Pine 'n' Dine, and every waitress called him "sir."

Bret lowered the phone and zeroed in on Chloe again. "You're my new ten o'clock."

"Okay. Where do I—" She hefted her briefcase awkwardly.

Bret glanced over the two rows of desks. He nodded toward the one behind Chuck's. "That one." It was littered with a hodgepodge of newspaper sections, a phone directory, a vintage-looking computer monitor, and a telephone Chloe could only hope was actually plugged in. "How about if you get yourself situated, have a cup of—" His eyes darted to a coffeemaker on a small cabinet against a wall, with about an inch and a half of coffee at the bottom of the pot. It looked lonely and cold.

Chuck sidled to the exit, sending what might have been an apologetic nod in her direction.

Bret took no notice. "Could you make a pot of coffee?" he asked her. "I'll get with you at ten. Sharp."

As if that were settled, he turned away and headed for a side door at the other end of the office, at high speed, dialing the cordless phone as he walked. Leaving her alone in the newsroom. With the coffeemaker.

If her new boss had paused long enough for her to draw a breath, Chloe would have been tempted to object. Probably just as well. His quick departure gave her time to remember her mother's advice whenever her dad or her brothers were being sexist: *Pick your battles.*

So, Chloe laid her briefcase down on top of the desk Bret had indicated and got to work.

Her first day as a full-time reporter, and her first assignment was to make a pot of coffee.

For the next hour, Chloe watched Bret Radner with a mixture of apprehension and fascination.

She'd only met McCrea in person twice, and she missed him already. The editor had definitely been a no-nonsense type, brief and to the point; she'd learned to keep her e-mails to him short, because sometimes he'd miss a question if she surrounded it with too much extraneous detail.

Compared to this guy, McCrea was a model of patience and leisure.

Bret made his way in and out of the newsroom with the speed of a tornado, but no tornado was ever so purposeful. The air around him practically crackled as he wore a path between the editor's office and the desk across from Chuck's, making and taking phone calls in quick, clipped tones. Physically, he wasn't as imposing as either of her two brothers, but even from across the room, he intimidated the heck out of her.

He got over to the coffeemaker moments after the pot had finished perking and poured a cup, with a brief glance in her direction, before he vanished through another door, this one at the back of the room. The *Gazette* didn't look that big from the outside, but obviously the building branched off in all directions.

Midway through the hour, Bret got the call he'd apparently been waiting for. "Ned? Where the heck are you?"

He'd come to a momentary stop in front of the desk across from Chuck's. Standing with one arm propped on the desktop, he said, "I don't get it. Your wife's in labor, not you."

Chloe studied his face for any sign that he was joking. She saw no change in his expression.

Then, as the person on the other end responded, he grinned—an expression she'd never seen on him before. "Same to you." The grin faded as he eyed the desk blotter calendar in front of him. "This is early, isn't it?" Another pause. "Okay. Keep us posted. Give Debbie my best."

He switched from the cell phone to the telephone

on his desk. Chloe wasn't sure what had happened to the cordless handset. "Jen? Could you get me McCrea's list of freelance photographers? Ned's going to be out for a while. Debbie's in labor. Yeah, two weeks early . . . Do you know if we have an account with the florist?" He nodded. "But hold off until we hear how it goes."

As he hung up, Chloe volunteered, "Two weeks isn't that bad."

He looked at her as if surprised to see her still there. "So he told me."

And he sped off to the reception area.

Chloe sipped her coffee and returned to the task of straightening—or finding—her desk. The newspapers covering the top ranged in age from two weeks to two years old; she set them aside for recycling. The phone did, in fact, have a dial tone, and the computer hummed to life when she turned it on. The drawers were filled with curious archeological artifacts: stray tea bags, broken pencils, absolutely no working pens, and half-filled memo pads with scribbled notes dated three years ago. Had it been that long since they had another reporter?

She thought Bret might forget her, but he returned to stand in front of her desk promptly at ten. "Okay. Let's back up and start from the beginning." He extended his hand to her again. "I'm Bret."

"Chloe." She leaned across the desk to shake his hand again and got the same brief, firm squeeze as before.

Did he remember her? He gave no indication. Good.

Bret leaned back to sit against the top of Chuck's desk, arms folded in front of him. Chloe wondered if he realized what a closed-off posture that was. She wondered if it was intentional.

"So," he said. "This is your first full-time news gig?"

"Yes."

"Okay." He closed his eyes briefly, as if he'd just witnessed a ten-car pileup. "Basics."

Then his eyes opened, and the onslaught of instructions began.

"Workday starts at eight. Deadline is two thirty, but we've never taken that literally. It was designed for the best of all possible worlds, and this isn't it. But unless you have an appointment, which you'll let me know about, you need to be back at your desk by then. We're short-staffed here, as you can see, so I need boots on the ground pretty quick. By the end of two weeks, I'll expect you to be filing ten stories a week . . ."

Without taking her eyes from Bret, Chloe felt around on her desk for the pad of paper she'd left there. Thank God she'd brought her own pens.

Bret nodded. "Yes, put that at the top of your list: always have a notepad ready."

If he saw any irony in that statement, Chloe couldn't tell, because as soon as her pen was poised, the torrent of information resumed.

"When you're doing a phone interview, use a headset and take notes on your keyboard, not by hand. It's faster and it's way more accurate. And when you quote someone, make darn sure it's what they said. No paraphrasing."

That was almost insulting. "I would never—"

"Good. No profanity of any kind, even in a quote. We're owned by Liberty Communications, which owns over four hundred newspapers across the country. They're very conservative, and believe me, we want to keep them happy."

By the time Bret came to a stop, she'd filled five pages with scribbled notes. She only hoped she'd be able to read them.

He pushed up from Chuck's desk. "Generally I'll be meeting with you on Mondays to go over story proposals for the week. We've already lost too much time today, so have at least five ideas ready for me tomorrow morning. Meanwhile, I'll get you some press releases to write up into news briefs. That should keep you busy."

As Bret retreated to the office formerly occupied by McCrea, Chloe sat back, took a deep breath, and exhaled. She had a feeling it would be her last chance for quite a while.

She could do this.

Writing for a newspaper hadn't been her first choice for a job, but then, her career plan hadn't been especially well thought out. She'd had the conversation dozens of times in college.

What's your major?

English.

Oh. You want to be an English teacher?

No. A writer.

Oh, like a newspaper reporter?

No. Probably something in marketing . . .

That had been vague enough to shut them up.

She'd been told what a versatile major English was, everything from pre-law to marketing. Somehow she'd believed it. What she really wanted, she supposed, was a solid day job so she could pursue something more creative on her own time.

Chloe knew what she was good at. She excelled at writing, and she loved it. She just didn't know how to make a living at it. Especially in Tall Pine. So, six months into her stint as a waitress, when the *Tall Pine Gazette* had advertised for freelance reporters, she'd cracked. As it turned out, she enjoyed it far more than she expected. But writing a few stories a month certainly didn't earn enough for her to quit the Pine 'n' Dine.

Now she had this, while it lasted.

Ten stories a week for the next three months. Including interviews and research, as well as writing them. Not to mention coming up with enough story ideas that would pass muster with her new boss.

She could do this.

It was this, or back to waiting tables.

Bret closed the door of McCrea's office behind him and resisted the urge to lean back against it and bar out the outside world. With glass walls, that wasn't an option. So, keeping his back straight, he closed his eyes and pinched the bridge of his nose.

He'd been wrong about one thing: her eyes weren't blue.

There was some blue in there, but they were more of a deep gray, with a hint of green if you looked long enough. Like the ocean on a stormy afternoon. Especially when he'd asked her to make coffee. And now he remembered her snarky joke about the Unabomber. So, not a china doll.

But she still didn't look much like a reporter, unless you counted the ones you saw on TV shows, with that bright smile and that shiny briefcase. Pretty enough to make him wonder, again, if McCrea had been thinking straight when he hired her.

He wouldn't invest much time in her—couldn't afford to—until he knew whether she was going to last beyond the first two weeks. He'd set the bar pretty high. But no higher than McCrea had set for Bret when he started here.

She'd pan out or she wouldn't. And he wouldn't let a pretty face sway his judgment.

Connect with

Visit us online at
KensingtonBooks.com
to read more from your favorite authors, see books
by series, view reading group guides, and more.

for sneak peeks, chances to win books and prize packs,
and to share your thoughts with other readers.

facebook.com/kensingtonpublishing
twitter.com/kensingtonbooks

Tell us what you think!

To share your thoughts, submit a review,
or sign up for our eNewsletters, please visit:
KensingtonBooks.com/TellUs.